MW00526668

MELODY OF FLAME

BOOK TWO

THE WILDSONG SERIES

TRICIA O'MALLEY

LOVEWRITE PUBLISHING

MELODY OF FLAME
The Wildsong Series
Book Two

"Keep the little fire burning; however small, however hidden."
– Cormac McCarthy

The Fae Realm

Danula

The Light Fae ruled by the Goddess Danu

The Elemental Fae

The Royal Fae Court of the Danula oversee
the Elemental Fae

Water Fae

Earth Fae   Fire Fae

Air Fae

Domnua

The Dark Fae ruled by Goddess Domnu

PROLOGUE

THE TRUE FATED MATES,
   Once shall meet.
   Standing at love's gate,
   Their marriage complete.
   Unknown to both,
   Their paths are chosen.
   They've taken the oath,
   Their hearts now spoken.

GOLDEN EYES, as though lit from within, stared at her through the flames of the bonfire. Sorcha Kelly prided herself on never stepping down from a challenge, so she met the man's gaze dead on, lifting her chin in acknowledgement. A smile quirked his lips, and heat seared her core as he raised a hand and beckoned to her with one finger. Pushing her instant attraction aside, Sorcha raised an eyebrow in disdain. The man had another thing coming if he thought she'd answer to a summons of that nature.

Queen of her own destiny, Sorcha turned away from the

fire, and followed the increasingly heavy beat of drums that made her insides thrum. The music was impossible to resist and Sorcha bounced to the rhythm as she made her way through the festival grounds, laughing as a random woman grabbed her hand and pulled her into an impromptu series of complicated Irish dance steps. Dance was Sorcha's love language, and she fell naturally into step, laughing and tossing her cherry red curls over her shoulder. Music, laughter, and creativity were her fuel, and this weekend's festival for artists filled her soul.

Billed as the "Burning Man" of Ireland, the Ring of Fire Festival encouraged artists of all types to commune together for the weekend to create art that would set souls on fire. These types of events were like catnip to Sorcha, and she'd packed up Betty Blue, her trusty camper van, and made her way to the festival tucked in the Irish hills with her gear in tow. She'd freelanced for years in the performing arts, mainly in dance and acrobatics, but was currently working on a new skill that had piqued her interest – fire dancing.

The art had risen in popularity both with photographers and audiences who wanted live performances at their events. Sorcha had been booked for everything from weddings to photo shoots and was finally beginning to eke out a steady stream of income. For the first time in years, she was allowing herself to embrace her art, and her lifestyle, without the heavy weight of guilt placed on her from her family.

With six sisters, Sorcha was but an afterthought in a long line of disappointments for her father. She'd watched the rest of her siblings try to live up to his expectations and quickly realized it was a game she'd never win. She was fairly certain the only thing that could win her father's approval would be if she could go back in time and be born a male. While she had many talents, time travel was not one of them, and she'd cut her losses and hit the road shortly after she came of age.

Oh, but she loved her life now! Sorcha laughed as the dancing woman plopped a kiss on her cheek, and she gave a small curtsy before wandering back to Betty Blue to fill her insulated cup with wine. Once there, she paused, leaning back against the cool steel of her car, and studied the scene.

The sun had long since descended, and the full moon shone brightly on the bonfires that dotted the hills. Fairy lights were strung up between campsites, and music and laughter rose to the gently sparkling stars above. Everybody here shared a common interest – to create – and the joy and love found among these people made Sorcha feel like she was burning from within. Aptly named, this festival, she mused as she took a sip of her wine.

"You ignored me."

Sorcha jumped, wine sputtering from her lips, as she turned to see the golden-eyed man standing beside her. He'd approached as lightly as a breeze, and Sorcha took a few seconds to study him more closely to see if she could get a read on him. She'd traveled alone for years now, and her instincts had kept her safe thus far.

"Sure and you can't be thinking that the way to a woman's heart is to beckon her with a single finger?"

"Oh? Do you prefer to be the one who makes the demands?" The man gave her a silky grin. The light dancing in his golden eyes told Sorcha this exchange amused him.

"I do prefer to be in charge, thank you very much. Do you have a name then? Or shall I just call you a cheeky lion?"

At that the man threw his head back and laughed, the huskiness causing Sorcha's toes to curl, and she found herself strangely entranced. While dressing in costume was encouraged for the festival, Sorcha got the impression that this man wore his regular clothes. Red leather pants, a fitted long-sleeve black t-shirt, and a tawny head of gold hair with gilded red highlights contributed to her impression of him looking like a lion. It was the eyes though, that made her take a second and then a third look. He must wear color contacts, and the effect his golden eyes had was both startling and arresting. Sorcha drew closer. Starkly handsome, with sharp cheekbones and a chiseled jaw, this man carried himself with a confidence that wouldn't be easy for most men to pull off while wearing screaming-red leather pants.

"That would certainly be a first. My name is Torin. And what is yours, my enchantress?" The words purred from his lips, their heat searing straight to her core.

"Sorcha." She took a sip of her wine, as her throat had gone dry, while Torin studied her with the same intensity with which she watched him.

"And isn't that the perfect name for a woman of your nature? I find you impossibly beautiful."

The words, simply delivered, struck Sorcha with their sincerity. Tears threatened, and she forced herself to break his gaze and look over at the festival for a moment. *Quirky?* Yes. *Interesting.* Most definitely. But beautiful? No, Sorcha had never fallen prey to those types of compliments before. While it might be just another line to get her into bed, the conviction with which his words were delivered resonated deeply within her.

"Are your eyes real?" Sorcha turned once more to Torin.

His lips quirked, the sulky half-smile that had captured her interest across the fire before, and he reached out a hand.

"Dance with me?"

"See if you can keep up," Sorcha said, raising her chin in a challenge once more. Downing her wine, she tucked the cup behind the wheel of Betty Blue and grabbed Torin's hand. A shock of heat rippled through her, and she gasped when his hand tightened on hers instead of releasing. Turning, she met his eyes in the moonlight and read the invitation held there.

Sorcha swallowed, not ready for the question he posed, and instead pulled him into a circle of people who danced around a large bonfire to a haunting Celtic melody. The pipers stepped forward, increasing the speed of the song, and Sorcha closed her eyes to catch the beat. Torin's hands circled her waist, and then he pulled her into his arms. Sorcha floated along, allowing herself to be pulled into a fluid dance, the heat of his touch invigorating.

Time seemed to slow, as they fell into an ancient rhythm where music propelled them forward, twisting and turning, their bodies brushing, their gazes caught on each other. Torin matched Sorcha step for step, challenging her with his movements, his tawny eyes searing hers. As the night drew long, Sorcha found herself caught in whatever spell he was casting.

The flames will dance,
Fire lights the dark,
To give love a chance,
Takes only a spark.

His voice husky, his eyes clouded with lust and something much more tender, Torin traced a finger over her lips as he sang. Intoxicated with him, Sorcha accepted his hand when he drew her back to Betty Blue, where she found herself pulling him onto her bed, twining her body around his as sinuously as they had danced together. Caught in a spell, the two feasted on each other's bodies, the pulsing of the drums mirroring the pulsing of their hearts, as lust and fire drove their most intimate of dances. Flames licked through Sorcha's veins, desire all but smothering her, as she met Torin's appraising gaze as he took her mouth once more. Light flashed, and Sorcha started, but Torin took her under once more, drawing her attention back to his touch. Only near dawn, once sated, did they fall apart, gasping for breath.

Sorcha blinked at the ceiling of her van, where she'd tacked up a hauntingly beautiful print of the sun slashing her fiery rays across a stormy sea, and turned to speak to...

Nobody.

Torin was gone. Gasping, Sorcha sat up and clasped her shirt to her naked chest, a trickle of sweat slipping down her back. Had she imagined the whole encounter? Her mind scrambled to make sense of the last few hours, for everything in her screamed that her meeting with Torin had been real.

Heat spread along her palm, to the point of pain, and a deep-rooted urge compelled Sorcha to open her hand. When a single flicker of flame, no larger than that from a small candle, winked to life and hovered over her palm, Sorcha closed her eyes against the panic that threatened.

Had she danced with the wrong man that night?

1

THE SIGHT of Mother Jones Flea Market always made Sorcha's heart sing. When she had time, she loved nothing more than an afternoon filled with digging through stalls to find a curious trinket or a vintage outfit to be used in her act. With her schedule, Sorcha found she only made her way through Cork about once a month these days, but she always made time for a stop at Mother Jones. A smattering of cheerful posies framed the dark blue entryway, and familiar excitement welled as she entered the building. The scent of cedar mixed with vanilla from a candle burning cheerfully on the front counter hung in the air, and Sorcha beamed at one of the regulars who worked there.

"Hi, Sorcha. Have a new gig you're working then?"

"Hiya, Talia. I've got a wedding booked for later tonight. But I *am* working on a new routine. I'm not sure what I want to add to it yet...but I'm thinking either a hoop or a baton..." Sorcha pursed her lips and tilted her head as she thought about it. Idly, she reached out and ran her hand over a wool scarf that hung around the neck of a fake stuffed sheep.

"And you'll be lighting a perfectly good piece of art on fire? Is that what I'm hearing?" Talia mock glared at her.

"No, no...I promise. I would never light a vintage piece on fire." Sorcha raised a hand as though she was taking an oath. "I'm thinking more for the acrobatics side of things. Tonight, I'll be working with fire but also doing various poses...I believe in a life-size martini glass? I have to scope it out when I get there. They wanted a circus-themed wedding. Something about how the last moment the bride had with her father was at the circus. I believe it's their way of incorporating him in their special day."

"Well, that certainly sounds fun now, doesn't it then? Imagine that..." Talia shook her head. "A circus wedding."

"I'm happy so long as I get paid," Sorcha chuckled. "But I do like performing at weddings as the mood is generally a pretty happy one."

"Well, a fresh lot just came in yesterday and was unpacked this morning. I haven't gotten around to categorizing it all yet, but a few of the sellers are wandering around and placing their bits and pieces in their stalls. Let me know if you find a showstopper in there – I'd love to see what your ideas for it are."

"Sure, and I'll do that. I have a good feeling about today." Sorcha rubbed her hands together in anticipation. Thrifting was a sport to her, and a steady hum of adrenaline filled her as she began to wander the narrow rows among the stalls. The market was set up so that individual sellers could each have their own space to showcase their wares, and it created a jumbled – and happy, in Sorcha's opinion – space filled with all sorts of treasures.

"No way," Sorcha breathed, bounding to a clothing rack. A sequined motorcycle jacket hung on a padded hanger, and Sorcha immediately slipped her purse and her coat off and dropped them unceremoniously on the floor. She slid her arms into the sleeves of the jacket and turned to stand in front of a dusty full-length mirror. The jacket fit her almost perfectly, though the arms were a little slouchy. Sorcha shoved the sleeves up, rolling them a bit, and turned back and forth to study it from various angles. Rose-gold sequins covered the sleeves and the back of the jacket, and the trim was made of worn grey leather. Sorcha fluffed out her hair – still the brilliant cherry red from the dye job she'd done herself – and studied her reflection. She was a tiny thing, with nary an ounce of extra fat on her due to long days of dance and acrobatics training. If she cut her hair short, Sorcha was certain she'd pass for a boy. Straight up and down, with the smallest hint of curve at the waist, Sorcha was slim, all muscle, and always bouncing on her heels. Energy always seemed to crackle through her, and she greeted life with enthusiasm and a smile, doing her best to bury the tough parts that would steal her joy.

"I wouldn't normally go with this pink color with my hair…" Sorcha said out loud.

"It works," Talia called to her, sealing Sorcha's decision. With a peek at the price tag, the heavily discounted coat was quickly added to her bag. Thrilled with the find, though she hadn't gone in to look for jackets, Sorcha grabbed her coat and purse from the floor and wandered to the back of the market where the doors to the storage room were. There, several people milled about, cutting open boxes and unwrapping items.

"*Banphrionsa.*"

Sorcha turned at the words, a ripple of awareness moving across her skin, her pulse kicking up. She'd never learned Irish, skipping out on the summer classes that her sisters had attended, so the meaning of the word was lost on her. A man stood in a shadowy corner, by a stack of half unpacked boxes, wearing a woven emerald-green cloak. Perhaps this man was a gamer, for his getup had a live action roleplay feel to it. He looked like he was about to embark upon an epic quest, and Sorcha's lips curved. She truly loved weird people, and proudly categorized herself as one, so she was more than happy to wander to his area.

"I didn't catch what you said, sir." Sorcha tilted her head, trying to see the man's face, but his hood was pulled so low that she could only catch a glint of silvery eyes. The items on the table beside him didn't seem to match his vibe, and Sorcha squinted at the rose-patterned tea set on the antique side table.

"A gift."

Looking back up, Sorcha's mouth dropped open at the staff the man held out to her. Excitement thrummed through her as she reached for the staff...or was it a walking stick? No, it was definitely a staff – like the one a wizard would brandish high up on a mountain cliff as he over-looked his village far below. Intricately carved with stunning Celtic knot-work, the top showcased a worn gold heart the size of her hand, which also incorporated the same delicate knot-work design. Sorcha's mouth went dry.

She *needed* this staff. Already her mind was bouncing ahead to all the ways she could use it in her performances, and the heart at the top would be particularly nice for when she was performing at weddings. Yes, this was exactly the item she'd been looking for today, and her smile widened.

"Absolutely brilliant. What a beautiful staff. How much is it? Is it quite expensive? I suppose it must be for this craftsmanship." Sorcha pressed her lips together as her hands closed around the staff. Two things happened simultaneously – the lights blinked out and heat raced up Sorcha's arm as though she had put her hand on an electric fence. Okay, perhaps that was a bit dramatic as she didn't go flying across the room or anything like that, but she did get a sharp shock.

"Och," Sorcha said, transferring the staff to her other hand. She shook her palm. "Sure, and that's some nasty static electricity here." Voices rose across the room and Sorcha blinked in surprise when the light returned. The man in the green cloak was gone.

"Well now, where'd he get on to? I didn't even hear him leave." Sorcha looked over her shoulder to scan the room. A few people glanced around in confusion before returning to unpacking the boxes. Unsure if she should put the staff back, or if she should take it with her, Sorcha paused and considered.

She leaned the staff against the table and let go of it – deciding that she would go ask Talia about this seller. However, the minute she turned, she was hit with a wave of dread so awful, that her stomach twisted, and she held a hand to her mouth for fear of vomiting. Turning back, she eyed the staff. Taking a step closer, Sorcha noticed the sickening feeling lessened. When she reached out and trailed a finger over the intricate carvings, the sick feeling dissipated completely.

"Right, then." Sorcha closed her eyes and steadied her breathing. The last man to disappear in front of her had forever changed her life – opening her mind to new worlds and possibilities – and now she wondered if this was connected to her chance meeting with Torin.

She still dreamed of him.

As time passed, Sorcha's dreams about Torin had inten-

sified, instead of lessening, to the point where either she
looked forward to sleep each night to see him once more or
she drank herself into oblivion to escape the clutches this
man had on her heart. The dreams were...well, it was like
she was being wooed in real time. They picnicked together,
they spoke of their interests, they traveled, they danced in
dimly lit night clubs. It was as though she knew this man –
what made him laugh, what made him wince, what
annoyed him...and yet, he *wasn't* real. Not really. Because
she couldn't find him, could she? Which was why some
nights, she drank just a little too much so that she could
escape Torin's visits in her dreams. Not only had he master-
fully seduced her in a way that no other had, but he'd left
her with an ability that she'd yet to find an explanation for.
Even now, holding this staff, Sorcha could feel the thrum of
power cascade through her body – like an inner river of
light – and she'd honed her skill over the past two years to
be able to produce fire at will.

It still astounded her, but this newfound ability had also
served to make her one of the most sought-after performing
artists in Ireland. Sorcha was careful not to reveal her gift or
her curse...depending on how one looked at it. But after
coming to terms with having, well, *magick*, she'd quickly
decided to use it to her advantage.

"That's a beauty, isn't it then?"

She jumped as Talia spoke from behind her.

"It is. The seller is an odd fellow, isn't he then? What
with the cloak and all?" Sorcha turned, staff in hand.

"Not sure who you're meaning, doll. But I'll ring it up for
you. I'm certain we've got a record of it somewhere."

"He told me it was a gift." Sorcha surprised herself with
her words. She was honest to a fault, never wanting to take
advantage of someone. But she knew that she wouldn't be

able to afford the price on this staff, and it absolutely needed to be leaving the shop with her today.

"Did he? Well, isn't that generous?" Talia shrugged. "Well, let's mark it down anyway and I'll get your phone number just in case there's any issues, yeah?"

"Sure and that's grand. I was surprised myself," Sorcha admitted, carrying the staff to the front of the flea market. Even when she leaned it against the counter to dig in her bag for the sequined jacket, Sorcha found she didn't like taking her hands off the cane.

"That jacket is to die for. Great finds today." Talia pulled out a notebook and made a few notes before tapping away at the computer. "I don't see a listing for the staff, or frankly, a seller's name. But that sometimes happens when we get a fresh lot of items in. Can I grab your phone number?"

Sorcha hesitated, surprised that she wanted to give a fake number, but then forced herself to give the right phone number. She wasn't a liar, and if this belonged to someone else, well, that was just the way of things. She'd have to accept it. But for now? It was coming back to Betty Blue with her.

"What will you do with the stick? Twirl it like a baton?" Talia asked, after she'd given the change to Sorcha.

"I'm not yet sure, to be honest. It's just too pretty to resist though, isn't it? I'm thinking I'll have to watch some videos of dancers with a cane and see if I can incorporate it."

"Is that what you do then? To get new ideas?"

"Oh, for sure. I YouTube everything. There's so much history in dance and performing arts. Remember, there's no new story lines – not really. They're just told in different ways. It's the same with dance and performance. I look to the past and then put my own spin on it."

"Well, it sounds fab. Have fun!" Someone called to Talia

from the back of the market, and she scurried away with a little goodbye wave for Sorcha. Sorcha grabbed the staff and all but ran from the market, feeling both elated and nervous over her find.

A part of her heart – the part she tried to ignore – hoped that maybe it was a gift from Torin. A man whom she'd never really gotten over – and one that she still searched for.

One day she'd find him again – and, when she did – he'd have some explaining to do.

2

"DONAL, I don't have time for this. We're needed. The Fire Fae are revolting, and we have to figure out why before they torch all of Ireland."

"Sure and we have a bit of time for fun now, don't we?" Donal, Torin's right-hand man flashed a grin from around a thin cigarillo. The acrid smoke hovered in the air, heavy with the promise of rain, and the lingering threads of twilight cast a warm glow over the arched red door of the pub. Torin had found Donal there, regaling the locals with tall tales, and making eyes at more than one pretty lady who'd wandered through the doors. Torin's impatience grew as he waited his friend out, knowing full well that he needed Donal's support in subduing the Fire Fae.

"Fun? You've been having fun for weeks now. I've barely had a minute with you in months. I can't say you've been particularly on point with your duties, either."

Wounded, Donal brought a hand to his heart, but the cheeky glimmer in his eyes showed Torin he wasn't too bothered about the criticism.

"You're always on about 'duty this' and 'duty that' – when do you ever relax?"

"When the world isn't burning down around us?" Torin threw up his hands. "Sure and you know that I'm always up for a bit of a party when I can. But now's not the time. I need your help, Donal. The Domnua are near, and they are stirring up trouble with all the Elemental Fae. I don't think this is the time to be treading lightly."

"So? Go on, then." Donal shrugged, and dropped his cigarillo to the ground, tamping it out with the sole of his leather boot.

"What's with you lately?" Torin asked. As Royal Court Advisor to the Fire Fae, Torin was in charge of overseeing all aspects of the Fire Fae's world, making sure they followed the rules set forth for the Elementals by the Danula, while also ensuring their needs were met and provided for. In doing so, the Danula Fae were able to keep a healthy balance to the natural order of the world and the humans were none the wiser for it.

Until the Domnua, also known as the Dark Fae, had decided to crawl out from their pitiful realm and cause trouble. Now Torin was faced with making sure the Fire Fae didn't switch allegiances from his people to the Dark Fae, and – oh right – stop them from burning down Ireland in the process. Donal was almost as powerful as Torin, though he lacked some accuracy in his magicks, and had proven through the years to be an adept and helpful addition to his team. But lately? He'd been gone more often than not, and Torin had allowed the absences because he understood that everyone needed to blow off steam from time to time.

"Don't you ever get tired of being at the beck and call of the queen?" Donal surprised Torin by asking.

Torin studied his friend, sensing something deeper

lurking beneath the question, and took his time answering. Leaning back against the stone wall of the pub, Torin glanced up as a few fat drops of rain splattered to the street in front of him. Relief filled him as he scanned the murky clouds that hung low on the horizon. The Fire Fae, while magick, still couldn't break the rules of Elemental Law. Which meant that a solid rain would put out many of the small fires they'd begun in protest just that morning. If they continued to light fires in protest, Torin would be forced to call on Nolan, the leader of the Water Fae, in a counterattack, and soon they'd have an all-out Elemental war on their hands.

Which is exactly what the Dark Fae wanted, Torin mused. It was just their style. Create chaos, wreak havoc, and in the middle of said confusion, make a play for power. The Danula needed to stop this uprising before it exploded into something that the Goddesses would weep over.

"She is chosen by the Goddess Danu to lead our people and she does so with a firm and fair hand," Torin said, returning to the conversation.

"Sisters." Donal made a small tsking noise with his mouth, before drawing his eyes up to the sky. "So much fighting because two sisters couldn't get along."

Torin raised an eyebrow at that. The complicated history of Goddess Domnu and Goddess Danu was rife with legends, betrayal, and centuries-old curses that were forged in the beginnings of their worlds. To sum it up as something so simple as two sisters having an argument was...well, it was concerning to say the least.

"Goddess Danu has shown herself time and again to be on the side of the light. She wants our people to thrive, as well as to protect the humans from the harm that could come to them if the Dark Fae infiltrate this world. She trusts us with enforcing that the natural balance of both worlds is not upset or used for evil. Think how many lives have been saved because of Danu and the Danula Fae who follow her."

"Maybe it would have been wiser to just let everyone fight it out and fend for themselves." Donal straightened, and pulled another cigarillo from a small leather pouch, glancing around before lighting it with a small flame from the tip of his finger. He shot Torin a devilish look. "You know...survival of the fittest and all."

Torin released the breath he'd been holding, seeing now that Donal was just winding him up a bit.

"Maybe. I, for one, am grateful that is not how it has played out. We've lived a nice life, relatively free of dark days, and I can't say that would be the same if the Dark Fae roamed freely here, as they wish to do." Torin circled a finger in the air at the street. "While we find humans endlessly entertaining and resilient, I fear the Dark Fae do not. And then where would you be without the pretty lass with the wistful eyes who was smiling at you this evening?"

"Sure and that's a point in our favor now, isn't it? The ability to come here at will when we like," Donal grinned.

"Not all of us, as you know the Fae can become addicted to humans. But enough of us slip through to monitor the way of things. The Dark Fae do as well. We need to find their portals, but they move them so frequently."

"Look..." Donal raised his chin at where a stream of cars pulled into a parking lot across the street. People got out and, with a glance to the sky, raced inside, as laughter and shouts carried on the wind to them. "It's a wedding. The blonde lass with the mournful eyes is singing at it tonight. Shall we go? I do love a good party."

"Donal. We're needed..." Torin trailed off as the skies opened and rain exploded from the clouds in an outpouring that could only be described as violent – or exuberant – depending on how one thought about rain. Torin would choose exuberant, because that was exactly how he felt, knowing that the rain would quench the fires that the Fire Fae had set in protest.

"Come on, mate. I need this. One night of fun and then I'm all yours. I'll go with you to talk the Fire Fae down. You know they love me and I'm sure that whatever is upsetting them is something that can be remedied easily."

Duty warred with friendship, and Torin paused as he thought it over. It had been a while since he and Donal had spent any real time together, let alone a night where they weren't discussing anything that had to do with their royal duties. They'd been friends longer than he'd been a Royal Court Advisor, and there was something to be said for that deep-rooted bond. Because Donal hadn't been as present as of late, and had seemed a touch off, Torin decided that tonight friendship would win out. If anything, it would make their royal duties easier moving forward if he could reconnect with Donal and strengthen their bond once more.

"Alright, mate. One night. Let's have ourselves a pint or three and maybe you'll get the moody-eyed one to sing just for you." Torin slung an arm around Donal's shoulders, relieved to see a genuine grin widen his friend's face.

"It's not me who has trouble making the ladies sing," Donal elbowed Torin in the side and Torin fake doubled-over before darting with Donal through the rain. Laughing, Torin cloaked them in Fae magick as they slipped through the doors and into a large reception room decorated with thousands of string lights, dangling metal discs, and minia-ture disco balls that caused light to dance across the room in an almost dizzying array of sparkle.

"It's amazing what the humans can do without magick," Torin said.

"Right? Their ingenuity is fascinating to me. A whiskey for us then?" Donal spied the bar.

"Let's." Torin followed Donal through the throngs of people who were moving around the room, finding tables, and grabbing food from waiters passing by with trays in their hands. The mood was lively, as befitted a wedding, and more than one woman gave Torin an appreciative smile which he ignored. Donal could have the lasses tonight, as Torin didn't really have the time nor inclination for women in his life at the moment – not when the Dark Fae were stirring up trouble. But, if he was being honest with himself, something he rarely tried to do and was relegated to the deep hours of the night after several rounds of whiskey, only one woman would do for him.

Sorcha.

Her name alone caused heat to throb through his veins. He'd left her that morning – that fated night sealing their bond – not out of callousness but out of sheer self-preservation. Torin had been wholly and thoroughly unprepared for what had transpired between them. Since then, he'd searched for her, often hearing her song call to him in his dreams but had never been able to find her when awake. That also annoyed him. Torin had strong magick and tracking a human – particularly one he'd claimed – should have been no issue for him. And yet. Sorcha must not have wanted to be found.

The single fact that he couldn't find her after all this time made Torin think that perhaps Sorcha wasn't human like he'd first thought. Perhaps she, too, danced in another realm and evaded him with ease due to her own powers. He had questions, and someday, Sorcha would provide answers.

In the time since, however, his attraction for other women had become all but obsolete, and Torin had been with no other women since her. Not that he'd tell Donal that particular fact, or he'd be the brunt of his jokes all night.

Humans had a tendency to naturally gravitate toward a Fae, whether they were aware of the Fae being a magickal being or not. Most weren't, as the Fae didn't reveal themselves lightly, and instead the humans were granted a night of passion they'd remember forever. In some ways, Torin likened it to cats pouncing on toys with catnip inside of them. There was something about Fae magick that entranced the humans, and Torin would be lying if he said he hadn't enjoyed the benefits of that a time or two in the past.

"One for down the hatch, one for mingling…" Donal held up a glass of honey-colored liquid to Torin. They tapped their glasses.

"Sláinte," Torin said.

"What is the folly of humans that they toast to their health while they drink poison?" Donal asked. Alcohol had a different effect on the Fae. While they enjoyed the benefits of it, rarely would it cause extreme drunkenness and their bodies were better suited to processing the toxin than humans.

"I suppose it is the same as those who dance while the world is burning…" Torin shot Donal a heavy look, but his friend merely threw his head back and laughed.

"Och, mate, we need to find you a lady tonight. You're wound too tightly. Let's mingle."

Torin replaced the empty glass with a full, smiling his thanks at the bartender, and followed Donal as the first notes of music filled the hall. A cheer rose as the bride and groom walked out onto the dance floor, the bride in a cotton-candy poof of a dress, her joy evident on her pretty face. Something about the way the groom looked at his bride tugged at Torin's heart, and he turned away, uncomfortable with this display of affection. It wasn't love he sought anymore, it was relief from the dreams that plagued him. If he couldn't have Sorcha, at the very least, a good night's sleep would do. Instead, she invaded his dreams each night, leaving him aching each morning, and he had grown bitter toward the possibility of new love.

An hour later, even Torin had to admit that the couple's happiness was infectious. Almost the entire party had stayed on the dance floor, and even though he wasn't inclined to take a lady home with him that evening, Torin had danced with almost every woman in attendance. He loved to dance, as did most Fae, the beat of the music moving through him so naturally that he barely had to think about his next step as he did his best to keep up with Donal who fed him a steady stream of drinks. The night had taken on a warm glow, and the hanging lights sparkled over the crowd when the music stopped.

"And for a special surprise..." The band leader's voice fell away. Time slowed. A shiver of awareness rippled across Torin's skin, and his gaze narrowed onto the one thing he ached for but could not have. Until now.

Sorcha.

She walked confidently onto the stage, as though she was born for it, an inviting smile on her lustrous face. Light exploded from her, reflecting off her sequined costume, and her flame-red hair dropped in long coils down her back. She looked like a candle that had lit itself. She needed no man to give her light – for she was her own flame. Torin was halfway across the room before he even realized he was moving.

Her words at the microphone were lost to the thrumming in his ears, and he only stopped when Donal moved in front of him, his friend's face filled with awe.

"She's magnificent," Donal said and Torin's lip curled.

"You'll not touch her." It was but a whisper and lost to the music that swelled in the room as Sorcha stepped forward and performed a complicated dance maneuver with a large hoop before swinging herself inside of it. The crowd gasped as Sorcha whirled on stage, a spinning delight of sparkles and elegance, and when the hoop erupted in fire the crowd gasped. Still, she twirled, her lithe body hung suspended in an endless loop of flames and flashing sequins, and Torin couldn't pull his eyes away. She was everything. His madness. His future.

His fated mate.

Torin barely restrained himself from jumping on stage and carrying her away that instant. Ignoring Donal, he wound his way around the dance floor and through a small side door that led to the back of the stage. He needed to speak with her as much as he needed his next breath, and Torin couldn't be sure how she would react when she saw him.

He owed her an explanation. One he wasn't sure he even knew how to give.

Sorcha swung through the curtains, a smile lingering at her lips, sweat caressing her brow. Her mouth dropped open when she saw him.

"Torin," Sorcha gasped.

"Wife." Torin shocked them both by saying. Wife? Where had that come from? Mentally kicking himself, Torin made to step forward as confusion slid across Sorcha's stunning face.

A scream tore through the crowd as Donal burst through the stage door.

"Domnua," Donal panted, his eyes landing on Sorcha. A gleam entered Donal's eyes, causing the hair at Torin's neck to stand up, and he stepped in front of Sorcha.

"Go. We must protect the humans."

"And what of this one?" Donal's eyes were still trained over Torin's shoulder on Sorcha.

"I've got her." Torin's voice held a warning, one which Donal heeded, before disappearing through the same door which he'd first come through.

"Fire!" Another scream from the crowd, and Torin turned to grab Sorcha and drag her to safety.

Her hoop lay on the floor, a few rogue sequins from her costume glinting in the dim light, the space where she once stood now empty.

3

IT WAS ONLY INSTINCT that had Sorcha turning and running at the first screams, for if she had allowed her brain – or her heart – to catch up, she'd have been frozen to the spot.

Torin.

The shock of seeing him once again, after countless nights of dreaming of him, his taste still fresh on her lips, had caused her heart to spill open. Desperate with need, she'd wanted nothing more than to cross to him and throw herself in his arms. It was as though an invisible thread connected the two, and the force with which she wanted him stopped her from crossing to him. That and the complete pandemonium that erupted in the reception hall.

What was he doing here?

Sorcha dashed into the crowd instead of away from the building, following her natural instinct to help others. She coughed against a wall of smoke that hit her, thick and vile, and automatically she covered her mouth with her hand. Sweat dripped down her brow and her eyes widened at the sight that greeted her.

The curtains of the stage she'd just performed on raged

with flames, and one side had already dropped to the stage, covering the band equipment and causing a loud pop to shake the room as sparks flew from an exposed electrical cord. The crowd was cut in half, clustered around the exits, and several people shouted for calm as people rushed to escape the inferno. Tears flooded Sorcha's eyes as she scanned the room searching for anyone left who might need help.

They would think this was her fault.

She'd been the one to use flames on stage, hadn't she? It was the only explanation, and likely a viable one. Though Sorcha was exceedingly careful when performing with fire, who was to say if a rogue spark had landed upon the curtains? There was no other explanation really, and fear gripped Sorcha as she simultaneously realized two things.

Her career was over.

And evil was near.

Her lungs seized as she gasped for another breath through the smoke, but she couldn't tear her eyes away from where sinuous silvery beings slid through the crowd, hunting for all intents and purposes, knocking over tables and grabbing terrified humans before tossing them aside like bags of trash. Sorcha gasped as one woman skidded across the floor and banged her head against the bar, going limp. Without another thought, Sorcha raced past the silvery beings and crouched to where the woman lay huddled on the floor.

"You have to get up," Sorcha gasped, shaking the woman's shoulder. Turning the woman, Sorcha gasped to see she was easily eighty years old, and blood trickled from a cut on her forehead. The woman moaned, blinking up at her, and Sorcha did the only thing she could do. Crouching, she gathered the woman into a fireman's hold and pulled her over her shoulder. Many people underestimated Sorcha's strength, because she was just a little thing. But years of training had filled her slim body with sleek muscles, and she used those to her advantage now, hurrying to the door with the woman over her shoulder.

By some stroke of luck, she made it through the now empty doors and into blessedly cool night air, where people huddled in groups in the parking lot.

"Gram!"

This, a shout from the bride, and soon Sorcha felt the weight of the woman removed from her shoulders. Straightening, she gasped, welcoming the night air like a soothing balm into her burning lungs.

"You saved her." The bride wept openly in front of Sorcha as a group carried the woman away.

"I couldn't leave her. I need to..." Sorcha struggled with her words, glancing back to the reception hall. She took a few more shaky deep breaths. "I have to go see...to make sure..."

"You can't be going back in." The bride grasped her arm. "That's madness."

"I have to make sure that nobody else..."

"You can't. You'll die."

"But what if I...if it's my..." Sorcha couldn't even say the words, but the bride saw the pain in her eyes.

"It's an accident. The fire brigade is almost here. Listen to the sirens..."

"I'm sorry. I can't stay. I have to know." Sorcha wrenched her arm from the bride's grasp and raced back inside, ignoring the shouts of warning behind her. She'd never live with herself if someone were to die this night because of her own mistakes. Grabbing a napkin from a table by the door, Sorcha doused it in a pitcher of water and tied the dripping fabric over the bottom half of her face. She dropped in a crouch to the floor of the smoke-filled room to try and see any bodies that might be lying on the floor. Slowly, she crab-crawled across the room, trying to see under the tables, hoping not to spot anyone else left behind.

"Oh!" Sorcha exclaimed as the sprinkler system kicked in, water exploding from the ceiling, instantly drenching her as sirens wailed. Had it only been minutes since she'd run from the stage? Either there was a delay in the fire safety system, or the seconds had felt like hours. Straightening, Sorcha wiped at the water that blasted her face as she tried to make sense of what was happening on the dance floor.

A group of men – the same men who had darted through the crowd – surrounded Torin. Fear clutched Sorcha, its icy claws digging in her gut, and she moved to take a step forward when an arm circled her waist. Turning to wrench herself away, Sorcha froze when the arm tightened, and a hand covered her mouth tightly.

"Shh, darling. You'll distract him."

Sorcha slid her eyes to the face that hovered near hers. It was the man who had burst onto the stage seconds before she'd registered that the room was on fire. Torin had spoken to him as a friend, hadn't he? She relaxed slightly, understanding his words to be true. Sorcha knew as well as any how the slightest distraction – or miscalculation – could result in injury. It was why she forced herself to train in a room full of other athletes, teaching herself a level of focus that wouldn't allow for mistakes.

Mistakes like lighting a wedding on fire.

Her gut churned, sickness rising in her throat, as the oddly glowing men circled Torin. What was this trick of the eyes that made them glow that way? Was it the smoke that still hung heavy in the air? Sorcha stiffened when one man darted forward and Torin caught him in the side with a dagger, already moving forward to handle the next man who jumped at him. It was a fluid and effortless dance, or so it seemed to Sorcha, as Torin dodged blow after blow, twisting and turning so that his knife did more damage than she'd ever seen before. She choked against the man's hand, trying to pull her face aside so she could drag more air into her screaming lungs. The men...their blood.

Their blood was silver.

Surely she was hallucinating by now – an aftereffect of smoke inhalation perhaps – as the men would explode in bursts of silver liquid when Torin impaled them. She must have inhaled more smoke than she'd realized, as surely her mind was playing tricks on her. There was no way a man would just disintegrate on sight, not from a single blow to the body, which meant...

A warning cry had her eyes darting to the left, where a slew of silvery men poured from the backstage door.

"No, no, no," Sorcha gasped, finally managing to wrench her mouth away from the man's hand. "He'll be killed. There's too many."

"Maybe. Maybe not. He's got strong magick, our Torin."

Magick. The words landed dully in her mind, as though her brain was fuzzy from sleep and still trying to decipher dreams from reality. A shiver of anticipation rippled through her as the man's words fully registered and she remembered Torin's comment before all hell had broken loose.

Wife. He'd called her his wife. The surprise on his face had likely mirrored her own, and now Sorcha's mind scrambled to keep up with the pandemonium that erupted in front of her as well as the implication of what the man holding her had just said. She wished she could process all of this at her own pace, because it was as though her brain had locked up, refusing to accept, refusing to move forward, so all she could do was stare at the battle that raged between one man and hundreds of...

"What are you?" Sorcha whispered.

"You don't know? I'm surprised by that, darling. We're Fae, of course."

Fae.

The truth of it slammed into Sorcha so hard that little spots danced in front of her eyes, and she had to force herself to take shallow breaths to calm her racing heart.

"Though she be but little, she is fierce." Sorcha whispered her favorite Shakespeare quote to herself, a phrase she'd contemplated getting tattooed on her wrist. The words calmed her, forcing her to take stock of the situation. Panic wouldn't save her this day, but her own street smarts could. "We need to help him."

"I don't think he'll need it. Maybe. We'll see how this plays out." The man seemed wholly unconcerned about the possibility that his friend might get hurt.

"Who are you?"

"I'm Donal, Torin's fellow advisor. We're Royals, well, he's Head Advisor to the Fire Fae."

"The...Fire..." Sorcha's words were but a whisper as she looked down at her own hands. Fire. Torin had gifted her with fire the night they'd been together. Never once had she considered using her newfound power to harm another, but now she might. Her teeth clamped as the new wave of silver men...well, Fae, she guessed, surrounded Torin and attacked. This time, he didn't rely upon his dagger, instead unleashing a wave of magick that disintegrated the inner circle immediately in an explosion of silvery blood.

"Why didn't he do that before?" Sorcha demanded.

"Magick requires a give and take. When you pull from the universe, you have to be careful how much you use and how often. It can upset the balance of things."

"But...if it's necessary?" Sorcha pressed her lips together, worry for Torin filling her.

"Who gets to say what is necessary? What is just? Do you think the Dark Fae don't have families? Don't know how to love?"

"I can't say, as until about a minute ago I didn't know any Fae existed, let alone all different kinds."

"That's foolish of you," Donal said, causing Sorcha to snap her head around and meet his dark eyes.

"How so?"

"You're Irish, aren't you? It's not uncommon for talk of the Fae to run through Irish stories."

"Myths," Sorcha insisted, turning back to where Torin blasted through another wave of Dark Fae. "They were supposed to be just myths."

"There's always truth in legends, darling."

The way he called her darling sent a shiver through Sorcha and she moved to step away, but his arm stayed tight at her waist.

"Let me go. I'm over my initial shock."

"You're safer here."

"You should be helping him. We both should be." Sorcha tugged at his arm, but it was like a vice across her waist. Fury at being restrained rippled through her and Sorcha reached for the power that hummed through her. Closing her palms around his arms, for the first time ever, she used her power to harm.

"Damn it." Donal dropped his arms and Sorcha darted away, putting space between them. Sirens sounded from outside as the Fire Brigade arrived and shouts from the parking lot carried as the doors to outside opened.

The Dark Fae turned in unison, the shouts alerting them to humans, and their gazes landed on Sorcha at once. She could feel the moment they shifted their intentions, moving as though they were of one mind, bearing down upon her. Sorcha lifted her arms, calling upon her power once more, only to gasp when she was grabbed from behind.

"Donal! Protect her!" Torin yelled over the din of commotion and the shouts of the Fire Brigade, as the Dark Fae advanced.

But Donal did nothing, instead allowing the Dark Fae to swirl around them, surrounding them. As one, the circle of silvery men turned their backs to Sorcha, looking out to Torin, and a sickening feeling filled her stomach as she realized what was happening.

"Torin. *Run.*" Sorcha didn't know if she screamed it with her mind or out loud, but Torin heard her. For a second, she saw the pain of betrayal flash across his face as he looked over her shoulder at Donal before disappearing into thin air as the Dark Fae sent a wave of magick across the reception hall, shattering glasses and splintering tables.

"Why?" Sorcha demanded, raising her hands, but a strange sucking sensation pulled at her body. Dizziness overwhelmed her, and then she knew no more.

4

SORCHA CAME TO WITH A SPUTTER, gasping for air, her lungs burning from the smoke she'd inhaled earlier. Instantly, she tried to jump to her feet only to find her arms and legs bound. She schooled her breathing, another wave of dizziness threatening her sight, and closed her eyes while she tried to process her surroundings. Somehow, she'd been transported from the reception hall to a cave of sorts. The rough edges of a damp rock wall pressed into her back, and the smell of musty earth mixed with smoke from a small fire in the corner hung in the air. There had to be an opening, Sorcha guessed, as the smoke from the fire wasn't overwhelming.

Which meant she had at least one way out...if she could remove the restraints. Sorcha kept her eyes closed for a moment longer, knowing she'd need her strength, and forced herself to calm her pounding heart. Panic wouldn't help her now, and she needed a clear mind to try and figure out what to do. The problem was...there was just *so* much to process.

The Fae *were* real.

There were good *and* bad Fae.

She'd been kidnapped.

Torin – a man she dreamed relentlessly about – was Fae. He was alive. He was in this world. And somehow, he'd given her power. Fae magick. *She* held Fae magick. The last thought caused a warm trickle of excitement to slide through her. Sure, she'd been learning to use this strange gift that Torin had given her, but she'd never been able to fully understand just what had occurred during the intensity of their lovemaking. Had Torin given her the power to make fire? Or had he unlocked something deep inside of her that brought forth *her* own unknown ability to create fire at will? Over the past months, Sorcha had sought out books and research that might lead her closer to an answer, but there had been nothing definitive for her to go on.

And she certainly couldn't tell anyone her secret. It was almost unimaginable, bringing something like that up over a pint at the pub. She'd been close to telling one of her sisters about it, but at the last moment something had stopped her from revealing her truth. There was no telling the response she'd get, and until she could better understand what had happened to her, Sorcha had kept her secret safe.

Only to have her world blown open in one very catastrophic evening. Sorcha dearly hoped that nobody had been seriously injured in the fire, though she was certain she'd scanned enough of the room to make sure that nobody else had been trapped there. Except Torin.

The look on his face when Donal had betrayed him... Sorcha's stomach twisted. Pain, sharp and searing, had flashed through his eyes before he'd disappeared from sight in some magickal way. Was that what had happened to her when she'd felt that strange sucking sensation? Had she also been transported in some weird Fae magickal way that she couldn't begin to understand?

"I know you're awake."

"I wasn't trying to hide that fact," Sorcha bit out, keeping her eyes closed as she took a few more deep breaths. It was a tactic she used to center herself before a performance as it helped her to clear her mind. Distractions were not welcome, particularly when working with fire.

"What are you doing then?" Donal asked.

"My lungs hurt from the smoke. I'm just catching my breath." A thought occurred to her, and she blinked her eyes open to look at where Donal crouched in the corner by the fire. He was a strong man, of sinewy build, with dark close-cropped hair and obsidian eyes. His face was all angles, with a cleft in the chin, and his mouth formed a small V when he smiled at her. "The fire wasn't my fault, was it?"

"No, darling. It was not. However, it was an easy enough diversion and so we used it to our advantage."

"We?" Sorcha asked. Relief pierced her, and Sorcha was happy to know that it wasn't her own mistake that had caused the fire to happen. She could still trust herself to perform. That being said...who would believe it wasn't her after this? It wasn't like she'd be able to tell the world that the Fae had set the fire – not without being laughed at.

"The Domnua and I."

Sorcha just shook her head at Donal, radiating confusion. He whispered something into the fire, and it grew larger, and a trickle of fear slipped through her.

"The Domnua are the Dark Fae. Although I don't know that we should really relegate things to dark and light, now, should we? If anything, most things in life are shades of grey, right?" Donal quirked that V smile at her again. "However, for ease of explanation, we'll call them the Evil Fae."

"And you and Torin are a part of the Evil Fae?" That thought didn't sit well with Sorcha, and she glanced down at her bound arms, resting on her sequined lap, and hoped she didn't carry dark magick in her now.

Donal threw his head back and laughed, using a long gold stick to poke at the fire.

"No, Torin is Danula. The Good Fae." Donal made quotation marks with his fingers. "The Good Fae oversee the Elemental Fae which are their own separate factions of Fae. It's basically like different cities all existing together in a country. Each city has someone who oversees things and makes sure the rules are followed and the needs of the people in the city are being met. That's what Torin does for the Fire Fae. He's part of the Royal Court of the Danula. As am I, actually. I work with him to make sure the Fire Fae's needs are met."

"And the...bad Fae?" Sorcha couldn't remember their name.

"The Evil Fae have been unfairly banished to a different realm and don't get to hang out in the country with the rest of the Fae." A bitter look hugged Donal's craggy face.

"Sure, and that had to have been warranted, no? You don't just banish an entire population unless something bad happened, right?" Sorcha pulled her ankles apart slightly, testing the ropes.

"It's open to interpretation." Donal shrugged one shoulder. "I always took it as two Goddesses having a fight and then they created this unnecessary split and here we are."

"Goddesses..." Sorcha's gaze darted to Donal.

"Don't you ever read?" Donal made a tsking noise with his mouth.

"I've been too busy trying to make a living. Why don't you bring me up to speed? Seeing as how I'm now involved in whatever this all is...at the very least you could tell me how I got roped into your issues. Because, let me tell you, I'm really not interested in being a part of whatever pissing match you have with the good or bad Fae or whatever."

Appreciation lit in Donal's eyes, and he rocked back on his heels as he studied her.

"I like a woman with spirit. Tell me you like broody men with a dark streak to them?" Donal offered her a sinuous smile and Sorcha shuddered.

"I'm not dating these days, sorry."

"Ah well, perhaps I can change your mind along the way." His grin widened at her look of disgust. "Don't worry, darling. I don't force myself on anyone. What's the fun in that? What you'll give to me – you'll give willingly."

She'd rather walk over broken glass than give herself to Donal, but Sorcha ignored his comment. "So, the goddesses?"

"Right, the Goddess Danu started her own faction of Fae called the Danula who are currently the top power in our little Fae world. Goddess Domnu, her sister, went off with her Dark Fae, and they've been fighting for power and various treasures that hold insurmountable magick for, well, centuries now. This is just the latest of battles. Well, sure and it's not quite a battle yet, now, is it? But it will be. By the time we reach that, the hope is that the Domnua will have stirred up enough discontent with the Elemental Fae that they'll join them in overthrowing the Good Fae."

Sorcha's eyebrows rose. She shifted against the uncomfortable wall, her limbs already stiffening from being tied, and thought about his words.

"But what do the Bad Fae want? Say they do accomplish their uprising or whatever...where will it lead them?" Keep him talking, Sorcha reminded herself. She took another long slow breath, hoping the pain in her lungs would subside soon.

"Power, of course." Donal stood and walked to her, and she flinched when he laid a hand on her chest, directly between her breasts. Her thoughts scattered, and she could only gaze up at him, frozen in place. Something washed through her, like a cool wave, and the ache in her lungs eased. Sorcha blinked at Donal in confusion.

"What...did you just..."

"Yes, I eased your pain for you. You should be able to breathe more easily now." Donal lingered with his hand pressed to her skin, where the deep V of her costume cut between her breasts. When Sorcha didn't react, he removed his hand, winking at her. "As I said...I don't take."

"Thank you," Sorcha whispered, hating that she had to be in debt to him. But her lungs really did feel better. Did this mean he didn't plan to harm her?

"So, as I was saying...power is what the Dark Fae want. You see, it takes quite a bit of their magick to be able to transport between realms and to walk freely in Ireland. This country used to be theirs, you know. When it was Innisfail. Now, we're hunted when we are able to slip through to this world."

"We?" Sorcha asked. He'd just told her he was Torin's right-hand man.

"Of course, darling. I'm not actually part of the Good Fae. I'm Domnua." He grinned at her, and Sorcha winced, remembering Torin's ravaged look.

"Which is why Torin looked..."

"Ah yes, that's unfortunate now, isn't it? He's a good lad, that one. I enjoyed having a pint with him, I won't lie about that. We'd have endless nights carousing in the streets, having our pick of women. You human women do love the Fae. We give you unimaginable pleasure, you know…"

Sorcha's mind flashed back to that night with Torin. Hours of pleasure that never seemed to abate, wave after wave of satisfaction coursing through her body, her skin vibrating like an exposed electrical current.

"Ah, you do know. I suspected as much, when Torin saw you again. That was the night he changed, you know…" Donal tapped a finger to the cleft in his chin. "That makes more sense now."

"Changed how?" Sorcha refused to speak of that night – not to Donal – not to anyone. It was a moment that she relived in her dreams, crystalized in its perfection, and nobody would be allowed to tarnish it for her.

"It used to be us, you see? We were the ones calling the shots. We'd make decisions together, party together, find women together…but after his night with you. No more. Something in him shifted. He kept his own council. Made decisions without me. Didn't go out anymore. I never saw him with a woman again."

The thought shouldn't have pleased Sorcha, because she barely knew Torin, and yet somehow the thought of him staying single warmed her. It hadn't been much different for her, she realized with a start. The few men she'd attempted to be with had fallen flat in comparison to that one night with Torin, and she'd resolved herself to a life of singlehood in lieu of suffering through bad dates.

"So, all of this is because you're mad at Torin? Because you lost your drinking buddy?" Sorcha leveled a look of censure at Donal.

"Ah, well, sure and I wish it was that easy. Alas, I'm not the sentimental sort and Torin was just a tool to be used."

Donal cocked his head as though listening to something she couldn't hear.

"I still don't understand why I'm here. This..." Sorcha raised her bound hands and made a little circling motion in the air. "Fae stuff has nothing to do with me really, does it now? Can't you keep it to yourself and let me be on my way? I want no part of this. You know something that I've learned along my travels?"

"What's that?" Donal was clearly amused with her, which suited Sorcha just fine. If she was entertainment, she could keep him talking and not focused on whatever it was he planned to do next. If she could time things right, she might be able to draw on her own power of fire to break through these ropes and make her way out of...well, wherever they were. One thing at a time.

"Sweep in front of your own door." Sorcha raised her eyes. "Your troubles are your own, Donal, and I don't meddle in other people's business. It never bodes well. The Fae can sort themselves out without involving me. Please let me go."

"I wish it were so easy." Donal cocked his head again and stayed silent a moment, his chin bobbing as though he was having an internal conversation. "But you, much like Torin, have become a useful tool for my purposes."

"I can't imagine how I'd be of any use to you. I'm a simple performer, Donal, with nothing to add to your fight."

"That's where you're wrong, darling. You're a distraction...a lure. Torin's going to have to make a choice now. Come after you or subdue the Fire Fae's uprising. What do you think he'll choose? Love or loyalty to the crown?"

Sorcha's mouth dropped open and then she did something unexpected.

She laughed.

She laughed until tears ran down her face and once more, she was gasping for air. Donal cocked his head at her and came to crouch by her side.

"I amuse you?"

"Oh...sure and you're a dramatic one, aren't you then?" A laugh sputtered from her lips again, and a whisp of irritation passed across Donal's face.

"I'm not sure I'm understanding your meaning then. Dramatic? To perform on stage?"

"No...I'm just..." Another giggle and then Sorcha shook her head. "It's...you're all high and mighty and world is ending and..."

"The world won't be ending. A new world would be beginning. So, the world as you humans know it would be. But for us? It's a birth, not a death."

At that, all humor fled Sorcha's body.

"You honestly believe this, don't you?"

"And you honestly believe that we won't prevail?" Donal shook his head and made that tsking sound again. "Humans are such fools. You can show them something a thousand times and still they'll believe in dreams."

"A life without dreams is an unlived one."

"Ah, now who is the dramatic one?" Donal ran a finger over her cheek.

"Torin won't come for me." Sorcha needed Donal to understand that fact. "We barely know each other. If you think I'm useful bait for whatever your plans are, you're wrong."

"You don't know, do you? What you are to him?" Amusement sparked in Donal's glittery eyes. "Well, now, things just got a little more interesting."

"What do you mean?" Sorcha shifted against the rock pressing into her back, annoyance and frustration making her want to do something – anything – to push back against this man.

"There's no time now. We must move. The portal is ready."

"Excuse me?" Sorcha's eyes widened when Donal stood and grabbed her arm, lifting her into his arms as effortlessly as if she were a stack of books. "Wait...no...where are you taking me?"

"Be quiet. I must focus now."

"But..."

"If you say one more word, you will die."

Sorcha gulped back the words that bubbled up her throat, fear racing through her as Donal strode across the room and...directly toward the fire. Flames surrounded them, the heat unimaginable, and panic replaced fear at the first brush of pain against her skin. A scream rose, caught in her throat, as Donal carried her into the fire.

5

SWEAT DRIPPED DOWN HER BACK, making the sequins of her costume scratch against her skin. Sorcha shifted and tried to pull herself from Donal's arms.

"Be still." It was an order and one which Sorcha immediately followed as she opened her eyes to see that they were not in the middle of a fire, no, they were somewhere else entirely. Somewhere not of this world, Sorcha realized, her pulse kicking up as she blinked up at the red-hued sky. At least she thought it was the sky, but she couldn't be sure. Donal carried her forward, following a curving grey stone path partially enclosed by stone walls on either side. Outside the walls, the hills loomed, but the grass was grey and dark, and the water that kissed the red horizon was black. It was Ireland, Sorcha realized with a start. But as though all the color had been sucked out of the landscape, aside from the odd reddish hue to the sky.

"Where are we?" Sorcha asked as Donal came to a stop at the end of the path and set her on her feet. Sorcha was surprised to find the ropes that bound her wrists were gone, and immediately she stretched out her legs, as she could feel the tension of the day settling into her muscles. Absently, she rubbed her wrists as she looked around, the scent of burnt grass carrying to her on a soft breeze. "Is this the dark realm you spoke of? Is this where your people live?"

"Not quite," Donal said, plopping down on the wall and crossing his arms over his chest as he looked around. "It's an in-between place. A resting spot between realms."

"Why do you need to rest?" Sorcha asked, taking a cautious step away from Donal. Perhaps there would be a way to distract him so that she could run back the way they'd come and through...well, through the fire she supposed...and back to her world.

Her world. A hysterical laugh threatened to escape, her mind still scrambling to keep up with all the new changes she was being forced to process. A part of her desperately wished this was some wild whiskey-soaked dream, and she'd wake up in the back of Betty Blue shortly.

"Mmm, we don't. Not necessarily, I suppose. It's more that we don't always know what's going to greet us on the other side of a portal, so it's safer to have a spot to wait for a bit."

"And where does this particular portal lead us? Are we going to the Dark Fae, then?"

"No, you wouldn't survive in that world for long. You're still useful to me at the moment," Donal said, shrugging a shoulder nonchalantly. Sorcha wasn't sure if it was the shrug, or the fact that he was so confident about her inability to stand up for herself, but anger began to roil deep inside of her. Usually, she'd push that emotion down, but today she welcomed the feeling, opening to it, and the power in her blood responded.

"No man – Fae or other – will use me," Sorcha hissed. Even as Donal stood, surprise flashing across his face, Sorcha raised her arms and threw a massive wall of fire at him. Not waiting to see what happened next, Sorcha turned and ran back up the path, tossing fire behind her as she went, not certain she was strong enough to escape Donal, but not willing to accept her fate without a fight.

Pain seared her side, and Sorcha glanced down to see a rip in her costume and blood welling. Fear spurred her on, and her breath heaved as she ran for her life – not knowing what would come next. The end of the path neared, and Sorcha could just make out the arched entrance into the craggy rock cave. If she could just reach the opening, maybe she could block it and give herself time to...

A flash of pain – bright and sharp – caused Sorcha to stumble, blood welling from a tear in her thigh. A few more steps...

Pushing forward, Sorcha swallowed against the bile that rose in her throat and tried focusing on pulling at the thread of power that wound through her, firing off another wall of fire behind her. Rocks tumbled from the wall of the mountain in front of her, and Sorcha realized what Donal was trying to do. He wanted to seal the passageway in order to stop her from escaping. Which meant – if she *could* get to it – she could go through the portal without him. He didn't want her to escape. The thought propelled her forward, and a scream ripped from her as another stream of fire glanced off her shoulder. Little dots danced in front of her vision, and fear began to claw at her, threatening her resolve as she neared the entrance to the cave. She stumbled again, this time falling to her knees, the rock scraping the delicate skin there.

"No..." Sorcha whispered, tears pricking her eyes.

Torin ducked through the arch to the portal, his tawny eyes instantly assessing the scene. He was by her side – far faster than any human – and Sorcha was lifted, the air hot with fire around her, and then she was inside the dark passageway to the portal. Once more, flames surrounded her, as Torin stepped directly into the fire, but Sorcha no longer cared.

He'd come.

He'd damn well better have come, she realized, fury tearing into her. Torin was the whole reason she was in this position. If he'd just left her alone that night at the festival, she'd never have been pulled into this...well, whatever this was. When cool air, misting with rain, brushed over her, Sorcha twisted in Torin's arms and shoved his chest – hard. He stumbled back a step and Sorcha dropped to her feet, gulping air, relieved to be back in her world. At least that's where she hoped she was. Running back a few steps, Sorcha lifted her hand in the air, signaling Torin to stand back, as she turned in a circle and took in her surroundings.

A few gulls circled lazily in the misty air over cliffs that dropped straight into the sea and the grass carpeting the rolling hills was a normal shade of Irish green. The scent of damp earth after a fresh rain mixed with salty ocean air, calmed Sorcha. Relieved, she stumbled closer to the edge of the cliff and stared down at the water, blinking at the tears that clouded her vision. Her adrenaline had spiked, and now that she was back in her world, fatigue crept over her like a heavy blanket. She wanted nothing more than to curl up in the grass and sleep for two days, waking as though none of this had happened.

The Irish landscape worked its magick, the familiar soothing her tension, and as her senses righted themselves, she realized she was injured.

And so very angry.

She couldn't bring herself to look down at the wounds she knew still bled, not sure if she was ready to accept what the damage may be, and instead she trembled at the edge of the cliff, her fury and fear the only thing holding her upright.

When the water in the cove below them began to radiate a brilliant blue light, Sorcha's mouth tightened, and she let rage win. Magick was still at play, it seemed, and she wanted nothing to do with it.

"You." Sorcha bit the word out, knowing Torin stood only a few feet from her. A part of her appreciated the silence he gave her, as some men would have immediately started trying to explain the situation or rush to patch up her wounds. Instead, Torin had stepped back and allowed her to collect herself, trusting Sorcha knew what she needed.

One point in his favor. But that was all she was willing to give him at the moment.

"Sorcha." Her name on his lips was like coming home, and Sorcha hated how much she wanted to collapse into his arms and cry until she had nothing left inside of her. More tears threatened, and she tried to hold them back. This moment…it was the beginning, and it was the end. The end of all she knew about her world, and the beginning of something that she didn't yet understand.

She was tied to Torin. In some inexplicable way. If she turned, and went to him, her life would never be the same.

But would it be anyway? Had too much already transpired that Sorcha could never go back to the woman she was before this night? Her career was likely over. The Dark Fae knew of her and wanted her as a pawn in some game. And Torin…well, he'd danced through her dreams for hundreds of nights. The reality of him wouldn't change what she already knew to be true.

Her life, as she knew it, *was* over.

It was moments like this that could drop a person to their knees, Sorcha thought, and winced against the increasingly steady throb of pain at her side. When faced with the writing on the wall, some people would spend the rest of their lives refusing to read it, as the comfort of the familiar was worth more than the promise of reality. They died that way, too, hugging their carefully crafted stories to themselves, never realizing that had they just turned the page, a whole new world could have been theirs for the taking.

The water of the cove rippled far below where they stood, the gorgeous blue light dancing merrily through the waves, as though the cove had some sort of divine message for her and Torin. Turning, she locked eyes with Torin, the punch of him no less than the first night she'd seen him through the flames of the bonfire.

"What have you done to me?" Sorcha whispered, tears rolling down her cheeks as the rage built. "How dare you come to me...and...and...disrupt my life as though the consequences are nothing? As though my life is of no importance to you and your stupid Fae royalty? You...you..."

"Sorcha." Again, her name on his lips made her want to prowl across the grass and crawl into his lap like a cat curling into a sunbeam on a couch. The need was so strong, that Sorcha had to actively work to stop herself from crossing to him, the promise of his touch like a siren's call. He will make you feel better, her mind screamed at her, and it was only her stubborn streak that held her back from crossing to him.

"I loved my life," Sorcha said. "Don't you understand

that? I was happy! *Happy*. Until you came along. That night...you did something to me. Something that I still don't understand. And I haven't been happy since. Not truly. I'm different now, and I don't know why. I can't seem to understand what's happened, I've never had answers, and you just...you *left*. You up and left with not a word. And now... this? You'd already destroyed my heart. Don't you see? But tonight? Now? You've ruined everything for me. Everything. I have no career anymore. There's Dark Fae running loose. People are getting hurt. Weddings are being ruined. There's..." Sorcha hiccupped as the pain in her body built along with the fear for her future.

"I'm sorry," Torin said. Still, he didn't move closer, even though Sorcha could now feel blood dripping down her legs from her wounds. "I didn't mean to leave you that night. Truly. It was...and still is...one of the most important moments of my life. Meeting you, Sorcha, changed my path irrevocably."

"You left!" Sorcha whirled, flinging her hands in the air in rage, and a small stream of fire flew from them. Torin dodged, his eyes growing wide, and Sorcha gulped back her instinct to apologize to this man. This Fae.

Fae or man, whatever he was, but God help her – she wanted him. Even now, when her fury knew no bounds, and her fear threatened to drown her, she wanted him in a way that she couldn't begin to understand.

"Aye, I did. And for that, I'm sorry. I'll spend the rest of my days making it up to you, if you'll only forgive me. Sorcha, my love, come to me. Please let me heal you." Torin held out his arms.

"I...I can't." Sorcha was openly crying now, the pain almost debilitating, but she knew she couldn't take the first step to Torin. He'd already torn her life apart, blowing open anything she knew to be real in this world, and she had nothing left to give him as Donal's evil Fae magick began to work its insidious way through her veins. But, even then, knowing her life was draining, Sorcha had to stand for one last thing.

Herself.

"You...you left me. You've used me as a pawn in some battle between dark and light, and I don't want any of it, you understand? I don't want any part of this. You had no right to step in like some all-knowing God and play with my life... my future...like that. People were hurt tonight because of you. Good people, I'm sure."

"And more will be hurt if you don't accept what is." Torin's words twisted Sorcha's heart with their truth. "Please hear me when I say that I never meant for you to be hurt. That I will protect you to my last breath."

"But you didn't." Sorcha looked up through her tears. His tawny eyes held sadness, his face creased in worry, and his muscular body was tense, as though he was poised to move the instant she gave an inch. She gestured to where blood ran down her body. "You didn't protect me, did you?"

"A fact that will haunt me the rest of my life. Sorcha, my love, you have to let me heal you. It's too much. Please... don't do this to me. I can't...I *need* you."

"How?" Sorcha laughed, gasping for air as the dark magick and heavy wounds caused her legs to weaken. "How can you even know that? We had one night together. You don't know me. You can't possibly want me – a simple woman from a small town. A woman who travels around in a beat-up van, following her art, letting her heart lead." Sorcha stumbled forward, almost to the cliff's edge, pain throwing her equilibrium off.

"I know that I need you with me because I claimed you that night." Torin's lips were at her ear, his arms wrapping around her body, and Sorcha's world went black.

6

"HOW IS SHE?" Torin demanded, as soon as Bianca exited the small bedroom, closing the door firmly at her back.

"She still hasn't woken but seems to be resting more peacefully now. Your magick is working, and her wounds have closed. Now, I suspect it is more a bit of exhaustion that has taken hold."

"She'll live." Torin's voice cracked, surprising them both, and warmth entered Bianca's eyes. She stepped forward and laid a hand on Torin's arm, squeezing it gently.

"Sure and she's a strong one at that. Your Sorcha will be just fine then."

"Thank you," Torin said, swallowing against the lump in his throat. He wasn't afraid of feelings, oh no, one couldn't lead the Fire Fae and be uncomfortable with large swings of emotion, but the thought of losing Sorcha again now that he'd finally found her had almost dropped him to his knees.

The portal had taken them to Grace's Cove, for which Torin was thankful. There, he'd been able to call on friends of the Fae, like Bianca and Seamus, who had been instrumental in helping the Danula Fae to subdue the Domnua through the years. Bianca, though technically human, was honorary Fae and had been awarded her own special set of powers after the quest to find the Four Treasures years ago. Recently Bianca and Seamus had been instrumental when the Water Fae revolted, and Torin was grateful they'd been immediately available when he'd sent up a call for help from the cliffs of Grace's Cove.

She'd nearly fallen over the edge.

It had taken all his willpower to let Sorcha leave his arms after they'd traveled through the portal. He'd been so focused on running a spell to close the portal behind him, that he'd let her go when she'd shoved him, bouncing from his arms in a fit of tears and rage. He'd been able to tell that she needed space but seeing her like that – covered in blood and the light glinting dully off her ripped sequined costume – had almost destroyed him. However, when she'd started to lose consciousness and had stepped too close to the edge of the cliff – Torin had drawn the line.

Now, they were at Bianca's friend's house – a woman who ran a pub in town – and Torin had been pacing in front of the bedroom door while giving Bianca space to tend to Sorcha. She'd removed the bloody sequined costume and now it hung limply in her hands – sparkles mixing with dull rust-colored blood stains – and Torin took it from her. Even touching Sorcha's discarded clothing caused a ripple of awareness inside of him and he sighed, knowing how close he'd been to losing her.

"A whiskey?" Seamus asked, gesturing to him from where he stood by the kitchen counter. The cottage was cozy, with a few bedrooms, and a main living area which opened to a small kitchen.

"Aye..." Torin's head came up and he grabbed Bianca's shoulders. "She's awake." Without waiting, he turned and

followed Bianca into the bedroom, his gaze immediately
going to the bed in the corner where Sorcha blinked at
them, a weary expression on her face. She looked like a
child in the large bed, her eyes huge in her white face, the
bright red of her hair standing out starkly against the crisp
cream linens. She was but a tiny thing, though packed with
muscles, and the blankets cocooned her as though she was
in a nest of clouds. Her eyes landed on Torin, and it felt like
a knife ripped through his core when she looked down and
away, shuttering her emotions from him.

"Well, now it's good to be seeing you awake then. I'm
Bianca, and I've been the one tending to you." Bianca smiled
cheerfully, and poured a glass of water from a carafe at the
bedside table for Sorcha. Sorcha eyed it with suspicion
before looking to Bianca.

"No magick?"

"Nope, just plain old spring water for you, love. I'm
human, by the way, and I suspect you're dealing with a big
mess of emotions after running into this lot, am I right?"
Bianca gestured with her thumb at Torin. Her words
annoyed him, but it must have hit the right chord with
Sorcha, because a small smile flitted across her face.

"You could say that," Sorcha said, her voice raspy. She
accepted the water and drank until Bianca stopped her.

"Little sips or you'll be sick. Fae magick is tricky on the
body."

"Where am I?" Sorcha's hands clenched the covers,
pulling the blanket further up her chest, and she burrowed
back into the pillows.

"Grace's Cove. A lovely little town on the west coast."

"I mean...like..." Sorcha raised her eyebrows.

"In Ireland. Not in any magickal realm," Bianca clarified
with a small smile, easing onto the edge of the bed. "When

Torin sent up the cry for help, we were lucky to be here and ready to assist. We'd already come this way because of the word that the Fire Fae were revolting."

"I..." Sorcha's eyes went glassy with tears and Torin stepped forward, wanting nothing more than to soothe her pain away.

"This one's brought me up to speed a bit." Bianca nodded at Sorcha. "He's made a right mess of it all, hasn't he then?"

"I wouldn't say this is all my fault..." Torin trailed off when both women turned to him with matching looks of accusation. Well, then. It seemed he'd been judged and found wanting.

"Will I live?" Sorcha asked, her trembling voice breaking Torin's heart. How he ached to go to her, but he understood it wasn't what she needed or wanted right now. He had his work ahead of him, if he was to win back her trust, and he hoped he'd be given the time to do so. Duty called, and yet he'd left it all behind when Sorcha had been taken. He'd put her first, over the call from the Royals to protect the Fae, and in doing so had put his own future and that of his people in jeopardy. Would she even understand what that meant? Would it matter to her? Already he felt the sting of censure from the queen, and his people, and still he stayed...needing to know that Sorcha would heal.

"Yes, you'll be just fine. Luckily, Torin has studied enough healing magicks that he was able to pull you through, and I called on a few friends here in Grace's Cove who could help with the rest. You should be just fine with minimal scarring. But you will need a little time to rest up. How are you feeling?" Bianca asked.

"I..." The covers rippled as Sorcha moved her legs and then ran her hands down her body. "Honestly? Not too bad.

I'm really tired. But I don't feel pain – and that's weird, isn't it? I should feel pain. Particularly where he hit me in the side." Confusion crossed that enticing face of hers.

"I took the pain," Torin said, wanting her to look at him with anything other than anger. Her eyes flew to his, a question in them.

"You took the pain?"

"Aye." Torin bowed his head. "I took it into myself. It's part of healing magicks. You can redirect the pain from the body, or you can take it in. I took it...as a penance of sort. For not finding you sooner. For leaving you at all. For letting you get hurt."

"Well, that wasn't very smart of you," Bianca said, interrupting his meaningful confession. Annoyance flashed through Torin.

"Right?" Sorcha laughed softly. "If you could send the pain elsewhere, why would you take it into your body?"

"Particularly if your people need you right now?" Bianca shook her head at Torin, making him feel like a toddler being scolded, and then shot a conspiratorial look at Sorcha. "Men. They're all the same, aren't they? Fae or human. They'd rather throw themselves on their sword in dramatics than offer a simple apology."

"Well at least some things are consistent between the worlds," Sorcha smiled.

"I did apologize." Torin realized he was dangerously close to stomping his boot on the wood floors. "A very heartfelt one, mind you."

"Is that the right of it?" Bianca looked to Sorcha, who nodded.

"He did. That much is true."

"So, if you apologized, why take the pain on? Self-flagellation isn't an appealing trait, you know." Bianca tapped a finger against her lips. A giggle escaped Sorcha, and Torin's brows rose when a snort followed.

"Are you...laughing at me?" Torin asked, torn between happiness at hearing her laughter and frustration at being the reason for it.

"And women are supposedly the dramatic ones..." Bianca sighed.

"Right?" Sorcha said, easing herself slowly up so she was sitting against the pillows. Bianca had found a simple men's white t-shirt for Sorcha to wear, and the fabric bagged loosely around her shoulders. "Sure and I didn't ask for you to be taking such a sacrifice on. Not that I had any idea of what goes into healing with magick and all, but it seems a silly thing to do. If there really is a battle looming, wouldn't you be needing your strength?"

"I wasn't...it was..." Torin raked a hand through his hair, his annoyance growing. Both women stared owlishly at him, waiting for him to finish speaking. "I wasn't thinking clearly, okay? I didn't know a safe spot to direct the dark magick to, and I knew I'd be in even more trouble if I shot it out the window and hurt someone outside."

"Wait...I'm just..." Sorcha held up a hand and then pinched her nose. "Explain, please."

"When you heal someone with your hands, in the olden ways of doing things long before modern medicine all but destroyed the practice, it was essentially to pull the sickness from the body. When doing so, the sickness needs a place to land – an outlet if you will. The practice allows for it to be directed to an inanimate object, like the ground or a tree or something like that...and then it is neutralized. Taking it into your own body is an option, but not a recommended one. In fact, I suspect you're not feeling so great right now, are you then?" Bianca narrowed her eyes at Torin.

"I'm fine," Torin bit out. Sure, he wasn't feeling particularly top notch, but he had enough magick and power to soften the brunt of the dark magick he'd ingested.

"Says the man with sweat on his brow." Bianca threw up her hands. "Goddess, save me from stubborn men. I swear, had I known you'd taken the damn pain for yourself you'd be lying in bed as well. As it is, I'll be asking you to get off your feet while I get Seamus to put on some soup."

"Seamus?" Sorcha popped up.

"My husband. He's Fae and the love of my life. Don't get any designs on him, or I'll have to fight you and we don't want that." Bianca winked at Sorcha. "He's a dreamboat, but he's *my* dreamboat. Understood?"

"Don't worry about me, I've sworn off men," Sorcha promised Bianca, gripping the comforter tightly. Torin's annoyance rose further, and he glowered at the both of them.

"You. Sit down. Now." Bianca gestured to an armchair in the corner of the bedroom. Torin strode to it and pulled it to the side of the bed, ignoring Sorcha's eyeroll. One way or the other, they'd have to see their way back to each other. Torin already knew what Sorcha meant to him, but it seemed the lass wasn't interested in learning about what was right in front of her eyes. "I'll get sustenance for you both and then we're going to have a little chat about how we move forward from here. Understood?"

"Yes," Torin gritted out. Sorcha nodded and Bianca bounced from the room, shaking her head and muttering insults about stubborn men.

"I'm glad you're safe," Torin said, reaching out a hand and then dropping it to the covers when Sorcha just eyed him warily.

"Am I?" Sorcha laughed softly, shaking her head and

glancing to the window when a fat drop of rain exploded against the pane. "I'm not sure I'll ever feel safe again knowing what I do of this world now."

"You should. I'll look after you," Torin said, his voice thickening with emotion.

"No, thank you." Sorcha turned, spearing him with the intensity of her gaze. "I can't trust that you'll be there for me, which means the only person I can rely upon is myself."

7

"I NEED MY STUFF," Sorcha said, after she'd downed a bowl
of vegetable soup and some delicious brown bread still
warm from the oven. Seamus, who had turned out to be a
delightful beanpole of a man with a shock of red hair and
nothing but adoration for his wife, had accepted her praise
for his culinary prowess with a faint tinge to his cheeks. The
man was adorable, Sorcha realized, and immediately
warmed to him and Bianca. Torin, however, was an entirely
different problem and one she wasn't sure how to handle.
Sorcha didn't like being on uneasy ground with someone,
and typically was quick to resolve issues with anyone in her
life. This, however, was something larger and much more
confusing for her than a normal spat with a friend. Her feelings twined together like necklaces knotted in a jewelry box,
and she was having trouble unraveling how she felt.

On one hand, her instant attraction to Torin was undeniable. Sure, and it was a liar she'd be if she couldn't admit
even *that* much to herself. The pull to Torin was so strong
that it was almost palpable, as though he was a spotter
holding the rope to her safety harness when she was

walking the high wire. Even with her eyes closed she could feel when he'd leave the room and walk about the cottage, her senses somehow able to track his movements. Sorcha didn't know what to make of it, nor of the fact that she'd been so happy to see him that she'd almost readily forgiven him for ducking out on her after their first night together.

Except...she just *couldn't*. Even with how she lived, where love 'em and leave 'em was largely accepted as part of the free love creative lifestyle, Sorcha had never been so unkind as to roll from a lover's bed without a word and leave. It wasn't the friendly thing to do after a night of intimacy, and when said lover happened to be magickal Fae and had left a parting gift of the power to make fire – well, it was even worse. Sorcha had spent almost two years convinced she was going crazy, or worse, that she'd let the devil into her van that night. She'd done her best to use her newfound power to her advantage, but the niggling worry that she was toying with evil had never left her. Since that night with Torin, Sorcha had become unsettled and uncertain, and had forced herself to work through the insecurity, building up a name and a brand for herself. Because that is what survivors did, Sorcha thought. She could have let madness claim her, prattling on about making fire with her hands to passersby on the street corner, or she could use the power to her advantage. She wouldn't feel bad about it, but that didn't mean she trusted the man who gave her this ability.

Now, she found herself hopelessly attracted to Torin, healing from nasty Fae wounds, and deeply uncomfortable with being used as some pawn between the Fae. It was a world she didn't understand, and she suspected the learning curve was steep, so Sorcha did what she'd always done when a situation made her uncomfortable – she left.

Well, at least she tried to.

"You can't just be walking out the door in a t-shirt now, can you?" Torin demanded, his hands on his hips as though he was a teacher reprimanding a student. Sorcha had waited until everyone was sleeping and had slipped to the front door, gathering a small satchel of items to take with her. Unfortunately, the Fae's hearing was excellent, and he'd jumped awake before she'd even turned the knob on the front door to the cottage.

"It's longer than some of the dresses that I wear," Sorcha said, inching the strap of the satchel higher on her shoulder.

"It's pissing rain out," Torin shot back, his face mutinous. "Where, exactly, did you think you were going at this time of night?"

"I want my stuff," Sorcha reiterated.

"What's going on?" Lights blinked on in the cottage and Bianca and Seamus stepped out of their room, their eyes soft with sleep.

"Sorcha was thinking she'd be leaving us in the wee hours of the morning. In this," Torin pointed a finger to where Sorcha stood barefoot in the oversized man's t-shirt. Now that Torin held a spotlight to her actions, Sorcha was beginning to see how foolish she looked. Nevertheless, her stubborn streak kicked up.

"I want my stuff. My entire life is in a van in Cork, and they'll impound the van if it just sits there for too long. It may not mean much to you magickals, but it's the only home I have and everything I've ever worked for is in it. I need to go get Betty Blue."

"Is that your van's name? I like it." Bianca came forward and wrapped an arm around Sorcha's shoulders, her warmth instantly comforting.

"It is. She's...all I have." Sorcha was surprised when her

voice cracked, so she lifted her chin higher and stared daggers at Torin.

"You have your life, don't you? Something you'll be losing fairly quickly if you step out the door like that." Torin raked a hand through his hair, making the gilded strands stand up, his tawny eyes furious. "Foolish woman..."

"Foolish, am I?" Fury ripped through Sorcha, and she stepped forward, stabbing her finger into Torin's muscular chest. Touching him caused excitement to lick through her, and Sorcha was shocked to find that being close to him instantly made her mind switch gears. She looked up, up, up to meet his eyes, to find the same fiery need echoed there. Sorcha licked her lips, swallowing against her baser urges, and stepped back, breaking the moment. "You don't get to decide what is important to someone else. I'm in charge of my life – not you."

"You're mine and I won't allow you to make stupid decisions."

"Oh no," Bianca whispered to Seamus, shaking her head ruefully. "He's done it now."

"Stupid, is it?" Sorcha batted away Torin's claim that she was his. She'd never gone to university, as she'd had little funds to support that path and with her agile and creative mind, Sorcha had never been able to decide upon one track to study. Still, it was a sore spot – the idea that a person lacked intelligence if they didn't attend university – and she lifted her chin at Torin. "The only stupid person I see here is you – the one who left a woman behind that clearly has some significance in this little Fae power battle of yours – not to mention..." Sorcha held up a finger when Torin started to speak, "gifted with some sort of powers and then left her to her own devices. For all you know I could've lit the whole of Ireland on fire with nary a thought to the consequences. And yet, *you* left me. And I'm the stupid one?" Her breath hitched in her chest as she punctuated the words with little jabs of her finger in the air. She didn't want to touch him again, knowing if she did she might lose track of her anger and focus on how much she wanted him. Which made no sense, really, because she'd only spent one night with the man.

"Told ya," Bianca hissed, clucking her tongue softly. "Torin has a lot to learn about women, it seems."

"He does have a few other things on his mind, doesn't he, love?" Seamus asked, trying to stand for his fellow man.

"He'd accomplish them much more quickly by getting Sorcha on his side instead of pushing her away then, wouldn't he now?" Bianca said.

"Sure, and that'd be the smart thing to do," Seamus agreed.

"See?" Sorcha demanded. "Even Seamus thinks you're the stupid one, not me."

"Oh, I..." Seamus audibly gulped as Torin's golden eyes slipped to him. Torin's face was hard, and if Sorcha couldn't see the visible tick of his pulse at his neck, she would have thought him carved from stone.

"I do not doubt your intelligence," Torin bit out after a long moment. "But I think your current course is stupid. A stupid choice does not mean a person lacks intelligence. We often make choices based on our emotions. Feelings aren't rational, even if they do drive our actions. I'm merely pointing out that running out in the stormy night with no shoes and no way to get anywhere will likely not bode well for you."

Damn it. The man wasn't wrong. Sorcha bit her lip, caught between her anger and her own foolhardy choice.

"Sorcha. How can I help you?" Bianca asked, drawing her attention away from Torin.

"I need to get to my van. I need my stuff. I have book-ings...a life..." Sorcha shrugged a shoulder when she real-ized she might not have any more clients after what had happened at the wedding. She didn't know. She had no phone, no computer – no way to connect with any of the current news. She needed to get online and see what damage had been done at the wedding reception. If she could just get Betty Blue back, she'd feel more centered and in control.

"That life is over. You're mine now..." Torin glanced to where Bianca and Seamus were vehemently shaking their heads at him. Seamus made a cutting motion with his hand at his neck, but the damage was done.

"I gave you sex. I didn't give you ownership of my life." Sorcha threw her shoulders back. "No man will control my destiny, Torin. You'll need to get that through your thick skull."

Torin winced, as though visibly wounded, and confu-sion spread across his face as he looked at Seamus.

"But she's my fated mate...she needs to accept my claim..."

"Um..." Seamus pressed his lips together, rocking back on his heels as he considered the problem. "I think we both know that it doesn't always work that way." A look, heavy with meaning, passed between the two men.

"Fated mate? Not likely, boyo. Because I don't claim you back, you hear me?" A slow slide of panic started through Sorcha, and she whirled on Bianca, desperate. "I'm nobody's prisoner. I get to make my own choices, right?"

"Right, right. Shhh, it's okay. We'll sort this all out, I promise you." Bianca immediately pulled Sorcha into a hug.

"First stop will be getting to Cork. Now that you're healed up, we'll just pop on over and get your van for you."

"But...we can't...the Fire Fae..." Torin protested.

"Sure and they'll have to be waiting a minute now, won't they? Or you can go on without us then, Torin. We're going to get Sorcha's home, don't you see? Once she's settled, I'm guessing she'll be in a better spot to be discussing your future together."

"There's no future with us," Sorcha said immediately, though her heart whispered to her that she was a liar.

"Not everything should be decided at three in the morning on an emotional high. Am I right, love?" Bianca elbowed Seamus in the ribs, and he grinned, grabbing her hand and pulling it to his mouth for a kiss.

"She's right. Best to let some things simmer a wee bit. For now, let's get Sorcha to this Miss Betty Blue of hers, and we'll go from there."

"Thank you," Sorcha whispered, stepping back from Bianca's arms, relief palpable.

"Lesson for you, though, dear. Just ask for help next time and we can avoid some of these dramatics with this one..." Bianca widened her eyes and motioned her head to Torin who threw up his hands and stormed from the room. "Sure, and he's a volatile one, isn't he then?"

"He's head of the Fire Fae, my love, were you thinking he'd be the placid sort?" Seamus asked, teasing a laugh from Sorcha.

"Now that you mention it, I suppose not...well then, we're in for an interesting ride with him. You've got your hands full." Bianca grinned at Sorcha who immediately held her hands to the air.

"Not mine. I'm not claiming him."

"Yet!" Torin thundered from the other room.

Sorcha shot her middle finger up at the door, causing both Seamus and Bianca to break out in laughter.

"Well, then. Let's get ourselves sorted out. Next time, doll, let's leave after a proper night's sleep, eh?"

"I'll keep that in mind," Sorcha sighed.

8

PERHAPS MAGICK WAS MORE useful than she had realized, Sorcha thought as she watched Torin effortlessly unlock the door to Betty Blue. Sorcha had realized the problem once they'd arrived in Cork and had stood on the street, staring at where her cheerful camper van was parked. Her purse had been at the reception hall along with her phone, her wallet, and the keys to Betty Blue. Luckily, she kept a spare set hidden inside the van, so once Torin unlocked the door she crawled inside and into the back where she unlocked a secret compartment which held her iPad, a stash of cash, a few personal documents, and her extra keys.

"Right, that's us sorted out then." Sorcha popped her head out the driver's side door and brandished the set of keys. The day was new, the sun just kissing the sky, and the birds had begun their morning hymns. "Thanks for helping me out and all. Good luck with your, um, battles and all that. I'm happy to drop you somewhere if need be?"

"Maddening woman," Torin said, kicking a rock on the sidewalk and muttering curses under his breath.

"I don't think you can just be dropping us off and

heading on our separate way," Bianca smiled at her, her eyes twinkling with amusement. "You're kind of linked up in all of this now."

"How so? That's not even fair." Sorcha crossed her arms over her chest.

"Well, let's just use a few context clues." Seamus stepped in front of Torin, interrupting what was likely a torrent of anger. "The Fae waged an attack on a place you were working, right? Then, they kidnapped you to get a rise out of Torin. And...well, it worked, didn't it then? He followed *you* instead of his royal duties. The Fae now know that. Which means, you've kind of got a bullseye on your back. It would be foolish to leave you unprotected, Sorcha. And, frankly, I think you're smarter than that. This may not be the path you've chosen, but it's the one you're on now. You understand?"

It really annoyed her that he was right, the truth of his words churning in her gut, and Sorcha dropped back against the seat. Slamming her fist on the steering wheel, she pursed her lips as her mind whirled. Was there any place she could go that she'd be safe? Or at the least off the radar for a while?

"What if I fly to Spain for a while? Have a wee holiday?" Sorcha turned her head to look at the group.

"Sadly, they'd likely stop you before you got on the flight. You're useful to them at the moment, so if you wouldn't be minding, we'll just tag along with you in the van. That way we can offer up some protection while we figure out the next course of action." Seamus offered up a rueful shrug.

"So, I'm stuck is what you're saying? I'm along for the ride whether I like it or not?" Sorcha asked.

"Goddess, but you're a stubborn woman," Torin said

from the seat beside her, causing Sorcha to gasp and throw a hand to her heart.

"How did you get in here? And belted up at that?" Sorcha gaped at Torin, the man having just been on the sidewalk seconds ago.

"We'll just be popping in the back while you two have a wee chat," Bianca decided, sliding the van door open and looking around at Sorcha's home before climbing in. Sorcha had converted the van into a home of sorts, with a bench along one wall that could provide seats when the van was moving, but also could fold out into a bed when she needed it. Along the other side of the van were cabinets for storage, a table that folded up, and a small galley-style kitchen area for food prep. Above was a locked storage box that held her costumes, performing gear, and other various items that didn't serve an immediate and useful purpose for her day-to-day. It was a simple existence, and an uncomplicated one, which Sorcha had found suited her quite well.

"You live like a poor band roadie." Her sister Mary's words echoed in her mind as Sorcha watched Bianca and Seamus take stock of the van in her rearview mirror. Her relationship with Mary was complicated, often dancing between competition and camaraderie, more so than with her other sisters. They were the closest in age and had been thick as thieves growing up. Only in the past few years had they started to grow apart after Mary had gone off to Uni and had started to become a bit more worldly. What had once seemed an adventurous lifestyle to Mary now looked unraveled and risky, and Sorcha had stopped trying to defend her choices to her sister. Her life was her own and that was that. Still, she hoped they'd be able to reconnect at some point, as traveling was often lonely. Sure, her other sisters called up periodically and rattled on about their boyfriends or babies, depending on which sister was calling, but Sorcha often felt like she was just a place for them to vent about life and rarely did any one of them have the time or inclination to ask how she was doing.

She was the free one, after all, and it was a fact that Sorcha thought her sisters resented. She wasn't around to care for their parents, or to help babysit, or fall in line with her father's commands. No, Sorcha had removed herself from that mind-numbing existence, and had been happy with her choice to do so. Only now, as she stared at the magickal Fae man sitting next to her, did she start to question where her life choices had taken her. Maybe if she'd stayed home and married Patrick, the village barber, she wouldn't be looking down the path of a Fae battle.

But, oh, she would have missed out on learning that magick, and Fae, were real. And what a sad fact that would have been, Sorcha realized. Sure, danger awaited them – but she could just as easily be hit by a car crossing the road one day. If she was going to go down, maybe doing so in the middle of an unbelievable Fae world was the way to go. Resolved, Sorcha glanced over her shoulder.

"Seat belts are tucked around the side – yes, just there." Sorcha nodded to where Bianca pointed to the corners of the seats.

"I like what you've done with the space. Very efficient, but also comfortable," Seamus said, settling his lanky frame onto the seat and stretching his legs out in front of him. "You think you'd like to do this someday, my love? Tour around in a camper van? We could go around Europe. Eat all kinds of marvelous foods. Have some delicious wine in Italy."

"You had me at yummy food and wine," Bianca held a hand to her heart. "Someday, yes, I think this could be fun. Maybe. What if you have to go the bathroom?"

"There's a toilet."

"What? Where?" Bianca exclaimed.

"It's not one you'd use with other people around," Sorcha laughed. "But if you lift up the top of that back cabinet, you'll see it. There's a small storage as well in the van for sewage, and water, that kind of thing. You just have to find spots to empty it correctly."

"Well, who would've thought?" Bianca said, peering under the lid of the cabinet. "Sure enough, there's a small toilet in here."

"Enough!" Torin exclaimed, his voice like a balloon exploding in the van. Instantly, everyone quieted. "We need to move. Now."

"Oh, is there…" Sorcha glanced in her mirrors and through the windshield. The street was quiet, as she'd parked near the pubs, and all of them were still closed. "I don't see anyone out and about. It's still quite early, Torin."

"I don't care about people – I care about Domnua. I've bided my time with you enough now. We have to return to Grace's Cove. That's where trouble is brewing – I can feel it." Torin raked a hand through his hair, his face set in hard lines, and for a moment Sorcha empathized with him. It seemed like he was a man who liked to follow protocol, and that had flown out the window when he'd met her. However, it wasn't like he'd been on duty the night they'd been together at the festival. Heat filled her as Sorcha's mind flashed back to that night, their bodies tangled together, the taste of his mouth a sin she could commit over and over again. Torin turned, his golden eyes finding hers, and his mouth lifted at one corner as though he knew of her thoughts. The air thickened between them, heavy with promise, and Sorcha swallowed against the nerves that blossomed.

"Woo, boyo. Get me a fan, because I am burning up back here with the heat bouncing between you two," Bianca exclaimed. Sorcha jolted, warmth tinging her cheeks, and threw the van into gear.

"Where to?" Sorcha bit out, checking her mirrors and pulling out onto the road.

"Sure and I think he just mentioned we were on our way back to Grace's Cove," Bianca said cheerfully. "Must be all those hormones bouncing around that's making you forgetful."

Sorcha shot a warning look into the rearview mirror, catching the blonde's delighted grin, and glared.

"There's no use arguing with this one," Seamus added, poking his wife in the ribs as she giggled. "I swear she's a perennial matchmaker."

"It's not a matchmaker that I am – oh no. I just happen to see the match has already been made. I'm on the side of love, is all. I think love conquers all, doesn't it, my sweet deliciousness of a man?" Bianca leaned into Seamus's side, beaming up at him, and Sorcha returned her eyes to the road, refusing to look at Torin.

Love.

The word bloomed inside her heart, a delicate rose opening to the first light of sun, catching a drop of dew on its finely hued petals. Deceiving, a rose was, for within its delicacy lay sharp thorns, ready to draw blood if mishandled. Sorcha had never been one to have the patience for gardening, and love needed careful tending. This wasn't the way for her, of that much she was sure. Pushing fanciful thoughts aside, Sorcha cleared her throat.

"How come you can't just magick the van back to Grace's Cove?" They'd transported to Cork through the weird power that the Fae had, where it felt like her body was being sucked through a vacuum hose and she came out the other side dizzy and confused. "Wouldn't that be a touch more convenient?" As it was, they had at least a three-hour drive ahead of them.

"The larger the item you need to transport, the more you disrupt the natural way of things," Torin said, his tone clipped. He shifted in his seat, his long fingers tapping his knee, and Sorcha studied him. The man was always moving, it seemed, much like a flame flickering in the wind. Bouncing, tapping, or rocking back and forth on his heels. She'd noticed it because she was much the same and had been accused of being too restless back in her school days. Energy had always radiated through her, and Sorcha sensed that she shared that trait with Torin. Action was a siren's call for the both of them, which was likely why they'd ended up at the same festival together that night.

"And that's bad, right?" Sorcha asked, following the signs for the N22 that would take them toward Grace's Cove.

"It's not necessarily good or bad. It's just..." Torin brought a finger to his lips as he considered his words. "Fae magick is part of universal and elemental energy. Because everything is entwined and interwoven, when you use magick it pulls from other areas. However, there's also sort of a balancing that goes on, that generally smooths things out. I suspect I'm not explaining this well."

"So, big magickal moves can have big ramifications elsewhere?" Sorcha asked, shifting into a higher gear as the speed limit increased.

"Yes, somewhat. It also depends on the need. Grave needs are weighted differently than selfish ones. Magick in battle defending humans and other Fae from harm is allowed. Magickal use such as building a gold mansion for one man's use – not as welcomed by the Fae. Not saying it can't be done, but slowly repercussions would occur through the years. It's kind of a way to allow us to have power without being too powerful, if that makes sense?"

"I still don't grasp the intricacies of it all," Bianca piped up from the back. "I feel like the Fae use magick on a whim. I mean, I've seen more than one Fae pull a meal out of thin air or create magickal gifts. I'm not sure why that would be considered a need…"

"Ah, well, the Fae are partial to gifts and love a feast. Usually, those things are done with good intentions," Seamus shrugged.

"Still missing the logic there, but so long as you keep me well-fed, I'm happy," Bianca said.

"Right, so back to Grace's Cove…and then what?" Sorcha slid Torin a look, hoping he'd ease some of the tension that was currently working its way into her shoulders. God, she needed a workout. Between being injured and resting in bed, her muscles screamed for a good stretch. Normally, she had a routine she worked through each day – at the bare minimum – to keep her body conditioned. She wasn't consistent with much in her life, but keeping her body strong was one area she remained committed to.

"We'll see what waits for us," Torin murmured.

"Great…just great." Sorcha flipped on the radio, and a morning news program filled the van.

"Fire broke out at a wedding reception in Cork this weekend…"

Sorcha almost drove off the road at the announcer's voice, and slapped Torin's hand away when he reached for the radio.

"Luckily, nobody was injured though there were reports of a mysterious group having crashed the reception. More likely, the

fire can be attributed to the special guest of the night – Smoking Sorcha – a renowned fire dancer and performance artist."

"Smokin' Sorcha? Is that what you call yourself?" Bianca asked. "I like it – but I'll admit, I wasn't expecting it."

"No…" Sorcha winced at the name. Dread curled low in her stomach, and she knew that the moment she got to her computer, she'd see cancellations piling up. "They must've come up with that on their own."

"It does have a ring to it. Just ignore them – trying to sell a story is all they're doing." Bianca reached forward and patted Sorcha's shoulder.

"It's screwed I am. And that's the truth of it." Sorcha pressed her lips together in a hard line, focusing on the road, refusing to let tears cloud her vision.

"You're not." Torin reached over and ran a single finger down her thigh, causing instant heat to blossom at his touch. "It may seem that way, just now, but I promise you that you'll find a way out of this. *We'll* find a way out of this."

Sorcha ground her teeth together, not trusting herself to speak, and drove on toward Grace's Cove and her now uncertain future.

9

"I'M GOING FOR A WALK," Sorcha said as soon as they returned to the cottage they'd left just that morning. She was too keyed up to sit still and was afraid to open her iPad and read the messages she was certain were piling up in her inbox.

"Not alone, you're not," Torin said, rounding the hood of Betty Blue to stand by her. Sorcha looked up at him, their height difference so vast that he towered over her and blocked the light from the morning sun rising behind him. Rolling her eyes, she climbed into the back of the van and opened a cabinet to dig through her clothes. Though she appreciated the basic t-shirt and loose jeans someone had given her to wear instead of her bloodied costume, she wanted her own clothes. Pulling out a long-sleeved soft blue shirt, she stripped off the t-shirt she wore, and slipped on a simple tank bra. Her breasts weren't large, so she didn't need much support, and tank bras were comfortable for exercise as well as all-day wear. Turning, she put her hands on her hips and glowered at where Torin stood in the doorframe, his eyes having grown more golden with lust.

"Oh, so you're a voyeur now, are you?"

"Sure, and I didn't know you'd be changing back here, did I then?" Torin retorted. He licked his lips, and Sorcha instantly did the same, the pull to him so intense that she almost buckled under its weight. Her emotions careened wildly through her, a contrasting mix of needs, and she found herself rooted to the spot.

"It's my bedroom. This is where I change," Sorcha said, the words coming slowly as though she was drugged.

"Magnificent," Torin said, climbing into the van and crossing to her in two steps. Sorcha gasped when he sat on the bench seat, pulling her into his lap, cradling her as though she was the most precious thing in the world. "When I first saw you – I thought the same. And I didn't think it was possible for you to be even more radiant than you were that night. Our first night together. But not our last, I hope." He didn't move, and she held still, transfixed by his tawny eyes where little slivers of green were interwoven with the gold.

"Torin...I'm not..."

"You are, quite simply, the most breathtaking woman I have ever laid eyes upon. In this land and the next. When you stepped onto that stage the other night? You've trans-fixed me, Sorcha, and I'm under your spell. You've only to ask and I will bow to your demands. You are as much mine, as I am your humble slave."

"Torin...it's too much...I can't..." Sorcha gasped, feeling as though a fire of need was consuming her from the inside out.

"Just a kiss, Sorcha...it's all I'm asking for..." Torin stopped, his lips inches from hers, anticipation making Sorcha's breath catch. *Oh*, but she wanted him. As much as she didn't trust him or his world – she wanted him. What harm could a wee taste do? Succumbing to the need that had plagued her dreams since the day she'd first met him, Sorcha gave a subtle nod.

Instantly his lips were on hers, and Sorcha was lost. Like two sticks rubbed together to create fire, their need exploded between them, and Sorcha cried against his mouth as lust threatened to consume her. Understanding, Torin pulled back, softening his kiss, angling her head so that the intensity lessened. Here was an exploration, a welcoming, and Sorcha was pulled under as he expertly brought her along on a dance that she hadn't known she needed. Oh, but she did – so very much. She could die a thousand deaths in his kiss and still come back for more. Reaching up, she dug her hands into his hair, the thick strands soft against her fingers, and pulled him closer, wanting more of him. He opened to her, tracing his tongue over her lips, before slipping inside for a taste. The touch of his tongue against hers was an invitation, no – a demand – and one that Sorcha desperately wanted to answer.

Instead, she pulled back, leaning her forehead against his, gasping for air as she tried to settle the need that threatened to consume her. Too much had happened in such a short time for her to be making out with a magickal Fae in the back of her van. What she needed was a cold shower and about sixteen hours of sleep before she made any other rash decisions in her life. The last time she'd danced with this man, her world had irrevocably changed. Who was to say what this time would bring?

"Sorcha."

"I can't. I just...I can't." Sorcha stood, grateful he let her go, and grabbed the shirt she'd meant to pull on over her tank bra. With brisk movements, she changed into fresh underwear and a slim pair of denim jeans before pulling on her socks and hiking boots. Turning, she trembled when she saw Torin's eyes devouring her motions. "I need to lock up."

"Of course." Torin stood and walked with his shoulders hunched over as he exited the van. Once outside, Sorcha followed, sliding the door closed and locking it behind her. Still need pulsed through her and she had to steady herself with a hand on the van before turning. "I'm going for a walk."

"I'll join you."

"No," Sorcha raised a hand. "Please, I need to clear my head. I can't do that with you around me."

"Do you find me distracting?" A pleased look crossed Torin's face, which was just enough to pull Sorcha out of her desire and into annoyance.

"Don't be so full of yourself now. If a person wants to go for a walk, they should be allowed to do so." Sorcha put her hands on her hips.

"I can't let you go alone. It's not safe just now, as you well know," Torin explained, his patient tone annoying Sorcha further.

"Fine, I'll get Bianca to go with me then."

"Why bother them when I'm right here and willing to attend to your needs?"

Sorcha threw up her hands at that and stomped across the front lawn toward the hills that rose behind the cottage. The village of Grace's Cove was set among a lovely range of hills that extended high behind the houses that dotted the countryside and rolled down to water below. Their cottage was on the outskirts of the village, about mid-way up the hillside, and Sorcha followed a path that would lead her higher onto the hills. She wanted the burn of climbing, to feel her muscles stretch as she ascended, and she picked up her pace – not caring if Torin followed or not. She climbed in silence for at least a half hour, relieved that Torin didn't try to speak, and when finally her lungs begged for a break – she stopped to catch her breath.

Turning, she gazed out at the water – at the hazy line where sky and sea kissed – and took the time to steady her breathing. Sunlight warmed her cheeks, a few clouds dotted the sky, and for the first time in two days, Sorcha took an easy breath.

"It's lovely here, isn't it?"

Sorcha whirled at the woman's voice, surprise quickly replaced by fear. Instantly, she raised her hands up – ready to call on the magick that pulsed through her if needed.

At first glance, the woman looked like a princess out of her childhood fairytale books. With pink and lavender hair curling wildly around her face, a sparkly tiara, and a pink sequined dress – the woman was clearly magickal. And one of high authority at that, as she held herself in a way that demanded respect. Torin immediately dropped to one knee and bowed his head.

Was she supposed to bow? Sorcha was unsure of the correct protocol, so she just bobbed her head awkwardly instead, tugging on the sleeve of her shirt and feeling severely underdressed. Which was weird, because she was out for a hike and wearing appropriate attire, but nevertheless, Sorcha was uncomfortable.

"My Queen." Torin's voice rumbled behind Sorcha, the tone of it causing her to raise an eyebrow. It sounded professional and polite, something which had largely been missing in his interactions with her. "You honor us with your presence."

"Introduce me to your..." The queen sauntered forward, her eyes trailing over Sorcha. There was calculation in her look – but not malice – as Sorcha was more than used to being sized up by judgmental women she met in her line of work. There was something about pouring herself into a sparkly leotard and performing on a stage that often put other women on edge. Sorcha was pleased to read interest in the queen's eyes, but not judgment. Truth be told, she'd had enough to deal with that day and her control over her emotions was tenuous at best. It probably wouldn't do to have that boil over on the likely very powerful queen of a magickal realm.

"This is Sorcha. My fated mate that I have claimed – though she refuses to acknowledge the claim as such," Torin said. Sorcha's mouth dropped open and she whirled, her hands on her hips, embarrassment whiplashing through her. How dare Torin reveal their past to this impossibly elegant woman? It was nobody's business who she slept with – not to mention she still had no idea what the hell a fated mate was.

"Is that so?" The queen surprised Sorcha by throwing her head back and laughing – a sound which rivaled delicate wind chimes dancing in the wind. "Fascinating. I'm Queen Aurelia. I suspect I am going to be more than enchanted with meeting you, Sorcha."

"I can say the same," Sorcha said, which was the truth. If ever there was a picture of what enchanting would look like – it was this woman. The queen exchanged a look with Torin, and Sorcha couldn't quite catch the undercurrent that ran between the two Fae. Either way, now was her chance to be very clear with this fascinating creature the Fae called queen. In any other circumstance, Sorcha would have instantly asked her about the material of her gown and how it changed colors in the morning light, shifting from blues to greens and pinks. The material was like when the sun kissed a dragonfly's wings, and Sorcha itched to reach out and skim a finger over the skirt. The need vibrated beneath her skin, so she rocked back on her heels and twined her fingers together, trying to force herself not to fidget before the queen.

The queen held a finger in the air and made a little circling motion. The air rippled around them, and Sorcha turned to find Torin pounding his fist against an invisible barrier. His face was mutinous, but even in anger he was arresting – if not more so for it.

"What have you done?" Sorcha said, rocking lightly on her feet, her hands now raised in case of a threat. She was learning very quickly that being caught off-guard wouldn't do in the world of the Fae, though a part of her might die inside if she had to shoot a fire bolt at that lovely dress.

"I've given us some privacy is all. You know how men are...allowing their frustrations to come in the way of progress. Now, tell me – you've rejected Torin. Is he a poor lover?"

Sorcha gulped, her cheeks heating as her mind flashed back to the searing night they shared in her van. "No, I'm not one to be dishonest. He performs well in that area."

"Just well?" Queen Aurelia raised a perfectly arched eyebrow.

"Um, more than satisfactory," Sorcha cleared her throat.

"As he should. The claiming of a mate should be an intense bond, and rejecting it can have catastrophic consequences. This is very interesting. What makes you reject him?"

"I'm not...it's not..." Sorcha laughed and shook her head, turning to look at where Torin stood, his hands now at his sides.

"Are you okay?" Torin mouthed to her, and warmth

bloomed in Sorcha. She gave a curt nod and turned back to the queen.

"Tell me." An order issued, and one that Sorcha knew carried more underlying meaning than she understood.

"I don't know him. And I'm not sure I can trust him. We had one night together, and I know nothing about the man. He left me without a word, and also with a magickal ability I can't bring myself to fully understand...and that was it. Poof! Gone. Then – all of a sudden – I can command fire and the man who did this to me disappears without a trace. The next time I see him? My life...my job...is ruined. His track record for showing up in my life and forever altering its course is two for two now. I'm...uncertain. And I don't like that feeling. I don't like not knowing where I stand." Sorcha's voice faltered, and she swallowed against the tightness in her throat at the thought of what she'd lost.

"That's fair," Queen Aurelia surprised her by saying. She turned and looked out over the buildings that dotted the hills below them. Moody grey clouds gathered at the horizon, casting long shadows over the water. "Our men are so used to their mates responding to their call that I'm sure Torin doesn't know how to proceed with you. That being said, I'm surprised he bonded with you and left. It's highly unusual to do so. Particularly if a fated mate is human. You'd have...questions, I'm sure."

"A lot of them." Sorcha tugged at the sleeves of her shirt, pulling them down over her hands and crossing her arms over her chest as the wind picked up.

"I can answer them for you. But not at this time. You see...the delicate balance we maintain for our world and yours – it's being threatened right now. Torin is greatly needed. And yet, he tarries here. With you. That says something. To me. To the Domnua. And to our people." The queen's voice was sharp, and Sorcha hunched her shoulders as though she was being reprimanded. "He's broken protocol to follow you – into a realm he shouldn't have gone to, mind you – and still he stays here. With you. Against direct orders."

The weight of the queen's words pressed on Sorcha, and she pulled her head out of worries for her own future.

"He's put himself at risk for me, hasn't he?" Sorcha whispered, glancing to where Torin stood – a mutinous lion – and her stubbornness eased a bit.

"He's put himself, his people, and our future at risk by coming after you. Which means – he highly values you, Sorcha. I can't speak to why he left you that night, but he's risking everything by staying by your side now and not answering a royal summons. We've managed through one battle without him, but the Fire Fae are his domain to rule, and his absence is sending the wrong message. People worry he's abdicated – gone to the Dark Fae. Even more so when the signature of his energy was discovered in the portal there."

"He came to rescue me," Sorcha said, turning back to the queen. "His friend betrayed him. Donal. He's evil. He's been lying to you all along."

"Ah." Sadness crossed Queen Aurelia's beautiful face, and she looked down as she absorbed the news. "I had hoped it wasn't so. I'd heard tell of it – but I just couldn't bring myself to believe it. Donal's been a good addition to our court. Or so I thought. Now, though, I have to wonder where else we've been infiltrated."

"I'd suggest looking into that," Sorcha said, and realized most people probably didn't speak to the queen that way when disbelief crossed her face. "Seeing as how the bad guys really have it out for you."

"I'll do that," Queen Aurelia said with a whisper of a smile. "I like you, Sorcha. I appreciate strong women – I always do. Some women, well, they are threatened by confidence. But not me. I like to collect strong women around me. It keeps me sharp, and I think together we can all raise each other up. The question remains – what will you do? Will you accept Torin's claim and help us? You're too entwined now to walk away. The Domnua know that. I can't say it will be easy having your life changed so suddenly, and I know the appearance of Fae can be disconcerting for humans."

"I'd say..." Sorcha snorted at her word choice. Disconcerting was like when she walked into an occupied public restroom. Being kidnapped by the Dark Fae was more like taking a frying pan to the face.

"I'd ask that, at the very least, if you can't help us on our way – you won't seek to harm us. Trust me when I say to you that we are on the side of all that is good and light in this world and the next. The balancing of the Elements is a dangerous and delicate job, and if threatened – everything will suffer." Queen Aurelia nodded to a spot on the hill and Sorcha followed her gaze. A puff of smoke rose in the air, a dark tendril of doom, and Sorcha's stomach twisted. "Well, Sorcha – what will it be?"

Sorcha tore her gaze from the smoke and down to the unsuspecting town of Grace's Cove. Were they really in danger? And, if so – would her actions end up harming others? Already shaken from the events of the night before, Sorcha turned back to Queen Aurelia.

"I'll help."

"I suspected as much. I've always been good at reading people." Queen Aurelia waved her hand in the air and Torin was beside Sorcha instantly.

"Why would you do that? You can't just leave me out of these discussions," Torin fumed.

"I'll do what I like, Torin. I suggest you remember with whom you are speaking. Take care of Sorcha. I like her." With those words, the queen disappeared in the unsettling way that the Fae seemed to do, and Sorcha blinked at the now empty cliff beside her.

"There's trouble. Over there." Sorcha pointed to the hills.

"Let's get back to the house. Sorcha...we need to talk," Torin said, reaching out and wrapping his arm around her shoulders as they began to climb down the hill. "I have a lot to say to you and I'm sure you have a million questions. It's just..."

"Maybe it's best we don't speak at all for a while..." Sorcha's mind was oversaturated with information.

"At the very least...let me tell you why I left you."

10

AN INSCRUTABLE LOOK crossed Sorcha's face, and she shrugged one shoulder as though it was no big deal to her.

"You don't have to tell me. You aren't my first one-night stand, Torin."

But I'll be your last. Torin bit his tongue and paced his strides to Sorcha's as they followed the path down the hill.

"You deserve an explanation."

"Maybe I do. I'd be lying if I said I wasn't curious. But also, I hate that wanting to know makes me feel like one of those clingy women who can't handle a man walking away from her. I didn't have a problem with you leaving, Torin – even if the way you did it was quite rude. I'm a big girl – I can handle it. But you can't be expecting me to trust you is all. And, as far as I'm concerned, this whole fated mate nonsense? Well, it sounds like a relationship. Like…a serious one, at that. And for me? That's not a dance I want to dance. Particularly when I don't have a foundation of trust to build upon. Get what I'm saying? We're cool, though. I'm not mad at you anymore." Sorcha turned and gave him a sweet smile before patting him lightly on the shoulder.

She patted him on the shoulder.

Like he was a little child being dismissed by a mother who was too busy to look at the shiny rock he'd found to show her. Torin couldn't decide if he was more dumbfounded or enraged and took another moment to collect his thoughts as he scrambled over a loose portion of shale on the path. Normally, he would have exploded instantly when she'd all but dismissed him as a suitor to be forgotten, but he knew he had to contain his fiery temperament if he was going to have any chance of making headway with her.

He had no choice. If he didn't win her love, there would be nobody else for him. He'd already learned that no other woman held a candle to Sorcha – he'd barely looked at another woman after he'd left the festival that fateful night. In the moment – he hadn't fully understood he was claiming her. It had scared him, to say the least, and he'd struggled with what had happened ever since. He'd always understood the claiming of a fated mate was met with great seriousness and a long decision process. To have such magick happen in a flash, well, it had kind of rocked his world for a bit. He shouldn't have left her, and for that, he still felt guilty. Even if just for the fact that Torin well knew that a fated mate claim could leave the other with enhanced powers. It was part of the allure of finding a mate, after all, for true love made a Fae significantly more powerful.

Too powerful for some to handle even.

It was what had happened to his sister. Sighing, Torin pressed his lips together as he tried to decide how much to tell Sorcha. He wasn't used to explaining himself – to anyone but the queen, really – and so this was unfamiliar territory for him. Torin cleared his throat.

"How many times are you going to clear your throat before you actually say something?" Sorcha laughed at him, punching him lightly in the arm like they were buddies, and turned to keep walking. It was the last bit that had him committing to action. Grabbing her arm, he turned her. Time was of importance right now, but so was this.

"I'm not entirely keen on the idea of fated mates myself, if I'm to be honest," Torin said.

"Oh, well, that's grand. Makes two of us, doesn't it?" Sorcha shrugged again and started to turn, but Torin stopped her. The woman was maddening, wasn't she? She seemed ready to just brush him off and move on as though all this was nothing to her.

"Do you even understand what fated mates are?" Torin bit out. He pushed down his rising anger and reminded himself that Sorcha hadn't grown up in his world – she likely had no idea of the importance of this concept.

"Sounds kind of like what humans would call finding soulmates. But listen, that's a tough thing to believe in, you understand? My friend Sheila finds her soulmate about every six months or so." Sorcha laughed, turning to scan the horizon. The threatening clouds had moved closer, and Torin scented rain on the wind. At the very least, that would help with the fires that he knew were being started in protest. He didn't have long now before he'd go to battle, and he needed Sorcha by his side.

Without her, he was weaker.

It was a thought that really irked him, but he'd instantly understood it to be true when he'd seen her once more. The bond they had filled him, and when together it felt like he'd plugged himself into an electrical socket. He all but vibrated with energy now, being this close to her, but if she continued to deny the claim – well, this energy would then kill him. That was the tricky thing with love, wasn't it? It held the power to both build and destroy.

"Are soulmates a casual thing then?" Torin asked.

"Sure, and it gets bandied about like it's an easy thing to find for some, I suppose." Sorcha nibbled her lower lip as she thought about it, and Torin's thoughts went to the taste of her lips on his. Sweet, they'd been...with a hint of mint from the candy she popped in her mouth from a little tin that had sat on the dashboard of the van. "For some, yes, it's quite serious. For others, well, it's not even an idea they'll entertain. I think most people have different thoughts about it, really."

"In the Fae realm, fated mates are not really up for discussion in the sense of which you speak. They just are. They exist, and certain rules govern the relationships."

"Like government rules?" Sorcha squinched her nose in confusion.

"No, like...universal elemental goddess-type rules." Torin smiled. "Basically, if a Fae is lucky, they will hear their fated mate's heartsong. If both accept the claim, they are bonded in love and their strength grows. The bond is both a magickal and physical one. You feel it, don't you?" Torin cocked his head as he studied Sorcha. She absentmindedly rubbed her hand just below her rib cage, the soft fabric of her shirt pressing against her breasts.

"I, um..." Sorcha's eyes darted to Torin's.

"Right there? Where you're driving me crazy by rubbing yourself? I feel it, too." Torin tapped his chest. "You'll know when I'm close and you'll know when I'm very far away. Because of this connection, we should be able to find each other in times of trouble."

"But...you said both sides have to accept the claim? I haven't accepted mine."

"I still claimed you. Which means I opened my side of it. The bond is there...and it's right. It's just waiting. On you..."

Torin reached over and lifted her chin with his finger, so she looked up at him under spikey black eyelashes.

"Yet you said yourself you're not so keen on it. And *you* left. So, maybe we just, you know, give it back."

Torin laughed, shaking his head, and bent quickly to brush a soft kiss across her forehead. He wanted more but didn't want to push her yet. She deserved an explanation.

"Ah, well, it doesn't quite work like that. May I?" Torin tugged her hand, threading his fingers through hers, and a little pulse of energy zipped between them. When she didn't pull away, he took that as acceptance and continued down the trail. "I suppose I have a less than glamorous view of fated mates because of my sister."

"You have a sister? Parents?" Sorcha stopped, angling her face up at him in surprise.

"Did you think I just hatched from an egg somewhere?" Torin laughed.

"I don't know...I hadn't thought much about your life at all, really."

"Ouch, she wounds me." Torin rubbed his other hand over his heart. "Yes, I have a sister – *had* a sister – and my parents. A small family for the Fae, but that's just us."

"You lost your sister. Oh...I'm so sorry," Sorcha turned to him, and this time when she ran a hand down his arm, he enjoyed her touch because it showed she might actually care more than she was letting on.

"Yes, well. To her fated mate, actually. Sometimes, well, not all connections are good ones, you see? Both people need to be in the right place to receive and give love. My sister's fated mate, well, he..." Torin searched for the words to describe Joshuan. "He was a very charming Fae, of the Air Elementals, and loved nothing more than to flit from woman to woman. He had a deep need for constant attention, an inability to be alone with his own thoughts for even a second, and carried a lust for power. When my sister sang his heartsong, he responded – largely because she came from a more powerful bloodline than he did. It was an upward move for him."

"But...if he responds, doesn't that mean they bonded then?"

"He responded but didn't accept her claim." Torin spoke carefully, edging around the wound in his heart that had never fully healed.

"What happened?" Sorcha's words were soft, but she gripped his hand more tightly as they continued down the path and toward the little cottage tucked on the hillside where Bianca and Seamus were likely sleeping.

"He strung her along. Promising the claim was coming. All while he built connections in the Royal court and bedded as many other women as he could."

"Ugh, your poor sister. He sounds awful."

"He was. Is. His refusal to accept her claim burned inside her, consuming her, until madness claimed her."

"Oh my, did she...take her own life?" Sorcha skidded to a stop, her hand to her mouth.

"No, um...it's gradual, you see. That same magick that strengthens when a bond is made between fated mates. Well, if that magick is rejected – it will eventually kill you." Torin looked away, not wanting to see the look on Sorcha's face, knowing that his fate hung on her acceptance.

"Wait...what?" Sorcha gasped. "You're saying that if I don't accept your claim, that you'll go the same way as your sister? That this love magick or whatever will kill you?"

"Unless we *both* reject the claim." Torin finally looked down at her, sadness creeping through him.

"Oh, so you can just reject it then. That's fine, right?

Seems silly not to do that, no?" Sorcha winced when she realized what she'd unintentionally said about his sister. "I'm sorry. That came out wrong…I…"

"It's fine. When you both reject the claim, it comes with consequences, as love isn't meant to be taken lightly. Consequences like being stripped of all your magickal abilities. Some are fine living that way, but Joshuan didn't want to lose his powers or his newfound connections, and he also didn't want to give up my sister. She was too head-over-heels to listen to any sense. So certain was she that Joshuan would stop chasing other women and come to her that she waited and whispered his name on her lips during her last breath." Still, the thought enraged him. He'd very nearly killed Joshuan that night, except Donal and five other Fae had pulled him off the man. He'd had Joshuan banished from the Royal court, and still he heard rumors from time to time of him trying to wile his way back into the good graces of the queen. It was only the thought of his parents losing another child if he murdered a Fae out of spite that had stopped Torin from going after Joshuan. The queen had promised him that these things had a way of working themselves out, and that someday Joshuan would meet the consequences of his actions twofold.

"How incredibly tragic," Sorcha whispered.

"It is at that." Torin pulled his hand away from hers, uncomfortable with how much he was revealing of his own pain and continued to walk in silence. A low rumble from the clouds matched his mood, and the first drops of rain spattered lightly against his forehead.

"So…why me then? After all you've been through – why would you claim me and leave? I…I can't understand it."

Torin stopped and turned, looking up at where Sorcha stood above him, uncertainty clouding her striking face. He wanted to trace his fingers along the sharp angles of her cheeks, and kiss away the insecurity he saw lurking behind her gaze. Instead, he knew if he were to win her trust that full disclosure would be necessary.

"I didn't know I was claiming you. I was so caught up in the moment – in us. I knew I needed you the instant that I saw you, but I didn't really understand what that meant. Not until I was inside you. Until I felt our hearts connect, and I was so lost in my feelings, that I just...I claimed you. I allowed the magick in."

"You didn't even realize you'd done it?" Sorcha gaped at him.

"Sure and it frightened me, it did. After everything I'd gone through with my sister, well, once I realized what had happened – I left."

"You didn't even mean to claim me?" Sorcha's voice rose. "It was an accident?"

"Of course it wasn't an accident. You can't accidently choose your fated mate. It was an accident we met that night – but not that we're meant for each other."

"And then you just left?" Sorcha's voice continued to rise. Now her hands were at her hips, and pink patches mottled her lovely throat. "You knew you had claimed me and that it could, I don't know, kill you if I didn't accept it and you just left? For two years? Are you...completely fecking mental?"

"Right, so, this wasn't exactly how I thought this would go down when I told you this," Torin said, raising his hands in the air.

"Name me something more stupid than a man?" Sorcha seethed, shoving past him and stomping down the path. "Of all the stubborn, stupid, idiotic, bullheaded, asinine things to do...to leave when you knew the claim hadn't been accepted by me? Knowing it could kill you? I just...I can't.

Honestly, if I were to have a fated mate, I hadn't thought it would be one with such low intelligence that I would be embarrassed for him. I'm surprised you even manage to get dressed in the morning, I am. Let alone run an entire faction of Fae."

"Well, now, sure and that's not very nice, is it?" Torin raced after her, aggrieved at her response. Hadn't he just bared his heart about losing his sister?

"Nice? You want nice? You just told me you didn't even *mean* to pick me. How do you think that makes me feel? And then you follow it up with saying you left, knowing the magick could turn on you and *kill* you and to top it off – you dishonor your sister's name by doing so. I can't...I just can't."

"That's enough." Torin grabbed her arm and stopped her from walking forward. He leaned down until there were only inches between their faces. Her chest heaved, her breath coming in small little puffs, and she raised her chin at him. "I loved my sister. Very much."

"And yet you let her death be in vain by making the same mistake?" Sorcha asked, her words cutting through him.

"I honor her by choosing to believe that love is worth it – and can cross any hurdles – if you've claimed the right mate."

"And you were willing to gamble two years of your life – at the cost of maybe dying – before you finally decided to come back for me? Gee, that makes a girl feel good. Must've run through the rest of the women and realized I was your best shot?" Sorcha shook her head, and looked away, but not before Torin caught the sheen of tears in her eyes.

"Sorcha...I searched for you. I visited you in your dreams each night – the only way that I knew how to reach you," Torin said.

"Oh, please, I don't want to hear it. You just told me our bond thingy helps you find people. You obviously didn't look that hard for me. I can't...I can't begin to understand you. No, I don't think that I do."

"I could only find you in your dreams. Otherwise, you blocked me. And, honestly? I was confused, Sorcha. I didn't know that you could find and bond your mate in an evening. I didn't know what to think at all. But I also didn't want to reject the claim because, well, what if...?" Torin gripped her shoulders, willing her to understand.

"What if what?" Sorcha demanded, stomping her foot in anger.

"What if...this...*us*...is everything I've ever dreamed of?"

11

SORCHA TOOK her time in the shower, grateful for the use of a full bathroom and not her small shower set-up in Betty Blue. She leaned her forehead against the shower wall, allowing the hot water to run over her shoulders, easing some of the tension she carried there. Her mind whirled as she tried to process her emotions, as well as the new information she'd gained in such a short time. In all reality, she felt overly exposed, like a nightcrawler on a sidewalk who hadn't made it back to the dirt after the rain had dried. At any moment, Torin was going to say something that would crush her – and she'd had enough blows for the day.

Unable to stay still, Sorcha repeated a series of ballet steps in the shower while she washed her hair, her mind bouncing between Torin and her future. It was as though she was in a crystal snow globe that had been collecting dust on the shelf for years and now someone had picked it up and shaken it. Her thoughts drifted around like the glittery snow in the globe, and Sorcha stood frozen in the middle, unsure of what was happening. For years now, well, at least until she'd met Torin, Sorcha had prided herself on knowing her own mind and forging her own path. Her work was her comfort blanket, something she returned to over and over again, and she was proud of the name she'd built for herself. Now, that reputation likely lay in shreds and the Fae were real and...Sorcha banged her forehead lightly against the wall.

And...Torin was her fated mate.

There, she'd said it. Well, to herself at least. There was no use denying the bond between them, for she'd felt it every night she'd dreamt of him since they'd been apart. The problem was – could Sorcha bring herself to understand, or believe in, an entirely new future? One that held Fae realms, and magickal beings, and powers she likely hadn't even considered yet? When she'd read books about becoming a fairy princess as a child, she hadn't actually thought that was a potential career path for her. And yet, here she was.

You've already crossed the line. The thought slammed into her so hard that she stood still, gasping for breath, as the water pummeled her face. There was no going back, was there? Whether she had anything to do with Torin ever again or not – her world still had irrevocably changed. Because now she knew about the Fae, and they knew about her. The good ones and the bad ones. She didn't know what that meant for her future, but the queen had been very clear with her. Right now, she was a tool for the Dark Fae to use in their battles. No matter what happened with Torin, she was still on the Dark Fae's radar. Which meant nothing in her life would ever be the same.

Whether she wanted it to be or not was more self-reflection than Sorcha had the energy for at the moment, so instead she shut off the water and got out of the shower.

When her anxiety kicked up, she always tried to force her brain to focus on small tasks.

Toweling off. Making sure to get all the water that dripped down her legs.

Wrapping her hair up. Making sure to tuck the towel around her head nice and tight.

Breathing in...breathing out.

Sorcha gripped the side of the sink and leaned into the mirror, seeing the beginnings of a panic attack in the lines that creased her forehead and the widening of her eyes. *Move through the emotions,* Sorcha repeated to herself. Pulling on just her tank bra and underwear, Sorcha stepped into the small bedroom next to the bathroom. Grateful it was empty, she immediately flowed into a handstand. Holding herself there required focus, and she shifted on her hands, letting her weight settle into her shoulders and arms. Slowly, she lowered her legs into a split, and then brought them up high again, before lowering them once more. Arching backwards, she dropped lightly to her feet and flowed into a somersault that ended with her pushing back up into a handstand from the floor. The routine soothed her, forcing her to focus on proper form, and pushed away the panic that had bloomed inside her.

"Wowza," Bianca exclaimed from the door.

Used to distractions, Sorcha held the handstand split and swiveled her head to see Bianca – and now Seamus and Torin – peering through the doorway. Seamus's cheeks immediately pinkened in the most adorable way and he spun around.

"Sorry, I didn't know you were almost naked."

Sorcha chuckled. This was fairly covered up compared to some of the outfits she performed in, and she warmed even more to Seamus.

"That's some serious skills you have there," Bianca said.

"Stunning." Torin's one word comment fell like a benediction. Bianca hummed under her breath and made to take a step back.

"Bianca, I'd like to speak to you," Sorcha said, bringing her legs back up and flipping easily over onto her feet. "Without the men, if that's quite alright with you, Torin?" She stared pointedly at the man who still stood in the doorway, gaping at her.

"Go on then, you heard the girl." Bianca nudged Torin and then stepped inside, closing the door behind her. "Whether you meant to do that or not, it worked."

"Worked how?" Sorcha said as she pulled on her pants and unwrapped the towel from her damp hair.

"You have Torin eating out of your palm. I was certain he was going to toss me out of the room and barricade the door. That's a smitten man if I've ever seen one. Sure and he's dying to get his hands on you again."

"Well, that was *not* my intention with the little show you just saw. I was working my way out of a panic attack and exercise is one way for me to calm myself." Sorcha saw no reason to hide her issues. Frankly she didn't know many people that could go through what she just had and not be subject to their own moments of panic.

"That's a healthy way to handle it, isn't it then? You're better now?" Bianca perched on the bed, crossing her arms over her chest, concern radiating from her.

"Mostly. How did you do it?"

"Do what?" Bianca tilted her head at Sorcha in question. Sorcha buttoned up the blue plaid shirt she'd brought in from her truck, the soft flannel warming her, and picked up the wet towel from the floor.

"You're human, right? You don't have the soft magickal

glow of the Fae around you like the other two. How'd you..." Sorcha paused and made a little circle motion in the air, "you know...adapt to all this. The Fae. Magick. Get used to it? It's a lot to just...take in. And Torin seems to think I can just be like – sure, let's mate or whatever and on we go to battle Dark Fae. Like it's...like it's just another day."

"Well, for him it is."

Sorcha sighed and pinched her nose, taking a deep breath. Bianca wasn't wrong. Torin's world wasn't changing at all – but hers was.

"Right, I guess that's fair. But I'm kind of tripping over all the new things coming at me so fast. Now, I'll be honest – in theory I love these magickal new age kind of things. I love going to full moon parties and dancing around the fire and crystals...all of that. I even do a few ritual type things once in a while, like to ward off bad energy. I'll sage Betty Blue from time to time to protect her energy. But this? This is real deal stuff here, Bianca. Life-changing, knock me off my feet, type of stuff. How'd you deal with it?"

"Honestly? I just embraced it." Bianca laughed, and leaned back, her face going a bit soft as she remembered. "Well, now, sure and I'd say two things helped me embrace it. The first? I used to run mythology tours at the University. So, I already knew a lot about the Fae, well, at least what the humans thought they knew of the Fae. And the second? I had no time. We quite literally were thrown into battle. I was already a passenger on a quest to stop the curse of the Four Treasures long before I even knew it existed. By the time I'd been given the knowledge of what was going on, I was in survival mode."

"So you just went...with it?" Sorcha paused in toweling her hair.

"When confronted with evil – you have two choices. You

can lay down and die or go forward and fight. I'll always choose action over inaction."

"Me too," Sorcha said softly. The drive for movement had propelled her from her small town and to risk a new life for herself. The door slammed open, bouncing off the wall, causing her to start. Seamus filled the doorway, his eyes carefully averted in case Sorcha was still half-dressed.

"What's wrong?" Bianca jumped up.

"At ease, Seamus. I'm dressed." Sorcha threw her hair up in a messy bun on the top of her head.

"The Fire Fae have taken over the cove. They're trying to burn the portal in the secret cave. Gracie is there. She's alone."

"We go now. Transport?" Bianca jumped up. "I need my bag. Sorcha, shoes on! Get a weapon. Any weapon."

"What's happening? Who is Gracie?" Sorcha whirled as Torin ran into the room, a bag over his shoulders and handed her a wicked looking dagger.

"Use this if anyone gets too close. Use anything you can really." Torin wrapped an arm around Sorcha's waist.

"I don't have my shoes…" Sorcha gaped down at her feet as a pair of boots appeared. "Well, that was handy."

"Gracie is, well, she's the famous pirate Grace O'Malley. Reincarnated in her own bloodline years later. She's extremely powerful, and the cove is enchanted with her blood. But even so – she's not Fae. She may be magick, but she's not Fae. She'll do the best she can, but on her own? It's terrifying. We have to go now!"

Worry for Bianca's friend filled Sorcha as Torin muttered some words and the weird sucking sensation which meant they were transporting surrounded her. The pounding of her heart filled Sorcha's ears, and she held Torin tightly,

completely unprepared for what greeted her when they
materialized on a beach.

The cove was on fire.

The sight stole Sorcha's breath, as flames rippled across
the water's surface, seemingly immune to its natural effect
on fire. High cliff walls hugged the beach they stood on,
enclosing the flames that danced across the ocean's surface,
and a cry from down the beach tore her gaze from the
flames. A lone woman, her hair tumbling in a riot of waves
around her head, held her arms in the air as an army of dark
Fae approached her on the sand.

"The ones glowing silver?" Torin looked down at her,
making sure she understood him. "Kill them."

"Erm…" Sorcha didn't know how to kill anyone.

"Use fire. Use your dagger. Aim for vulnerable spots.
The neck. Heart. Gut. Through the eye to the brain. Whatever works."

"Oh man…" Anxiety roiled in her stomach and Sorcha
wondered briefly if she was going to be sick.

"The Fire Fae? The ones out there on the water? See
them dancing through the flames?" Torin pointed as they
hustled toward the army enclosing on the woman who
stood in front of a small archway cut into the cliff wall. That
must be the portal site, Sorcha thought and turned to see
where Torin pointed.

"Oh shite…" Sorcha breathed. What she'd first taken as
flames on the water's surface were so much more than that.
Thousands of people, well, Fae that is, filled the fire, their
skin flickering shades of red, gold, and deepest blue. Their
eyes were brilliant orange opals of fire, and their bodies
flowed and darted, like the wind hitting a candle flame.
Together, they created a wildfire of unimaginable proportions that writhed over the ocean's surface.

"Don't hurt them," Torin said. "Unless they truly try to kill you. They shouldn't. But otherwise, just...it's my job to protect them. Even when they revolt. I don't know that they fully understand what they're doing."

"Right." Sorcha nodded, respect for Torin's leadership blooming inside her. Glancing to the water again, she watched the Fire Fae's eyes land on her – tracking their movements – but they didn't come forward. Equally as wary, she realized.

"You catch that?" Torin called to Seamus and Bianca who pounded the sand next to them.

"Kill the Domnua. Be nice to the Elementals as needed," Bianca panted. Ahead of them, the woman cried out and the first line of Domnua fell at her feet.

Gracie cut a magnificent figure, Sorcha thought, instantly falling a little bit in love with her. There was something so starkly oppositional about the woman standing barefoot in a flowing housedress against the wall of evil Fae who surrounded her. She was a beacon of light in the darkness, a lighthouse on a rocky outcropping, stalwart and terrifying as she raised her arms once more and screamed to the heavens. Yes, this was a woman who commanded others, not afraid to stand up for what was right, and admiration for her courage brought tears to Sorcha's eyes.

"She's magnificent," Sorcha said as they skidded to a stop behind the wall of Domnua who were still so focused on Gracie that they hadn't seen Torin approach.

"The best there is. Let's help our girl out, shall we?" Bianca said and raised her voice in a war cry. Turning, Gracie's face lit with pleasure when she spotted their little group through the throngs of Fae. Whipping out a hand, she blew down another row of Domnua in the front as Torin blasted them with fire from the back. Realizing they'd been flanked, the Domnua turned, a confused mass, running in all directions and the group fanned out, picking them off as they scattered.

Well, the others picked them off. Sorcha just did her best not to get in the way. Only when one Domnua narrowed in on her, raising his sword, did she react and fire bolt him in the face. It wasn't pretty when he exploded into a ball of silvery goop, but Sorcha had to admit it was satisfying. Perhaps she had more of a bloodthirsty side than she realized. In seconds, another Domnua ran for her and soon Sorcha had little time for a thought other than of her own survival.

Battle was nothing like they portrayed it in the movies. At least, the ones she'd watched had the epic soundtrack in the background and momentous heart-pounding moments. In reality, Sorcha realized that fighting for her actual life was quite scary and very tedious. It never seemed to end. Wave after wave of Domnua appeared, seemingly from nowhere, and soon her shirt was soaked in sweat as she dodged, rolled, and ducked out of the way of the evil Fae. At least her acrobatic skills were helpful here, as she found the Domnua to be clunky in their movements and not as skilled at anticipating where she'd pivot to.

"Not very bright, are they?" Sorcha panted to Bianca who'd come to fight back-to-back with her.

"No, the evil ones rarely are, are they? I can't decide if that makes them more or less dangerous."

"That's an unfortunate truth, isn't it?" Sorcha gasped as four Domnua shouted her name from the cliffs above. They held a wiggling dog in their arms, brandishing it over their heads, and Sorcha's heart froze. She couldn't abide this. She broke for the trail, not caring if the Domnua were luring her in. It had only taken one glance at Gracie's horrified face to understand that this was her dog, and the Domnua were using it to lure Sorcha away from the group.

Fine, have it their way, Sorcha thought, as she pushed her muscles to the extreme as she pounded up the path.

They had no idea who they were messing with.

12

SORCHA'S LUNGS screamed as she drew closer to the top of the cliff where the Domnua brandished the struggling dog. Anger pushed her to move faster, but still she worried she wouldn't make it in time. Her heart wouldn't be able to handle it if they tossed the dog over the cliff.

"I'll just be giving you a bit of a boost." A voice at her ear almost had her tumbling backward off the edge of the path. A gentle pressure at her back kept her in place, and Sorcha's eyes widened at the woman who hovered at her side. Yes, hovered. Slightly transparent, glowing, and clearly not fully in this world – the woman bent over Sorcha's shoulder. "Lean into me. I've got you. Go get Rosie. I can only do so much to help that sweet dog."

"But..." Sorcha gasped as her feet lifted off the ground.

"*Lean* into me." The harshness of her voice snapped Sorcha out of her momentary confusion, and she leaned back, trusting this apparition to carry her to safety. Maybe it was stupid, but time was of the essence, and Sorcha trusted her gut. Even when said gut coiled in knots as her body swooped from the ledge and up the side of the cliff walls as though she was a gull diving for its dinner in the waters far, far, far below where she now hovered. Sorcha gulped. On the list of possible ways she could die, this particular scenario had never been a consideration. When her feet touched the grass on the top of the cliff, Sorcha sent a silent prayer upwards, while already lifting her hands to shoot off a ball of fire at the Domnua.

They clearly hadn't anticipated her to act so quickly, and the startled Domnua holding the dog dropped it to the ground when he brought his arms up to try and defend himself. Relief filled Sorcha as the dog rolled over the grass, finding its feet quickly, and she shouted to it.

"Go on, Rosie! Run!" Hoping she had the dog's name right, Sorcha dropped to one knee and sent off another round of fire balls at the advancing Domnua, taking two out in a very satisfying silvery explosion. The one that had been holding the dog stalked toward her, and Sorcha noted a silvery circlet at his forehead. This one must hold more magick, she realized, and steeled herself for an onslaught. With the dagger in one hand, Sorcha took a deep breath and called upon the river of power that coursed through her. Raising her eyes to the Domnua's, she smiled.

"You've miscalculated. Don't you see? You *never* hurt the dog." With that, Sorcha raised her hands to blast as much power as she could into this nasty Domnua, but before she could the Domnua stumbled.

Rosie was back. Instead of running, she'd circled back and now took her vengeance out on the Fae that had kidnapped her by sinking her teeth into its calf. The Domnua kicked its leg out, trying to shake the dog, but Rosie held on, her little furry body vibrating with rage.

"We don't deserve dogs." The voice at her ear again.

Sorcha didn't even look, so focused was she on the Domnua in front of her. "Let's take him down."

Together, Sorcha and the apparition sent out a wave of magick so powerful that the Domnua barely had an instant to register it before he too was destroyed in a silvery spray of goo. Immediately, Sorcha was up and racing to the dog and crouching by its side.

"Oh, you sweet thing. You came back to help. You shouldn't have. I had it covered, I promise. We didn't want you to get hurt," Sorcha said, stroking the dog's shaking body, accepting her haphazard licks. Finally, when Sorcha couldn't handle the slobber anymore, she laughed and leaned back on her heels. "You are going to have to stay up here, Rosie. I think you must belong to Gracie, and she needs my help."

"I'll take care of Rosie."

Sorcha looked up from her crouch and studied the woman before her. With white curling hair and a tumble of necklaces at her throat, she looked like every depiction of a wise woman she'd ever seen.

"Who are you?"

"I'm Fiona. And Rosie is a grand-pup of mine, you could say. As is my Gracie who is courageous to the point of foolishness. The Domnua are getting smarter. They weren't wrong in thinking that grabbing Rosie would distract Gracie. But it seemed they also wanted you."

"Yes, I heard them yelling my name." With one more stroke of Rosie's soft ears, Sorcha stood. "I don't know how you came to be here, but I appreciated the help."

"Oh, well...I'm around." A quick smile flitted over the ghost's face. "I need to get you back to the beach. I suspect you were used as a distraction, and I don't like you being unprotected up here."

"Yes, best to go. You're certain Rosie is safe?" Sorcha cast a dubious look back to the dog smiling up at her.

"Now that the Domnua don't have her, I can work a protection spell around her. She'll be just fine with me."

"Goodbye, Fiona. Thanks for the help." Sorcha began to run to the path and gasped when she felt that swooshing motion again which meant she was being lifted. "Oh, I don't think I can get used to this."

"It doesn't happen often, I can promise you that," Fiona said at her ear, and then Sorcha's stomach flipped over itself, and she bit back a scream as Fiona hurtled her over the side of the cliff, diving down the cliff walls and straight toward the battle that raged on the beach below them. Nope, it wouldn't do to throw up everywhere, though Sorcha briefly considered it as a possible battle tactic. At the last moment, she was able to swallow the vomit back as Fiona slowed her descent and dropped her gently onto the sand. Gracie raced over as Rosie howled from the top of the cliff.

"You saved her." Gracie reached down and hauled Sorcha up from the sand.

"Of course," Sorcha said. "Well, with some help from Fiona, that is."

"I'm in your debt."

"Nah, don't bother. I'm just happy she's okay."

"Nevertheless." Gracie whirled and muttered something under her breath before a pearlescent wave of magick shimmered across the beach and knocked out the next wave of advancing Domnua. "Your man is distracted because of this. You need to go to him. It was what they wanted. The further they lure him away from the portal entrance, the more likely they'll take control of it. I'll stand my ground."

"Wait, just you? But what about..."

"Just go." Gracie shoved her toward the water where

Sorcha could now see a circle of Domnua closing in on Torin. The flames on the ocean grew higher behind him, the Fire Fae agitated as they bounced from flame to flame, seemingly unsure of what their next move was. Did they even understand what they were fighting for?

Or against.

Her feet dug into the soft sand, slowing her progress, and panic built once more as Torin stumbled and went down to a knee. Still, he held his ground, lashing out with both magick and a deadly-looking sword, but for every Domnua he cut down, two more advanced. Panic flipped to anger, and a shot of adrenaline fueled Sorcha so that by the time she skidded to a halt behind the group, she was ready to destroy.

Without a word, Sorcha ruthlessly stabbed a Domnua in the back of the neck, while shooting out a bolt of flame with her other hand. Whirling, she took out two more Domnua that had approached from the back, gasping as she took a hit to her side.

"Torin!" Sorcha shrieked. Diving into a front flip and kicking a Domnua in the chest with both feet, Sorcha drove her blade into its gut as it fell.

"Sorcha!" Hope bloomed on Torin's face, and with a roar, he stood, magick crackling around him like someone had cut a live wire. With renewed energy to fight, now that he saw she was alive, Torin destroyed several more Domnua as he advanced to where Sorcha fought.

"See how he fights for you? You're his greatest weakness." A silky voice at her ear was the only warning Sorcha had before an arm locked around her throat. Gasping for air, she dug her nails into the arm, trying to release it from her neck.

"Fire Fae!" Donal shouted, his voice carrying from her

shoulder and bellowing across the water where the Fire Fae careened in chaos. "She is the one you want. It's her that stands in your way."

"Sorcha!" Torin shouted, terror flashing in his tawny eyes, as fire exploded higher into the sky, the heat now almost unbearable. Tears filled her eyes as she gasped for air, dizziness threatening her sight.

And then, there was nothing. Sorcha fell to her hands and knees in the sand, dragging air into her screaming lungs. Looking up, she pushed her sweaty hair out of her face to see Gracie smiling down at her.

"Well, now, that's a nice quick way to repay a debt, isn't it then?"

"Sure and I'm thankful for it. Is he..." Sorcha's gaze darted down the beach.

"He slipped away before I could take him out. Coward." Gracie spat and hauled Sorcha to her feet once more. "No time to dally, though. Fire's coming."

"Torin?" They needed to get away from the raging inferno that now threatened the edges of the beach. Smoke filled the air, clouding her vision, and a wall of heat pressed against her skin.

"I've got him. Go on then," Gracie ordered, but Sorcha ignored the command. Instead, she followed Gracie into the wall of smoke, ducking low to try and gain some air, and almost screamed when she saw Torin face down in the sand.

"I see you listen well," Gracie shouted over the roar of the fire.

"It's one of my best qualities," Sorcha quipped back though it felt like her insides were being torn in two. Together, the women hooked their arms under Torin's and pulled him up, switching position, and then dragging him haphazardly across the sand until they reached the walls of the cliff. There, they propped Torin against the wall and made sure he was breathing.

"I'm going after Bianca and Seamus," Gracie said, pulling her hair back from her face in a quick knot. "Stay here because if he comes to and doesn't see you – he'll be right back into the fire."

"I…" Her words rang true, so all Sorcha could do was acknowledge them with a quick nod. Gracie raced off across the beach, and admiration for this incredible woman filled her once more. She didn't even know who they were, and yet Gracie had laid her life on the line this day. It was courage in its most pure form, and remarkable to bear witness to.

Dropping to her knees, Sorcha brought her hands to Torin's face and wiped the dirt and soot away from his cheeks. Blood seeped from several wounds on his arms and his sides. Sorcha began to take stock of his injuries, trying to see what needed the most attention first. There were so many wounds, *too* many, and Sorcha pulled her flannel shirt off and ripped it into strips. Moving quickly, forcing herself to stay on task and not trip into the panic that danced at the edges of her mind, she bandaged as many of the wounds as she could. Still, it didn't seem to be enough.

A tear slipped down her cheek and landed on Torin's lips.

"Sorcha." Torin blinked up at her, a soft smiling playing on his mouth, his eyes filled with excitement to see her. "You're safe."

"I…yes, I am," Sorcha said, swiping the back of her hand across her eyes. "Torin, oh, I'm worried for you. You've taken a lot of hits."

Torin shook his head, looking up at her and then out

where the raging inferno crept closer. "I'm so very happy you're safe."

"Torin, we need you here. The Fae need you. We can't get through this battle without you. I need you to hang on just a little longer."

"Prettiest woman. Enchanting woman of my heart. I'll sing for you...my heartsong always."

Sorcha swallowed against the lump in her throat when his eyelashes fluttered closed once more. A cry sounded, aching and pure, hanging in the smokey air. Turning, Sorcha gaped at the water.

A thousand voices followed the cry, uniting in an effervescent harmony, the song cool and liquid like the water from which it rose. Hundreds of...mermaids it seemed, teemed in the water below the flames, engulfing the Fire Fae and the inferno they tended.

"The Water Fae are here..." Bianca skidded to a stop by their side, with Seamus and Gracie following closely. "How is he?"

"Not good," Sorcha bit out, transfixed by the nebulous beings that shimmered in the water, their power and song engulfing the flames. In a mere matter of moments, the Fire Fae had been subdued and the beach lay empty of Domnua. At the water, two people rose and hurried up the sand to them.

"Imogen! Nolan!" Bianca sprang up from Torin's side and ran to them.

At least they weren't more enemies, Sorcha thought, and turned back to press a hand to Torin's forehead. Gracie was already crouching at his side.

"Please don't touch him," Gracie ordered, her hands on the largest wound at Torin's side.

"Excuse me?" The order rankled, and Sorcha found she

didn't like another woman touching Torin's body. A thought to be filed away for later, she realized, when Gracie looked up at her with whiskey-brown eyes.

"I'm a healer. But I can't have you touching him when I work."

"Oh she's a healer as well, sure why not. Are you every-woman then?" Sorcha said, dropping to her knees to watch Gracie work.

"Something like that. A little bit of this, and a little bit of that. I can't heal all of the Fae magick in him, he'll need his own kind to heal him for that. But I can at least knit his wounds and stop the blood loss. It's not much but it will see him through until he gets better help."

"I..." Sorcha shook her head and then pressed her lips together. Her emotions were all over the place right now, and tears threatened with laughter. Uncertain of what to do, or how she was feeling, she kept her mouth closed lest she say something stupid.

Bianca turned to the striking couple who now stood looking down at them. "Imogen and Nolan – this is Gracie and Sorcha. Sorcha is Torin's fated mate."

"Um..." Sorcha caught Gracie grinning up at her.

"Is that right? He's a fine one at that," Gracie said.

"I'm not certain of that yet," Sorcha bit out.

"Methinks your heart has already decided," Gracie whispered, before turning back to her duties.

"The portal is safe?" Nolan, an extremely large and muscular man who carried himself with a similar air of authority as Torin did, spoke to Seamus.

"The portal has been protected. But not without a major fight. The Domnua are growing stronger, and they are getting better at riling up the Elementals. I was worried if we didn't get hurt by the Domnua then we'd die from smoke inhalation," Seamus said. Dirt streaked his face, and his red hair stood up at all angles.

"I'm glad we came when we did," Nolan said, his face a mask of worry. "It took a bit of convincing, as the Water Fae weren't certain about turning on the Fire Fae. But in the end, they understood the necessity of it."

"Let's get him out of here. It's not safe." Nolan bent and scooped Torin into his arms, annoying Gracie.

"You'll take care of him then?"

"We've got our own elixirs for the magick seeping through his veins. But time is what matters now. Are you with this group?"

"No, I'll stay here," Gracie said.

"She protected the portal," Sorcha spoke up, drawing the man's eyes to her. "She's not Fae. But she stood for you and yours. She deserves some protection."

"Noted." Nolan nodded curtly before turning.

The sucking sensation where Sorcha felt like she was being pulled through a vacuum cleaner came quickly, and then they were no longer in the cove.

13

THE GROUP STOOD in a cavernous hall comprised of white marble, long narrow windows, and free-floating balls of light that flitted around the room. Upon closer inspection, Sorcha discovered these balls were miniature fairies who grinned impishly at her as they danced by. Instantly she wanted one, or two, for her van – little sparkly companions to hang out with on road trips. Even now, she could see how they'd add extra excitement to her shows and how people would try to guess how she created the floating balls of light.

At the thought of her shows, her heart fell again. The Irish did love a good pun, and in her heart of hearts she knew that now she'd been dubbed "Smokin' Sorcha" along with the tragedy surrounding it – her career was over. It stung, *really* stung, and her mind still couldn't come to grips with the fact that she wouldn't be attending her booking this coming weekend. Or the weekend after that. Or any, really. What she needed was a chance to get online, so at the very least she could kindly and professionally respond to what were certainly cancellations, but there was no way for her to do so. Not from here. Wherever here was. No, every day that she showed silence to the world and didn't respond to inquiries would only add to her tarnished reputation. Not that any of that mattered at the moment.

"Where is he?" Queen Aurelia strode into the hall in a magnificent gown of shimmery silvery beading shot through with aquamarine threads. Her hair was pulled back in a series of intricate braids showcasing a delicate crown of quartz and aquamarine stones. Instantly, the group she'd traveled with bowed, even Bianca, and Sorcha hurried to do the same. Not that she pledged allegiance to the queen or anything, but it wouldn't do to be disrespectful either. "Guards, take him to the tower room. Prince Callum will attend to him at once."

"Wait..." Sorcha surprised herself by speaking. As she did, the queen turned back to her with a sharply raised eyebrow.

"Yes?"

"May I..." Sorcha wasn't sure how many protocols she was breaking. But she did feel it necessary that she stay with Torin. She couldn't say why, exactly, but it felt like she needed to be by his side. Bianca squeezed her arm, reassuring her.

"It's okay to ask, Sorcha. The queen is nicer than she seems," Bianca whispered at her side. Bianca had held her own during the battle, escaping with minimal scrapes and bumps, and it seemed Seamus was faring well, too.

"You'd like to accompany Torin during his healing?" Queen Aurelia guessed correctly.

"If it's not too much of a bother..." Sorcha ducked her head, bobbing it awkwardly in what she hoped was a sign of respect.

The queen held her eyes, a knowing light gleaming there, and then nodded once.

"Come with me." The queen turned without another word.

"Thank you." Sorcha squeezed Bianca's hand and then hurried after the queen who was almost all the way out of the room, her steps echoing across the huge hall. Sorcha fell in line as the guards carried Torin through a softly lit hallway, again with the floating sparkle fairies, that wound in a half circle until it stopped at an arched door with no handle or hinges. Leaning forward, the queen touched her palm to the door, and it shimmered with rose gold light before swinging open to reveal a set of white marble stairs.

Now *that* was cool.

Sorcha followed silently as they climbed the stairs, noting that a guard had swiftly stepped between her and the queen, so she wasn't climbing directly behind the powerful Fae. Smart, Sorcha thought. Even though Sorcha was a mere amateur compared to the magick these Fae held, it wouldn't do to expose their matriarch to any potential threats.

Walking through another doorway which the queen opened again with the touch of her palm, they entered a large circular room built in the same white marble. Along the wall stood a narrow worktable and several shelves. The man in front of them turned at their arrival. Sorcha blinked in surprise. Was every royal Fae just drop-dead gorgeous? Gilded hair, ocean-blue eyes, and a chiseled jaw made this man look like he'd just stepped from a Vogue cover.

"Callum, meet Sorcha. She's Torin's fated mate. She wished to accompany him during the healing." Queen Aurelia turned to her. "Callum is my son, and Prince of the Danula Fae. His talents run to healing magicks, though he's powerful in most areas. He'll see to Torin at once."

"Thank you," Sorcha said, dipping her head in the

awkward nodding bow she seemed to have adopted as her way of greeting royals.

"Can you tell us what happened?" Prince Callum asked as he turned back to the table and the bottles that lined it. Sorcha wasn't sure where to go or what to do, so she crossed to the bed in the center of the room where the guards had laid Torin. Gracie hadn't been wrong – she *was* a healer – and Sorcha was pleased to see many of the major wounds had stopped seeping blood. But his color wasn't good, his face pale in the soft light of the tower, and his eyes remained closed. Hesitantly, Sorcha reached out and slipped her fingers into his hand, applying gentle pressure so he would know he wasn't alone.

"I certainly don't know all the magickal players or anything, but I can give you a basic run-down," Sorcha said, watching Torin's face for any sign of awareness. "We arrived at the cove, and it was burning. As in...the water was on fire. I've never seen anything like it. Turns out it was the Fire Fae on the water. The...the bad guys? The Dark Fae?" Sorcha darted a questioning look over her shoulder.

"The Domnua," Queen Aurelia supplied with a small smile.

"Yes, those. They were there by the hundreds...if not more. Gracie – she's not Fae, but clearly magick of some sort, was standing alone on the beach. She held them off from entering the portal cave. I think you owe her – big time. She was..." Sorcha shook her head, her throat tightening again at the sight of this woman standing alone in her billowing dress before the forces of an evil army. The image would forever be seared into her brain. "Magnificent. Stronger than any warrior I've ever seen. I don't know that she would have lasted, but she kept them from taking over the portal until we arrived. After that, it was bedlam.

They lured me away to save a dog, I'm not sure what happened to Bianca and Seamus for a while there, the fire got so big I thought we'd die from smoke inhalation, and then..."

"Battles are incredibly difficult...emotionally and physically." Queen Aurelia surprised Sorcha by laying a hand on her arm, and a soft wave of calm swept through Sorcha. Perhaps the queen was soothing her with magick. "It's difficult to go through and even more so to recount."

Sorcha swallowed, her stomach still in knots over Torin, and nodded.

"When I got back to the beach, they'd overtaken Torin. I tried to help, but...Donal came back. He choked me, and I could barely breathe. I was about to pass out when Gracie saved me. Said she owed me for saving her dog. Like I'd let a dog get hurt," Sorcha shook her head with a rueful laugh. "Donal disappeared and the mermaids came. And...well, Torin was wounded. Badly. Gracie helped, again. She healed him where she could. Is there any way..." Sorcha looked at the queen. "Can you check on her? I just want to make sure she's safe."

"Of course, we'll send someone at once." The queen nodded to a guard who stood at the wall. "Please send a royal warrior to offer support to Gracie as needed. As well as our debt of gratitude." The guard disappeared instantly at her bidding, something Sorcha wasn't sure she'd ever get used to. The whole people standing in front of her and then not there in the next instant thing was a bit disconcerting.

"Donal has betrayed us." Prince Callum stepped to Torin's side, a small bottle in his hand. Taking a dropper from the top, he tapped it against Torin's lips, pushing his mouth open and then fed him a silvery liquid. Sorcha watched for Torin's throat to move, swallowing the medicine, and was rewarded when he did. Squeezing his palm more tightly, warmth filled her when he squeezed back.

"He has." Sorcha looked up at the prince. "He kidnapped me the first night, using me as a diversion at…" it was still hard to say it, "at the wedding reception that the Dark Fae set fire to. He's not a friend to your people."

"He spoke to you?" Queen Aurelia asked.

"He's…Dom…Dark Fae."

"Domnua," Prince Callum said, helping her out with the word. "He's Dark Fae? All this time? How did we miss it?"

"Something we'll be looking into very seriously," Queen Aurelia murmured.

"He seems to think they should have all the power," Sorcha said, her eyes still on Torin. The color in his face seemed to be returning, but perhaps that was just her being hopeful.

"A not uncommon sentiment among their people. The Domnua have no respect for order, instead caring only for their most basic and immediate wants – which they will classify as needs – and refuse to think of their impact on the world as a whole. A myopic bunch, they are, focusing solely on more, more, more with zero regard to the damage left in their wake. A rise to power would be catastrophic for all, but they're too blind to see the ramifications of the actions of their leader, Goddess Domnu. They follow her, drunk on the promise of more, not realizing they are setting their own houses on fire in doing so," Queen Aurelia's voice was laced with sadness.

Sorcha didn't know what to say, so instead she continued to squeeze Torin's hand lightly, hoping to see his eyes open soon. Whatever was going to happen between the two Fae realms was their own problem – hers was whether she would be going home or not. And, maybe, just a little bit –

whether Torin was going to be safe or not. She didn't want to claim him as her mate, oh no, she needed to go home and follow her own path forward. But the chemistry between them was undeniable and even if she wasn't sure where she stood with him – he wasn't necessarily a bad man. He didn't need to be a casualty in all of this.

"How did he mask it? For so long?" Prince Callum crossed his arms over his chest, a mutinous expression on his rugged face. Sorcha could all but feel his rage crackling around him, and she hunched her shoulders, not wanting to be on the receiving end of his fury. Donal must be fairly confident if he was willing to take on these two royals – who both exuded deadly confidence.

"And how many others are hiding in your ranks?" Sorcha spoke without thinking and then drew her gaze from Torin when silence filled the room.

"She's right." Queen Aurelia turned away from the bed and began to pace the circular room, the sound of her heels on marble echoing in the chamber. "If Donal managed to get this far – how many others? We…"

"Can people be turned?" Sorcha asked, not caring when both royals looked at her with surprise for interrupting.

"Turned? What do you mean?" The queen tilted her head, a subtle shake of her finger stopping a guard from crossing to Sorcha, presumably to shut her up.

"Like…can you be good Fae one day and then be turned to bad? Is there a way that maybe the bad guys got to Donal, turned him…like a zombie or something…and so maybe he wasn't bad all along?"

"A zombie?" Queen Aurelia's forehead crinkled in confusion.

"It's a human fairy tale. One of their stories. Where dead people come back to life and kill others by biting them.

Then those dead people become like them. Zombies. It's quite amusing, I must admit." Prince Callum shrugged one shoulder.

"That doesn't sound like an appealing story at all..." Queen Aurelia continued to look puzzled.

"It's just that...I'm wondering if people can convert. Or switch allegiances. Or do you have to be born into being dark or light...is it blood only?" Sorcha asked.

"That's a fair point she's raising." Prince Callum tapped a finger against his lips and rocked back on his heels as he considered her words. The fact that they were even entertaining her theory sent a little jolt of pride through Sorcha. She may not have known a lot about the Fae realm, but she did know a lot about people – having studied them in all walks of life. People changed all the time – their allegiances, their beliefs, and even their religions. It wasn't that far-fetched to think that joining a different magickal kingdom would cause a shift in power.

"Torin mentioned he'd been acting a bit odd of late. More distant. He seemed to think it was because of a woman." The queen turned to another guard in the corner. "I'd like you to alert the Royal Court advisors that we'll be holding a meeting shortly. I need to warn them, as well as assess if there have been any other unusual behavioral changes among our people. If so, we'll need to single them out and start tracking their movements."

"Yes, your highness." The guard disappeared into thin air.

Torin's fingers tapped hers and Sorcha glanced down to see his inky lashes fluttering against his cheeks, before his eyes slowly opened. He blinked a few times, his eyes darting around the room, before landing on Sorcha and staying there. A small smile quirked his lips and Sorcha fought the urge to reach over and trace her finger over them.

"Hey there..." Sorcha said and both royals were instantly at the side of the bed.

"Torin...you're home in the castle. You suffered some grave injuries but were able to hold on until we could administer aid," Prince Callum said, holding his hand to Torin's forehead.

"The portal?" Torin rasped and Sorcha turned to look for water, but a guard was already bringing a glass to the bedside.

"Safe. You've served us well this day. You bring honor to us, and we appreciate the courage you showed in battle today. And you were able to do so without harming any of the Fire Fae," Queen Aurelia said.

"Not that they didn't deserve it," Sorcha muttered.

"Why do you say that?" The queen's voice was sharp, and Sorcha put her chin up. This wasn't her queen, after all, and she could be as insubordinate as she wanted. Not that she really wanted to, actually, because the queen was pretty badass...but, still.

"Well, how come the Fire Fae are allowed to almost kill us with their smoke and flames but we have to refrain from hurting them? It seems unfair, doesn't it? Not to mention, a weapon they can use against us, no? If they know we won't hurt them – then they have nothing to lose," Sorcha pointed out. She realized she was already speaking of herself as a "we" with the Fae, and that thought didn't sit particularly well either. Uncomfortable with all of it, she shrugged. "I just don't think it's a fair fight then, is all."

"The Fire Fae have been manipulated by the Domnua. They don't fully understand what they're doing," Queen Aurelia said.

"They know they can kill, don't they?" Sorcha pressed.

"Yes, they do." Queen Aurelia bowed her head in acknowledgement.

"Well, maybe they need to learn that they aren't immune to loss either. Otherwise they'll just keep pushing and eventually they will kill one or all of us. And then where will you be?" Sorcha demanded and then stopped when Torin squeezed her hand tightly.

"Sorcha," Torin whispered, and Sorcha looked down at him, annoyed.

"What?"

"It's okay, darling. We're safe now."

Frustrated, Sorcha withdrew her hand and pressed her lips together, not wanting to say anything else that might get her tossed in royal jail or something even more disastrous.

"It's a point I will consider carefully. Thank you, Sorcha, for speaking freely with me. Not everyone has the courage to do so," Queen Aurelia said. Sorcha swallowed, nodding, afraid to say anything else lest she lose the small footing she'd gained with the Queen. "I'll be leaving you to him now. Callum, will you join me?"

"Of course." Callum turned and bent over Torin. "Your vitals are good, mate. But you need to rest, at least this night. We can discuss our steps forward tomorrow."

"But...what if I'm needed?" Torin tried to push himself up, but Callum pushed him gently back to the bed.

"You'll do no good to anyone in this condition. Nasty magick that Donal used. Let our counter-magick work through you and you'll be fine in the morning." Callum turned to Sorcha. "You'll stay with him."

It wasn't a question, and since Sorcha had no idea how to open the magickal doors to the chamber room, all she could do was nod her acquiescence.

"We'll have food sent, a bath, and change of clothes for the both of you. We'll speak again." With that, both royals left through the door they'd come through earlier. It sealed itself quickly behind them, virtually rendering Sorcha a prisoner with Torin, and she decided not to think too deeply about escape. If anything, she trusted Bianca to come get her as needed. Sorcha might not understand a lot of what was going on, but she knew the blonde was one of her people.

In Bianca I trust, Sorcha laughed to herself silently.

14

SHE'D STAYED by his side.

Torin slitted his eyes open, drinking in the sight of Sorcha, feeling at peace for the first time since they'd landed on the beach. When she disappeared during the battle, he'd almost lost it. His fury had known no bounds, and he'd killed more Domnua in the space of her absence than he had in years. He'd paid for it, that was for sure, but at the time he'd thought Sorcha was lost to him. Never had he seen a more welcome sight than Sorcha racing down the beach, her brilliant red hair streaming in the air, and her face set in stone. Sure, and his love was a ferocious one, she was, and she'd been a pleasure to watch in battle. He hadn't known, not really, what she'd meant to him until he'd seen how skillfully she'd ducked and dodged the blows from the Domnua. Sure as the sun rose in the east, she was a partner worthy of him, and that was the truth of it. Now, he just had to convince Sorcha that he was deserving of her. That would be a much trickier battle than the one he'd just fought, but one he was willing to tackle.

A trail of soot streaked across one of her alabaster

cheeks, and she no longer wore the flannel she'd gone into battle with. Instead, she stood before him in her dirty jeans, tank bra, and covered in cuts and dirt. Why had nobody tended to her wounds? Torin eased himself further up on the bed, so that he could prop against the pillows.

"You've been hurt," Torin rasped. His throat burned from smoke inhalation, and he greedily gulped at the drink the guard had handed him. Water, with a touch of Fae magick, instantly cooled the sting.

"Not so badly," Sorcha said. She glanced down at her side, and Torin saw the moment she realized she'd been standing in her bra before the queen this whole time. He bit back a smile as a flush of pink tinged her skin, and he wondered if this was how she would look in the mornings after an evening of lovemaking. He'd know, if he'd stayed around to find out, Torin chided himself.

The door slid open behind them, causing Sorcha to start. Whirling, she held up her hands and then lowered them when a troop of guards entered carrying platters of food, two large baths, and armfuls of fabric which Torin presumed were fresh clothing. Once finished setting everything up, they glanced to Torin who smiled his thanks.

"Wow, that's certainly convenient, isn't it?" Sorcha wandered to the table and lifted the cover to a platter, sniffing at the food beneath it. She doubted she could ever get comfortable with having people attend to her basic daily needs.

"It has its uses, yes. Will you help me up?" Torin knew he could stand on his own but wanted an excuse to touch Sorcha without her pushing him away. Immediately, she crossed to him and allowed him to hook an arm around her shoulders. Standing, Torin was surprised when a rush of dizziness made him wobble on his feet. So, perhaps Donal's magick had been stronger than he'd realized.

"Steady as she goes there..." Sorcha said.

"I'd like to bathe, if you don't mind? You look like you could use one as well. Then, I can see to your wounds."

"Really...just a few bruises and scratches," Sorcha said, winding an arm around his waist. The energy crackled between them. Could she feel the warmth that bloomed when they touched? Slowly, they made their way to the first copper tub, and Sorcha looked up at him, her eyes full of concern.

"Will you be able to lower yourself in? This tub is almost as high as I am, so I'm not sure how much help I can be."

"Yes, I should be okay. If you can just help me with my clothes."

Sorcha blanched, looking from the tub and then back to him, her pretty pink lips dropping open.

"Um...you want me to undress you?"

"You've seen me naked, Sorcha. I didn't think you were one to be shy around nudity?" Torin smirked at her, and her chin came up.

"I'm not shy. Honestly, as performers we change in front of each other all the time. It just caught me by surprise is all." Quickly, Sorcha unbuttoned his pants and shoved them down his legs, averting her face at his private parts, and then pulled what remained of his shirt from his body in little strips. The thought of her undressing around other men did a curious thing to Torin, and he found that he didn't like the idea at all – no he most certainly did not. He'd have to make sure that wouldn't happen in the future. Sorcha waited, her eyes on the ceiling, as he gripped the sides of the tub and then lowered himself slowly into the steaming water. Fragrant with eucalyptus and lavender, the heat of the water instantly soothed his fatigued muscles. Groaning, he settled back.

"Is that a bad groan or a good groan?" Sorcha asked, her eyes still averted, and Torin laughed.

"If I say it's bad, would you massage my aches away?" Torin asked, enjoying when her eyes narrowed in annoyance.

"Maybe I'd just push your head under and let you drown," Sorcha bit out.

"Now, now, that's not very nice, Sorcha. I'm wounded, you know..." Torin made a tsking noise.

"I'm thinking you're feeling much better than you're letting on."

"Why don't you have a bath as well? It looks like they've brought towels and fresh clothes," Torin said, letting his head settle back against the rim of the tub and luxuriating in the deliciousness of the bath.

"You want me to bathe with you?" Sorcha squeaked.

Torin popped one eye open and found her gaping at him.

"I'd be more than delighted to have you join my tub, my love, but there's also a second one just there."

"Oh, right..." Sorcha flushed, and amusement filled Torin. So, her mind wasn't all that far away from where his own thoughts had gone. Good. He wanted her to be thinking of him in a sensual manner. Flouncing across the room, Sorcha grabbed a large stack of towels and brought them back, draping two over the side of his tub while looking away. Turning her back to him, she stripped quickly, causing his blood, and other parts of him, to heat. Grateful for the cover of the water for his obvious reaction to the sight of the muscular lines of her back and her high tight bottom, Torin bit his lower lip. His hands gripped the sides of the tub tightly, and he willed himself away from standing up and scooping her into his arms. No, patience was what Sorcha needed, not brute strength, and he deliberately closed his eyes as she settled into her own tub.

"You can open your eyes," Sorcha said amidst the splashing of water. "Thank you for respecting my privacy."

"Of course," Torin said, and found he could just see her head over the edge of their respective tubs. "Though it seems silly when I've been inside you."

The flush he loved so much crept up her face and Torin smiled, enjoying the knowledge that his words affected her.

"That was then. This is now," Sorcha said, her head dipping as she used a small towel to clean herself. Torin wished he could do it for her, for it was torture to be this close to her and not be able to touch her. Tearing his eyes away, he looked up at the marble ceiling where a chandelier sparkled, green vines entwining its arms, with the vines crossing over the ceiling to create a forest canopy. The bath worked its magick, easing his pain, and soon he found himself refreshed.

"Is it always like this here? Bathing beneath chandeliers and forest-like ceilings?" Sorcha asked, breaking the silence between them.

"No, it's not. While the Royal Advisors do enjoy more luxurious accommodations, this is the prince's wing."

"What is your space like?" Sorcha asked and Torin turned to her.

"It's a small wing of the palace. Much like an apartment in your world. A few rooms. Some for sleeping, one for dining, one for work, and others for other pursuits."

"Like what kind of other pursuits?" Sorcha asked. Torin kept his eyes on hers, allowing the air to grow thick with tension between them, his meaning clear as he smiled slowly at her.

"Pleasurable ones," Torin supplied.

"I can't imagine having so much space." Sorcha quickly changed the subject, splashing her hands in the water. "It feels very decadent. Honestly? I'm not sure if I'd like it or not. But right now? This is really nice after the last couple of days."

"What was it like for you then? Growing up? Did you live in a small room?" Torin asked and Sorcha shot him a bemused look. Reaching up, she piled her dripping locks on her head, winding the strands in a haphazard knot, as she cast her eyes to the ceiling once more.

"No, my family has a small house. We grew up in the country, so we had more outside room than if we lived in the city. Still, with seven girls and my parents, space was tight. I grew very used to sharing everything that I owned and never getting a moment alone to myself unless I took to the fields or played in the old barn nearby." Sorcha sighed. "We didn't have a lot. Well, I still don't. But what I have is mine and nobody else's to take."

"Ah, that is why Betty Blue is so important to you," Torin said, studying the emotions that danced across her expressive face. "It's not just that she's your home – it's that you finally get to control your space."

"Correct. I can't tell you how difficult it is to even know yourself when someone is constantly interrupting every solitary moment you have. Where's the time to read or sing or daydream? I'd barely get privacy in the bathroom before one of my sisters would barge in and be nattering on about one thing or the other."

"Your family is close then?" Torin asked.

"No, we're not. Despite living close together, we are not

close. I...well, I shouldn't say that, I suppose. My sisters are close. I'm just not close with the rest of them. I don't fit, you see?" Sorcha tossed him a sad smile, making Torin want to go to her and give her a cuddle to soothe the pain on her face. "I never did. I think everyone was relieved when I took off on my own. I know my father was – one less mouth to feed."

"Do you speak with them still? Or visit?"

"I do, yes. I suppose there's some guilt there. My parents are aging, and my sisters bear the burden of it. I have a few nieces and nephews now, as well. I'm not around as much for them as I should be. But home? Well, it's not a happy place for me. It never really was. It's tough for me to go back. I feel like...I'm performing when I'm there."

"How so? Like dancing?"

"No," Sorcha laughed, shaking her head. "Like I'm playing the role of what they want me to be, but nobody ever sees me for who I actually am."

"I see you, Sorcha." The words were out before Torin could stop them, but the truth hung between them. She looked down, shuttering her eyes, but still Torin pressed on. "I've seen you in our shared dreams. I've walked by your side, danced with you, made love with you, and I see you. You're the lightning bolt that illuminates the darkest of nights. Fervent, sharp, and achingly beautiful. It's an honor it is to have met you, and it's sad I am that your family can't see that about you."

"Torin," Sorcha said, her voice a touch breathless. "I just don't know what to do with you."

"Dance for me," Torin said automatically, watching as her mouth dropped open.

"Dance for you? Right now?"

"Well, sure and I'd be overjoyed if you danced naked for

me, and I'd heartily support your decision if that's the way of things. But no. The water grows cool, and I'll return to the bed. Will you dance for me then, Sorcha? And show me who you are?"

"Maybe. Food first, methinks," Sorcha said, and twirled a finger in the air. "Eyes closed."

After they'd dried off and dressed – him in loose cotton pants and a soft overshirt, her in a simple tunic the color of a plump blueberry – they gorged themselves on the dinner that had been delivered. Torin kept the topics light, answering her endless questions about the Fae realm, and in turn asking his own of the human world. He didn't want to see the sadness shadow her eyes when she spoke of her family, instead listening as she told him about how her independence had fueled her life. Independence was deeply important to her, Torin quickly realized, and filed the thought away for later. Perhaps it was one of the reasons she remained so reluctant to accept his claim.

Shifting in the chair, Torin rubbed at an ache just below his heart. Though Callum had healed the dark magicks that Donal had used upon him, something else now grew. If Torin had to guess, his time was drawing near. He'd lingered too long, foolishly avoiding Sorcha, and now the magick of a claim unanswered was beginning its stealthy work. Once his sister had felt the magick – as in physically felt it – it had only been a matter of weeks before she was gone. If this was the case for Torin, he'd need to make a choice soon. Reject the claim, lose Sorcha, and most of his powers – rendering him useless to the Royal Fae and forever changing his role in the Danula Realm – or giving up his life for love. Neither was particularly appealing, and he cast his thoughts away from the dull ache and to where Sorcha stood.

"Do you really want me to dance for you, Torin?" Sorcha asked, an unusual look of shyness creeping over her face.

"I'd love nothing more in this world. But, first, if I can make myself more comfortable?" Torin nodded to the bed and Sorcha came to his side, offering her arm. Once more, he took it, just to be close to her, and allowed her to lead him to bed. Once tucked in and propped up on a mound of pillows, he smiled at her.

"Do I get to pick the song?" Torin asked.

"There's music here?" Sorcha whirled, looking around for speakers.

"You've only to ask and music shall play."

"Well, now, isn't that handy? In that case, I'd like to dance to La Vie en Rose."

The music swelled, a tune that Torin didn't recognize, soft and romantic with a lilting beat. Sorcha raised her arms over her head, her body curving slightly, her leg angled just so. He watched, entranced, as she flowed into the music, becoming an embodiment of the song, as though there was no line between where the music ended and her movements started. They were one and the same, and Sorcha became her own magick as she twirled through the room, effortlessly flowing through backbends and dips, arching lightly through wide-legged jumps, and flirty little twists. She was a butterfly in motion, her radiance undeniable, and his heart swelled watching her do something she loved. When she finished, coming to a resounding wide-legged split on the floor, her arms held high, her head thrown back so that her hair tumbled down her back, Torin cheered.

"Magnificent! Quite simply, my beautiful sprite, you take my breath away." Without thinking, Torin snagged her arm as she walked to the bed, pulling her quickly so that she tumbled next to him, her eyes alight with excitement, her breath coming in soft little puffs from her exertion.

"Torin..." Sorcha whispered.

"I want you with the same desperation that a hummingbird will beat its wings a thousand times over just for a taste of a flower's sweet nectar," Torin said, leaning close to Sorcha. "Won't you grant this ailing man just a taste?"

"Are you still not well?" Sorcha asked, pushing herself up on a pillow, concern crowding her eyes.

"I'm not, no." Torin shook his head sadly. "But a kiss would renew my energy immensely."

"Seems suspicious," Sorcha said. She narrowed her eyes at him, and he affected a puppy dog look, earning himself a quick grin. "Och, you're insufferable. One kiss, Torin. Just to heal you up."

"One kiss is a bounty for my poor soul..." Torin said, pleased when she leaned forward, making the first move. Her lips met his, hesitant, and Torin held still, allowing her to explore. The dull ache below his chest eased, confirming his suspicions, and he shifted, taking her mouth possessively. Drunk on her taste, Torin feasted on her kiss, demanding more of her. When she moaned into his mouth, opening more for him, Torin seized the opportunity and slipped his tongue inside, dancing lightly along hers, savoring this moment as though it was a glass of delicate fairy wine. Heat rushed through his body, and he shifted, pulling her closer so that she sprawled over him, her compact body fitting neatly against his. Sorcha gasped into his mouth when she felt his arousal, tearing her lips, wet with kisses from his, her eyes clouded with need. It took everything in his power not to push for more, but Torin saw the confusion that lurked behind the need. She wasn't ready.

One day soon, he'd get past her walls – but he wasn't there yet.

He only hoped he'd have enough time.

Pulling her into the crook of his arm, Torin dragged a featherweight blanket over their bodies, and let the silence settle over them. Nothing else needed to be said in this moment, and words would ruin the tenuous thread of emotion that hung between them. The lights dimmed in the tower room, and content with her nestled in his arms, Torin allowed himself to slide into sleep.

15

SORCHA HAD ALREADY WORKED her way through an hour of calisthenics the next morning by the time Torin opened his eyes, followed shortly by the door sliding open and a flurry of guards carrying trays of food. Perhaps the man really was still recovering from his wounds, Sorcha thought, watching him wince as he rubbed a hand across his chest.

"Are you not well?" Sorcha crossed to the bed.

"I'm just fine. How could I not be – with you by my bedside?" Torin captured her hand, tracing his lips over her palm in a whisper of a kiss, and tendrils of excitement curled through her. Easing back, Sorcha shot a glance to where the guards readied their food.

"I'm not interrupting anything, am I?"

Sorcha whirled to see Bianca, resplendent in a deep maroon tunic and pants, smiling from the doorway.

"Bianca!" Sorcha raced across the room and gave the other woman a hug, rocking back and forth in her arms. Pulling back, Bianca held her for a moment, studying her face.

"You look well enough then," Bianca said, her gaze darting over Sorcha's shoulders. "How's this one?"

"Milking it for all its worth, I'm sure of it." Sorcha raised her voice so Torin could hear, and he fell back against the pillows and brought a hand to his head, pretending distress. "See? Typical man. Dramatic when ill."

"Well, best gather your strength, dear, as it's back to Grace's Cove for us," Bianca said, and fear slipped through Sorcha. She was enjoying this little cocoon of peace they had, though she itched to get outside and explore. Being stuck in a room with nothing to do but sleep or exercise was enough to make her restless.

"Is it bad?" Sorcha asked, dropping down on the bed next to Torin.

"Not yet. There appears to be a lull of sorts. But we can't do much for the Fire Fae in this realm, as the Domnua are dragging them along for their fight in Ireland. It's best we're there to figure out our next steps, and perhaps we can be proactive instead of reactive this time."

"I'll be ready to leave at once," Torin said, sitting up.

"Breakfast first – then we travel. Seamus will meet us here shortly. Then we'll travel by guard to the portal and back to Grace's Cove."

"Have you heard word of Gracie? Her dog?" Sorcha asked. Nobody had followed up with her on the woman, and she hoped that Gracie hadn't faced any retribution for her courageous acts.

"She's right as rain, that one is. Rosie's cheerful as always. Gracie's husband, Dylan, is a bit peeved he didn't get in on the action and she's had to endure a few lectures, but otherwise, all is well."

"So that's it then? We just wait for the Fire Fae to do something? Or the bad guys to attack? That doesn't seem…"

Sorcha looked between them. "Like, am I the only one seeing that as not the brightest thing to do?"

"Ideally I'll be able to secure a meeting with the head of the Fire Fae and from there we'll be able to work something out. The Domnua have thus far blocked me from meeting with them, and the longer that I stay away – the more they believe whatever lies the Domnua are feeding them," Torin explained. His hair was a mess, standing up in spikes around his head, and Sorcha barely resisted walking to him and running her hands through it.

He'd visited her in her dreams last night. Much like the dreams she'd had of him through the last few months, but now, knowing he was close and having the taste of him on her lips again, well, the experience had certainly leveled up. At one point, Sorcha vaguely remembered waking up, moaning, pleasure rocketing through her as Torin drove into her over and over in her dream. But when she'd blinked her eyes open, embarrassment heating her skin as much as her desire did, she'd found him sleeping peacefully next to her, one arm thrown loosely across her waist. Now, in the bright light of morning, she wondered if he'd experienced the same dream. Was that how it worked? The magick of the Fae made it so they could dreamwalk together? She'd have to ask Bianca when they had a private moment.

Today, it felt like their bond had grown stronger. While before, Sorcha had been aware of their chemistry, now she was even more attuned of where he was in the room even when her back was turned. It was as though an invisible thread connected them, and Sorcha wondered if their kiss last night had meant something more in the Fae realm than she understood. She didn't like this feeling – not understanding the rules at play – and it made her already frenetic energy even edgier. She all but bounced around the room as she waited for someone to tell her when it was time to go, too keyed up to eat, and obsessively braided and unbraided her hair. Sorcha didn't like feeling trapped, and this waiting game was not one she was particularly enjoying.

"Ready?" Bianca called from the doorway where she'd been conversing quietly with Seamus. Torin had eaten a hearty breakfast, though he still seemed to be moving a touch slowly. Perhaps she was over-analyzing, and he was still just waking up. She didn't really know if he was a morning person or not, she realized, and that was something else to add to the list of why she shouldn't have feelings for this man whom she didn't really know much about. Was it possible to fall for someone in a minute? A day? A week? What was the timeline for love? For her, all of this was incredibly surreal, as though she'd be waking up from a dream any second now and heading off to her next gig in her trusty Betty Blue.

Thinking about her career made her sad again, and she hoped that once they were back to their world, she'd get a chance to check her email. At the very least, she suspected her sisters had been trying to contact her as she knew Mary religiously listened to the radio while she cooked her meals.

"Sorcha?" Bianca called, snapping Sorcha to attention.

"Right, sorry. Let's go."

Sorcha's hopes that they would leave the castle were dashed when they wound through a series of twisting hallways, until she lost all sense of direction and wouldn't have been able to find her way back if she tried. Had it been designed that way – so as to stop any intruder from easily navigating the castle – and if so, how did the guards remember where they were going? By the time they reached another door without a doorknob, Sorcha was thoroughly confused, and she found she didn't like the unease that came with being so completely in the dark about where she was. It was time for her to go home and that was that.

Once Torin had opened the door with the same magick the queen had used, they hurried through a natural tunnel made of craggy rock and to a fire which Sorcha now understood to be a portal. Did the fire always burn? Or was it lit knowing the portal would be used that day? Really, she had so many questions, but now was not the time. Forcing herself to breathe past the innate fear that accompanied stepping into a fire, Sorcha followed the others through the flames.

When the salty air greeted her on the other side, Sorcha drew in a deep gulp of it, as though she was drinking down a pint, the taste of Ireland on her lips. Home. It soothed her in ways she couldn't explain, as the air just felt right here, and having some control of her own actions again helped ease her anxiety. Torin fell in step beside her as they walked out onto the beach in the cove, and she matched her pace to his. Nobody would have known that a battle had been fought here just yesterday, Sorcha thought, her eyes scanning the pristine beach. A pair of gulls fought over a small fish in the sand, while another three chattered in the sky above them. The water lapped gently on the sand, and the high cliffs cocooned the beach as if they were giving the water a hug. Far above, a bark sounded, and Sorcha whipped her head up to see Rosie racing along the edge of the cliff.

"Can we go up?" Sorcha asked Torin. "I'd like to see Rosie if that's possible."

"Of course. But we'll need to walk it. I want to control our use of magick so as not to create too many ripples in the universe."

"What does that even mean?" Sorcha asked, and then skidded to a stop, reaching for Torin's hand without thinking. His palm met hers, warm and rough, and a fissure of pleasure curled through her. "Look!"

A brilliant blue light shone in the waters of the cove once more, much like it had the time before, and Sorcha was struck once again with just how many things there were in the world that she truly didn't understand. Bianca turned, a sugary smile on her face, and shot Sorcha a knowing look. What was that about?

"Sure, and that's lovely, isn't it?" Torin smiled and brushed a lock of Sorcha's hair from her face. Before she could pull back, he bent and brushed a whisper of a kiss over her lips, sending Sorcha's heart into a tailspin. "I dreamed of you last night."

"Wait..." Sorcha called, as Torin was already walking toward the path. "What did you...was it..." Distracted from the light in the water, she bounded after the group, not wanting to be left behind. Her skin tingled, remembering the contents of her dreams, and she wasn't sure if she could talk to Torin about it in the light of day.

Torin turned at the base of the cliff, the wind rustling his gilded hair, his eyes hot on hers. His handsome face creased in a languid smile, his look turning her insides liquid, and Sorcha almost whimpered as need rose within. Torin bent, his lips brushing the sensitive skin at her ear.

"The taste of you lingers on my lips this morning. I enjoyed our night together. Thank you for dreaming with me – it's the next best thing to being with you."

"Oh..." Sorcha breathed, her heart fluttering in her chest. "So...we have the same..."

"Yes, my decadent and delicious Sorcha. I dreamwalked with you." Torin nipped at her neck, his lips sending shivers across her skin, and Sorcha swallowed. Right, so her dreams weren't so private after all. Which meant...all these months...they were dreaming together? Shaking her head to clear it, she started up the path with Torin bringing up the rear.

"Do you mean to say that for months now, when I've dreamed of you – that, well, that was actually you? We were like, *you know*, in our dreams?" Sorcha stumbled through the words, but she didn't care about being articulate, as understanding dawned that she knew far more about this man than she realized.

"Yes, we were, *you know*, in our shared dreams." Torin's chuckle was a low timbre that rumbled through Sorcha.

"But we didn't just...*you know*...in our dreams."

"Sex," Bianca called from a few feet ahead of them. "It's called sex, you guys. You can just say the word. We're all adults here."

"Lovely. Just lovely," Sorcha bit out, her cheeks flaming.

"It's a zesty pastime, isn't it my love?" Seamus snatched Bianca's hand and peppered it with kisses until she dissolved into laughter. Pulling her ahead, Seamus flashed a grin over his shoulder. "I'll just keep this nosey one busy."

"I'm not nosey...but I'm right here, aren't I? What? Am I supposed to pretend that I can't hear them mooning over each other?" Bianca groused.

"A little subtlety may help..." Seamus poked Bianca in the back, urging her forward.

"Alas, the art of being subtle is a gift that has not been bestowed upon me, as you well know." Their voices faded out as they moved ahead while Sorcha tried to remember all the dreams she'd had of Torin. Sure, there had been a lot of the sexy dreams, but there had been others too. Ones that often left her waking up, tears in her eyes, a gentle yearning ache in her heart. They'd walked through fairy fields together, the flowers swaying in the wind, sprites bouncing from petal to petal. They'd swam with the mermaids, effervescent bubbles surrounding them, the cool water sliding across their skin. She'd learned he was a proud man, but kind – and enjoyed bouncing to the next activity as much as she did. He wandered a lot, his thirst for new experiences as boundless as hers, and together they'd explored their realms. She'd danced with him, oh so many times, showing him her new routines or in a sultry salsa rhythm in darkened nightclubs in Spain. They'd laughed over street performers, and Torin had surprised her with his own ability to juggle.

They'd cried over movies together and read passages of books to each other while relaxing on a blanket tossed on dewy grass. He had a knack for comedy, and loved stories or movies that made him laugh, yet at the same time wasn't afraid to shed a tear if moved by a haunting piece of music. Mercurial, brilliant, and enthralled with life – Sorcha struggled to blend the Torin of her dreams with the man who stood before her today.

He wasn't perfect, oh no, for who was really? Sorcha continued up the path, worrying her bottom lip, as she mulled over what she'd just learned. The Torin of her dreams was like when she first started dating someone and they were all shiny and new with no faults. At the beginning of every relationship was the only time that people were perfect, and wasn't that the truth of it? Because new relationship people weren't real – they hadn't shown their true colors to each other yet – so they really were just ideas. A polished version of themselves, like a fancy antique vase turned so that the chip in the rim faced the wall. The Torin of her dreams never would have left her the morning after their lovemaking, nor would he have left her unguided with this new power to navigate.

Had he though?

Sorcha skidded to a stop, so that Torin almost bumped into her, his hands coming to her shoulders.

"Are you okay?"

"Um...yeah, just thinking." Sorcha's mind whirled as she tried to reconcile her thoughts with her feelings.

"Anything I can help you with?"

"Maybe. I need a moment."

They continued up the path as Sorcha worked through what was bothering her. Dream Torin had showed her how to use fire. He'd shown her. Over and over, they'd trained with it, and she'd taken those lessons into her waking moments. He hadn't left her at all – had he? All these months, Torin had been wooing her in her dreams, guiding her on her path with magick, even when she didn't fully understand what magick was all about. She hadn't been left alone at all, which likely explained how she'd grown so confident with the use of her newfound power so quickly. Sure, she'd doubted herself when she was alone during the day, often questioning her own sanity, but at the same time reveling in her newfound power. It had been her little secret, one she could share only with Torin at night in her dreams, and she'd grown immensely confident because of it.

It was a gift he'd given her, and she'd been nothing but rude to him since the moment he'd reappeared at her side. Sure, it had been a chaotic few days, so who could blame her for her mixed reactions to his sudden appearance back in her life? The learning curve was a steep one with the Fae, but that didn't mean Torin hadn't been trying to help her all along.

"You never left me, did you?" Sorcha stopped at the top of the cliff, turning to look down at Torin. Her position on the hill made it so that she was the taller one for once, and he tilted his head up to meet her eyes. "You were there all along. All those dreams? The dates? The dancing? The long walks? That was really you, wasn't it? I know that you hate being wet, but you'll swim with me anyway. I know you consume books at a scary pace, but don't like sitting through lectures. I know that you love to dance but prefer to walk instead of run. That's you...isn't it?"

"Sorcha...my heart." Torin reached for her hand, pulling it to his chest. "I never left you. I'm not perfect – I tried to. I wanted to forget about you, I wasn't ready, you see? But I couldn't just *leave* you. I came to you at night because I didn't want you to be scared or lonely. Even as I tried to figure out why I claimed you, what our bond was, I never wanted you to feel alone."

"I don't need you to make me feel less alone," Sorcha shook her head. "Alone isn't scary for someone like me. But feeling abandoned is. I've never had someone pick me, understand? Not really. Nobody's put me first before. Not my family, not friends, not lovers...I'm always the afterthought. The wild one. The black sheep. The performer. The life of the party. Or...a burden. But that's just an act, don't you see? I wish...I wish I understood that you hadn't truly left me. It would have made it easier."

"And for that, I'll apologize a lifetime to you, Sorcha. It was my own personal failings that made me choose foolishly. I should have come to you sooner, but I was blocked somehow. I could find you so easily in my dreams, but never during the day. It was like the signal was turned off."

Sorcha looked up and to the horizon where fat puffs of clouds hovered over the crystalline water.

"Because I didn't claim you back?" Sorcha asked.

"Maybe, I can't say. Fae magick is tricky on a good day."

"But you kept trying to find me?" She brought her eyes back to his.

"I did. Not at first. I didn't want to accept that my party days carousing with women were over. You see...partnering up felt like, well, it felt like I was being caged. Which isn't a good feeling for someone like me. I didn't realize that finding my fated mate would actually give me the freedom I craved all along."

Tears rose in her eyes at Torin's words. His sentiment was one that she could greatly identify with, and he'd articulated her mixed feelings about relationships perfectly. Was what he was saying true? Could there be freedom in finding love and having a partner by her side? She'd compromised her entire life – up until she hadn't anymore – and now she wondered what sharing her future would look like. People always made it out like they skipped happily off into the sunset once they found love, but Sorcha never believed that to be true. A partnership was about balance, trust, and a lot of compromise. What would that look like with Torin?

Loud barking jerked her out of her thoughts, and she turned to see Rosie racing across the grass, ears streaming behind her. Pushing thoughts of her future aside, Sorcha dropped to her knees in the grass as Torin finished climbing to the top of the cliff. Rosie swiped her tongue across Sorcha's face, leaving a slick trail of drool behind, and Sorcha giggled.

"Rosie! Gross!"

The dog collapsed at her feet, flipping over on her back, wiggling in ecstasy as Sorcha rubbed her belly. Despite everything, a huge smile spread across Sorcha's face.

"She loves you."

Sorcha glanced up to see Gracie standing over her, an incredibly handsome man at her side. He had the polish of someone used to money, though his relaxed jeans and dirty boots looked like every other working man's clothes.

"And I her. I never got to have a dog growing up. Too many mouths to feed, my father always pointed out. But I really love dogs."

"Thank you for saving her. I'd be gutted if anything had happened to her."

"I had a little help..." Sorcha wasn't sure what she could say in front of the man by Gracie's side.

"This is Dylan, the love of many of my lifetimes. You can speak freely with him." Gracie leaned into his arms.

"I'm Sorcha and this is Torin," Sorcha introduced them. Still she crouched, running her hands through Rosie's soft fur, the dog soothing the emotions that churned inside. "I had help...a family member of yours, I believe? Fiona?"

"Ah, yes. She doesn't like to be left out of things, does she?" Gracie laughed. "Sure and we're grateful for her assistance."

"She lifted me in the air...as though it was nothing..." Sorcha huffed out a laugh, and Rosie jumped up to slobber her with another kiss.

"That magick isn't easy for her, what with her crossing over into the next realm. But she'll do it if needed."

"The Fae are indebted to you," Torin said. He bowed his head to Gracie, who returned the gesture. "If the time ever comes..."

"I'll be sure to reach out. Thank you. That being said... this was left. Presumably for you?" Gracie held out a scroll of paper and Torin took it, unraveling it.

"Banphrionsa. When the sun kisses the horizon, at the stone circle we shall be," Torin read. The paper shook in his hands, and he lifted his eyes to Sorcha. "I believe this belongs to you."

16

TORIN DIDN'T LIKE arranged meeting spots – at least not during times of war. And, they *were* at war, whether the queen would openly admit it or not. The Domnua, which had been thought to have been banished to their realm a few decades ago, had quietly been planning their revenge if Donal's betrayal was any indication.

"Why don't I go instead?" Bianca asked, her hands on her hips. They'd returned to the cottage, relief crossing Sorcha's face at the sight of Betty Blue unharmed, and had spent the afternoon creating magicks while educating Sorcha on the Fae realm. Particularly that of the Fire Fae, because if Torin was reading their note correctly – Sorcha might be a part of the prophecy.

That was annoying.

Torin shook his head, mentally chastising himself, as he gently rubbed at the cold ache growing across his chest. He could feel the magick working, its sinuous threads slipping through him, and he wondered just how much energy he'd have left before he'd be forced into a choice. The problem was – he needed his powers right now to protect Sorcha.

Even as his energy waned, his magick was still strong. If he renounced his claim to her, he'd be left defenseless. As would she.

It wasn't a spot he enjoyed being in – and now that the Fire Fae were likely claiming Sorcha as their princess, she'd need even more protection. Stuck, Torin shifted his attention back to the conversation.

"You're not going, my love. Why risk angering them?" Seamus rubbed the back of Bianca's neck gently.

"But then we'd know if it is a trap, right? If they jump me when I get there, well, we can know it was all a trap and we'll have protected Sorcha in the meantime."

"And put you in danger? I don't think so." Sorcha crossed her arms over her chest. She'd changed into tight-fitting jeans, a simple form-fitting blue long-sleeved shirt, and sturdy boots. "If the note is for me, well, then it's on me to go." A hint of something, a flare of recognition crossed Sorcha's face, and she opened her mouth before shutting it again. What had she been about to say?

"We'll all go." Torin cut off Bianca's rebuttal. He held up the vest he'd been working on. "Sorcha – you're to wear this."

"What is it?" Sorcha crossed the room and held up the vest. Made of intricate interlocking circles, the gold linked vest acted both as chainmail and was highly magicked. If anyone fired at Sorcha, she should be well-protected. He should have thought to make this available to her sooner, but they'd been going non-stop since he'd found her at the wedding reception. Torin stood and helped Sorcha slip the chainmail vest on. It fitted to her perfectly and looked stylish as well.

"Hey, that's fancy. Love the gold." Bianca crossed the room and ran a finger over the vest.

"I've one for you as well," Torin said, holding up another vest. Seamus and he didn't need the protection in the same way the humans did, and there was no way he would let Bianca also go into another potential battle without similar protection. Torin caught the relief that crossed Seamus's face and acknowledged his nod of thanks.

"I get one, too? Badass! I've always loved Fae magicks." Bianca chattered on happily, as though they weren't likely walking into danger, and Seamus helped her with the vest. "How do I look?"

"Fierce," Sorcha decided, tilting her head at Bianca. "I'm also loving this chain style. It looks so effortlessly cool, like just thrown over a t-shirt like that? I may need to incorporate this into a costume at some point." Instantly, sadness crossed Sorcha's face and she pressed her lips together in a tight line.

"I do feel very cool. I can still be cool, right? Even if I'm in my fifties?" Bianca strutted around the room, the light glinting off the gold of her vest.

"Never has there been a cooler fifty-year-old," Sorcha promised, a smile returning to her face. "I mean...you did just race into battle and like murder a bunch of Dark Fae. I don't think many people, at any age, can add that as bragging rights."

"You make a good point," Bianca agreed, laughing.

"It's time," Torin said, noting the light outside the cottage's window. Instantly the group sobered. Gracie had given them directions to the nearest stone circle, though Ireland was covered in them. They'd decided it was likely one of the more prominent ones that sat close to the cove, as the Fae seemed partial to those hills. It was but a short drive away, and they'd be taking Betty Blue. Torin had spent a portion of the afternoon, along with Seamus, running spells to protect the van and they were both fairly confident she'd hold up under any attack. Once they deemed their trusty chariot safe, they'd worked on adding layers of magick to the daggers the women carried, as well as any weapons the men would have. After that, they'd enjoyed a quick bite of vegetable soup and brown bread. It was the best Torin could do to protect himself and his little crew before they walked into...well, whatever this was. He dearly hoped it was just a meeting with the head of the Fire Fae where he could spend some time convincing them to pull back from the Domnua.

Torin had known Bran, leader of the Fire Fae, for years now. Prior to this, they'd had a fairly easy relationship, wherein Torin would meet with him quarterly and review any issues or concerns the Fae had. Occasionally, he'd have to issue sanctions or impose new rules if the Fae had grown too unwieldly, but overall, he'd always enjoyed his meetings with the Fire Fae. They were a lively bunch, as befitting their element, and the meetings often concluded with a party that raged through the night and he'd enjoyed the feverish attentions of more than one of their women. Those days were over now, as Torin only had eyes for Sorcha, and his heart hung open, weeping like a gaping wound as he waited for her to see what was right in front of her.

That they were meant for each other.

In some ways, he felt like the puppy they'd seen earlier that day, rolling over and showing his belly to Sorcha, desperate for any attention she'd give. The feeling wasn't a comfortable one for him, and he didn't particularly enjoy how vulnerable he knew he was to her. At the same time, Torin refused to sit around and wait for Sorcha to wake up to what they could have – no, *did* have – together. They'd had a moment at the cove earlier today, where it seemed he'd made some serious headway, and that she was finally realizing just how connected they were. After they were interrupted, there had been no time to revisit that conversation, though Sorcha had sent him several considering looks throughout the afternoon.

"You're sure this message is from the Fire Fae?" Sorcha asked him once again when they were on the road.

"Yes," Torin said. He could feel the Fire Fae magick on the missive, along with the faint whiff of smoke that accompanied anything they touched. Torin kept his eyes on the road ahead, scanning constantly for anything amiss, as they wound their way down the narrow road that twisted and turned along the cliffside. It was a steep drop to his left, and one he didn't wish to experience, so Torin deeply hoped that the Domnua wouldn't strike at this moment. When they finally turned from the road and bumped along a gravel lane into an empty field, Torin let out a small sigh of relief. He would have been able to cushion their fall, but not prevent it, and there would likely have been serious damage.

"Just there..." Bianca leaned between the front seats and pointed.

"Ah, sure, that's a grand circle isn't it now?" Sorcha said, pulling the van thirty feet away and then coming to a stop. "Should I go closer? Or pull it back more? I don't see anyone around."

"Here's fine. Let me get out first." Torin was already unbuckling his seat belt and opening the door. "I'll have a look around." He'd already explained to the group the protections they'd placed on the van, so the safest spot was inside. Torin slammed the door behind him and stood still, letting his senses open to feel for any Fae magick in the area. A soft breeze brought the scent of the ocean mixed with the damp earth to him, along with a whiff of smoke. The Fire Fae were close, though they'd yet to reveal themselves.

Perhaps they were being equally as cautious, and Torin couldn't blame them. They'd certainly been causing quite a bit of trouble for his people, and they'd almost killed him. It wasn't unusual for them to worry about his response.

Torin moved forward, approaching the circle as the last of the sun's rays slipped between the stones. Each stone came roughly to his shoulder, and moss grew among the cracks in their surface.

"Nice try," Sorcha called, and the sound of the doors opening made him glance over his shoulder. "You don't get to walk into the circle without us. We're a team, remember?"

"These are the people I govern," Torin said, his eyes scanning the hills. "It's my duty and honor to represent them, and you are not bound by such promises."

"Yeah, yeah, yeah. Very noble of you," Bianca said, coming to stand by his side, with Sorcha and Seamus fanning out. "But we do this together or not at all."

"I really think…" Torin began and then stopped at movement on the other side of the circle. Bran, leader of the Fire Fae, stepped between the stones and stood in the circle. A fierce-looking Fae, he'd worn his full battle gear for the meeting. Gold plates, molded in the shape of flames, fit his legs and stretched across the tunic he wore. A gold circlet, with a fire-red ruby in the center, nestled in his brilliant red hair. Cool blue eyes met his across the circle, and he bowed his head slightly to acknowledge Torin's rank. Torin didn't miss when Bran's eyes strayed to Sorcha or the subtle nod he gave to her as well.

"Bran," Torin said, stepping between the stones. The others followed, flanking him immediately, and a few of Bran's men stepped forward to mirror them.

"My lord," Bran said, nodding once more. Torin caught Sorcha's side-eyed look of astonishment, as though she was just realizing his position among the Fae. Biting back a small smile, he focused on the man in front of him.

"You've requested a meeting?" Torin asked, his words clipped.

"Yes." Bran paused, seeming to think about his words, his eyes once more straying to Sorcha.

"Is that it then? You two are just going to stare at each other all night?" Sorcha demanded, breaking royal protocol without realizing it, and once again Torin bit back a smile while Bran just looked astonished.

"What is it with men?" Bianca demanded. "All these heavy looks and long silences. Listen...Bran, is it?"

Bran nodded, his eyebrows almost reaching his hairline.

"We're not really all that happy with you, okay? The Fire Fae almost killed us. And, for what? Do you even know what you're fighting for? From my estimation, Torin's been a pretty fair leader to you. What have the Domnua ever done for you? Huh?" Bianca put her hands on her hips while Seamus laid a hand on her shoulder and whispered in her ear.

"Um..." Bran said, clearly unsure of how to proceed.

"Um, is right. They've done nothing, have they? Except place your entire faction into jeopardy by risking the queen's wrath, not to mention throwing the natural world out of balance. And again – for what? You think it is better to throw in with the bad guys than the good? You should be ashamed of yourselves. You owe us an apology. Seriously... I'm *really* mad about this." Bianca directed the last part to Seamus who was clearly trying to get her to quiet down.

"She raises some valid points, Bran. If you're displeased with the Danula's treatment of your people, you could have spoken with me about it. Falling in with the Domnua is an extremely risky decision. And now you're here...for what? Do you come to apologize?"

"We do," Bran said, bowing his head once more, before lifting it and addressing the group as a whole. "As you know, my people are a hot-headed bunch."

Bianca groaned at the pun, though Torin didn't think that Bran even realized he'd made one.

"Yes, I'm aware," Torin said, dryly.

"Our talisman has been stolen. We were led to believe it was by you, and that the Danula hoped to impose more restrictions upon the Elemental Fae. We heard the reports of the Water Fae uprising and were told that together we would be stronger if we united against you. We don't want to lose our voice, do you understand?"

"Why would you ever think you'd lose your voice? Haven't I always listened to you, Bran? And taken your concerns seriously? Even now, when your people try to kill us – I made sure no harm came to them."

"I know." A sheepish look crossed Bran's face, and he ran a hand over his brow. "Trust me, I know. I saw that. You had every right to hurt us – to defend yourselves against us – but none of you lifted a hand. Why? Why is that? We were led to believe..."

"By whom, Bran? Who made you believe these things?" Torin demanded.

"The Domnua. Donal, specifically. He...he spoke of knowledge of your Royal Court. As though he had the secrets to your plans."

"And what did he say those plans were?" Torin asked, exasperated.

"That once you gained the favor of our princess, you would take our talisman and step fully into power. We'd be helpless to make any of our own choices and you'd take our freedoms."

"And you believed that?" Torin demanded, throwing his hands up in the air. "Why in the world would I want to take your freedoms, Bran? I want your people to be happy. The entire world – the universe itself – relies on the elements working in balance together. What do you think happens when that balance is destroyed? If one element grows too powerful? Flooding. Wildfires. Famine. Hurricanes. The world...it fails, don't you see? It falls apart, ripping at the seams, and will implode upon itself. I don't seek to take your power, Bran. I seek to empower you. I'm shocked you don't see that."

"Donal is quite convincing. And you did exactly what he said you'd do."

"Which was what?"

"You claimed our princess. And now our talisman is gone."

"Wait...what?" Sorcha held up a hand, and Torin's heart caught. Though he had suspected that Sorcha might be the child of the prophecy, hearing the words from Bran's mouth was another thing entirely. "Are you talking about me?"

"Yes, your highness." Bran bowed his head in respect, while Sorcha gaped at him.

"Sorcha! You're a princess!" Bianca exclaimed. "How cool is that?"

"Surely you've got the wrong person," Sorcha said, tapping a finger on her chest. "I'm not...this isn't..."

"I can very much assure you that you are indeed our princess. Child of the prophecy, the one who shall return our power."

"I'm sorry, but you really must be out of your mind. Also, what are you talking about...return your power? Because I was *on* that beach. I saw you Fire people bouncing around in the flames on the water. You weren't looking all that weak to me. In fact, you almost killed all of us. That doesn't exactly speak to lack of power, now, does it? I think this all sounds like some made up crap that you are using to reassure yourself that you didn't screw up too badly." Torin watched as Bran's eyes shuttered and he lowered his head, accepting the censure from his princess. Sorcha might not see it, but both Bianca and Seamus stilled at Bran's reaction to her tirade. In any other circumstance, if someone had spoken to the head of a Fae faction like that – they'd likely be dead.

"I'm sorry, *banphrionsa,*" Bran said. Again, a flicker of... something...crossed Sorcha's face and she turned to Torin.

"What am I supposed to do here?"

"I believe him to be telling the truth, Sorcha." Torin kept his tone gentle, unsure how this news would make her react. She'd taken a lot of hits in the last few days, and learning she was secretly the Princess of the Fire Fae might just send her over the edge.

"Right, uh-huh, sure." Sorcha drew the last word out. "I'm a long-lost princess. Who has just been languishing in a little village, sharing a bedroom with her six sisters before taking off to travel around Ireland in a used van? Right, okay. Because that's how princesses are treated."

Bran, unused to being spoken to in such a manner, cleared his throat and looked to Torin for help.

"The prophecy speaks of children born both of human and the Fae world," Torin said. "The reason you haven't been found is that while helpful, the prophecy doesn't state exact times. It isn't like the wording specifies a certain date and in a certain year that a princess will be born. These are foretellings that span centuries, Sorcha. It makes it a touch difficult to nail down when a princess shall arrive. However, once certain events are in motion, it makes it easier for the Fae to decipher the meaning."

"And you've just now realized that I'm the one?" Sorcha directed this at Torin.

"I had my suspicions," Torin said. He saw no reason to lie, but now he second-guessed himself when hurt filled Sorcha's eyes.

"You thought I was a princess but said nothing to me? All this time?" Sorcha asked.

"I suspected, but I couldn't be sure. In fact, I wasn't until I received the summons today."

Bianca whistled, shaking her head. "Bad move, boyo."

"Even if you just suspected it, I feel like it would have been pertinent information to have, no?" Sorcha asked him, and the ache in his chest spread as he realized how deeply he'd miscalculated.

"It's been a busy few days. I didn't think it was worth bringing up until we knew for certain what we were dealing with."

"Even today? You couldn't have pulled me aside for a wee chat? Like hey…Sorcha, you might be meeting your people tonight? Oh, and, by the way – you're a princess of a magickal realm?" Sorcha flipped her brilliant red hair over her shoulder, the golden chainmail and haughty toss of her hair making her look every inch the princess she was.

"I realize that I've made a mistake," Torin said.

"As have I," Bran interjected, clearly seeing this meeting was about to go left.

"So, we have two men apologizing…a first, I'm sure of it," Sorcha said.

"Ouch," Seamus whispered, and Bianca elbowed him in the gut.

"And now what? What is the goal of you coming here today?" Sorcha whirled on Bran.

"We come asking for forgiveness and your help," Bran said, spreading his hands out in front of him. "We've allowed the Domnua too close, and we are now realizing the error of our ways. Unlike you, they have no qualms about hurting our people. They've already slaughtered many. Once we opened the door to them, they infiltrated everything. We're under siege. And without our talisman, our power weakens daily."

Torin could understand that feeling, as the ache in his chest pulsed softly.

"How can we help you?" Torin asked.

"Oh, now they want help?" Sorcha demanded, still furious about being kept in the dark. Torin foresaw a long night of placating her, which also pleased him a bit. He didn't mind a furious woman – quite often their anger could be turned into other passion – but he didn't like knowing he'd hurt her feelings.

"We'll help you – however we can. I promise to be in contact daily, and if there is anything the Domnua let slip to us…I promise you'll be the first to know," Bran said.

"I'll tell the queen," Torin said, and Bran let out a soft sigh of relief. "She'll send forces. But no more will you hurt our people. You almost killed your princess. In doing so, the Domnua would have taken total control of your people, and think where that would have landed all of us."

"I understand," Bran hung his head.

"We'll find your talisman. Do you suspect Donal has it?" Torin asked.

"I do. He's much cagier than I realized."

"What's so great about this talisman?" Sorcha threw up her hands.

"Whoever has it, ultimately will control the Fire Fae. Even you, Sorcha."

"Oh, great, just great. And you thought to let this item out of your sight?" Sorcha glared at Bran.

"It was taken during battle," Bran explained.

"I hate the Domnua," Bianca sighed. "Like damn cockroaches. No matter how many times you kill them, they just keep coming back."

Torin held Bran's eyes briefly, nodding once as a silent exchange passed between them. Discovering Sorcha was their princess was only one step of the prophecy. If she was killed, and the talisman was lost to the Domnua, they'd take over.

And likely burn all of Ireland.

17

"STUPID MEN. STUPID FAE," Sorcha muttered. She'd snagged a whiskey bottle from the cottage when they returned, and shooting a glare of warning at Torin, she'd stomped out to Betty Blue. Unfolding her mattress, she kicked off her boots and poured herself a glass of whiskey. Torin had already told her that her van had been protected with some sort of spell, so she was comfortable enough hiding there.

Muttering, Sorcha took a few sips of the whiskey, enjoying the heat that seared down her throat, easing some of the hysteria that threatened to bubble up. Sorcha stared at the artwork she'd tacked on the ceiling of her van, not really seeing it, as her mind whirled to make sense of this new information.

A child of human and Fae.

That part just...it didn't make sense. Did it? Would that mean one of her parents was not human? Sorcha brought the images of them to her mind. Her father – tall and glowering. Her mother – short, round, and tired. Always tired, she was. A memory rose from the depths.

"You're a changeling," Mary screamed, poking her with a

stick. Sorcha cried out, grabbing at the stick and missing it. She raced after her sisters, but as youngest of the bunch she couldn't keep up. The rest of her sisters streamed across the field behind their home, laughing and singing, and only Mary circled back to taunt Sorcha. "Stupid Sorcha, a changeling you'll always be. Never fast, or smart, or as loved as our sisters and meeeee." She sang the last bit, a glint in her eyes that only siblings taunting each other could have.

"I am not a changeling!" Four-year-old Sorcha cried. She didn't know what the word meant, but she knew it couldn't be good.

"Yes, you are. Father found you in the woods. I saw him," Mary cried, poking her again with the stick so that Sorcha began to cry. "Mother doesn't want you. She says we can't feed you. It's back to the woods for you."

"But, but..." Sorcha's lip trembled. She didn't want to go into the woods. It was dark and scary there.

"Girls! Inside now! Rain's coming on." Her mother's voice, sharp with warning, sounded across the field and Sorcha turned, running as fast as her little legs would take her, away from the forest. Away from her sister's words.

"Ma," Sorcha gasped, skidding to a stop at her mother's feet. "Mary says I'm a...I'm a..."

"Changeling," Mary sang from behind Sorcha. Her mother reached across Sorcha and slapped Mary across the face, causing her skin to go white aside from where a red handprint stood out on her cheek.

"You'll never speak of it," her mother hissed, and Mary's eyes filled.

"But..." Another slap, and Mary fled inside. Sorcha didn't dare speak. She'd never seen her mother raise a hand to any of them before. Her father certainly had, but never her mother.

"Wash your hands. Tea will be on shortly."

As the memory drifted away, Sorcha finished her whiskey. Leaning over, she poured another glass of the honey-colored liquid before rummaging in a drawer and pulling out a picture of her family. It had been taken at her oldest sister's wedding, several years ago, and it was one of the few photos Sorcha had of everyone together. For the first time, she really looked at her family. Her sisters were all tall and slender, unlike Sorcha's compact frame. Their faces were rounded, where hers was angular, and their hair ran to straight where hers curled of its own accord. Her stomach clenched as dread filled her. Could this story actually be true?

Banphrionsa. She'd heard it once before, hadn't she? In her favorite vintage shop in Cork. Her heart skipped a beat when she remembered the man who had called her princess and given her a staff. A staff that hadn't been listed for sale. A gift, he'd told her. Could...the staff be their talisman? In her head she'd been picturing a small rock or an amulet of sorts. Now, she wondered...

Sorcha jumped at the knock at her door.

"Go away!" Although, Sorcha would have to go outside her van and climb up to the top lockbox if she wanted to examine the staff. She'd put it there for safekeeping, and now was even more happy she'd insisted on going to rescue Betty Blue.

"Nope." Torin's voice reached her, muffled through the door. "I should let you know that I can open locks. So..."

"Ugh, fine." Sorcha rolled to the side and walked to the door, flipping the lock. She scooted backward and sat on the mattress as Torin's large frame filled the doorway. Her eyes widened when he slid the door closed behind him and locked it. Despite how upset she was, she couldn't help but remember the last time they'd shared this space

together. Twice now they'd shared passionate moments
here.

The mattress creased as Torin sat next her. He was so
large, his presence seemed to fill the space. Instantly, the
energy that bounced between them crackled.

"Whiskey?" Sorcha held up her glass, and Torin took it,
downing it in one gulp and putting it aside.

"I'm not used to explaining anything. To anyone," Torin
said, looking down at his hands. Sorcha realized he was
opening up to her, and she stilled the retort that rose on her
tongue.

"Okay," Sorcha said instead.

"I didn't say anything about you being a princess as I
didn't know how you would react, and I needed Bran to see
your reaction as well. Because I suspected that the Domnua
were using you against me, and I guessed correctly. If you'd
already known, Bran would have seen that and would have
thought we were colluding against him. Your surprise – and
your anger – showed him that we aren't working together to
take over the Fire Fae's power."

"So, you used me."

"Only for the greater good, Sorcha. And I wasn't even
certain of it, until today. Then I had too many preparations
to make to protect you in case of an ambush. But I mean this
when I say that I'm sorry." Torin turned, his tawny eyes
heavy with sadness and something more. "You're the very
last person I would ever want to hurt."

Sorcha read the truth in his eyes. She took a second to
think it over before she responded. What was more important? Hanging onto her anger with Torin or figuring out a
way forward? There was more at stake right now than her
feelings, and the weight of responsibility hung heavy on
Torin's shoulders. He'd been right to order that nobody

harm the Fire Fae. Now, knowing the evil that the Domnua were capable of, Sorcha realized what a delicate balancing act it was to be a leader of his nature. Behind the sorrow in his eyes, she also sensed just how tired he was. And in that moment, when she stopped focusing only on her feelings, everything fell away. Only to be replaced by one thing – need.

Reaching up, Sorcha brought her hands to Torin's face, pulling his mouth to hers. For months now, she'd hungered for his touch, and he was here, now. She didn't know what tomorrow would bring or what her future would look like after that – but she did know that she could only control this moment. A lovely liquid pull of lust rolled through her, and Sorcha smiled at Torin's lips. He took the invitation, angling his head to explore more, his tongue dancing with hers.

Much like a match being lit, Sorcha's desires exploded. Rolling, she pulled Torin over her, needing the weight of his body on hers. Torin never broke contact, his mouth plundering hers, his kisses taking her under as her body screamed for his touch. Sensing how close she was, Torin ran a hand down her side and cupped her through her jeans. She arched into his hand, needing movement, the friction of him to send her careening over the edge. A thin mewling sound escaped her, as she ground herself against his hand, wanting him everywhere at once. When Torin laughed down at her, breaking their kiss and concentrating on stroking her just right, she came in one long rush, her legs shaking with her need.

"I've missed you," Torin smiled again, a wicked glint in his eyes, as he bent once more to bring his lips to hers. Slowly he traced her mouth with his kisses, as Sorcha lay limp, her heart hammering in her chest, little pulses of pleasure still rolling through her.

Torin traced his tongue lightly down her neck, nibbling at the soft spot where her shoulder dipped. He blew a breath over the skin he'd just licked, causing a shiver to race through her, and Sorcha arched as his hand found the soft skin of her stomach.

"Have I told you how intoxicatingly beautiful I find you to be?" Torin asked, his breath warm at her neck, his fingers trailing slowly up her stomach beneath her shirt. Heat followed his hands, and her nipples puckered, her breasts growing heavy with the need for him to touch her. Slowly, so slowly that Sorcha began to protest, Torin lifted her shirt, pulling it so the sleeves almost came off her arms, but stopping short of removing it completely.

"What are you doing?" Sorcha gasped when Torin leaned over her, and she felt a tug at her wrists.

"You seem a touch impatient, and I'd like to savor this," Torin said, his eyes hot with need.

"Did you just tie my hands up?" Sorcha craned her neck, trying to see what she was affixed to and then gasped when Torin lightly pinched her nipple.

"I did, you delicious minx. Tonight…I get to feast."

Sorcha's mouth dropped open when Torin ripped her tank bra straight down the middle, exposing her small breasts to his gaze, her nipples standing hard at attention. He cupped her immediately, both of his hands rubbing gently across her sensitive skin, and liquid desire moved through Sorcha.

"Take…your clothes…" Sorcha said, her mind skewing blank as he brought his mouth to one breast, sucking gently, the wet heat of him tasting her sending a jolt of sheer lust through her core. Instantly, Torin was naked, and Sorcha blinked up at him.

"That's handy," Sorcha said, and he laughed, the warm

timbre tickling her skin. He was all muscle, tall and sinewy, and his arms rippled as he shifted on the mattress, to hover over her.

"First, I'm going to taste every bit of you. Then, after I've had a sampling, I'm going to return for the main course," Torin said. Sorcha squirmed, the sensation of being restrained making her both nervous and excited. It added to the thrill, she realized, as Torin took complete control of her body – and her pleasure. True to his word, he tasted every bit of her – licking down her thighs, nibbling at her stomach, kissing the delicate skin at her elbow. By the time he'd finished, he'd kissed everywhere but where she wanted him to touch her most, and her body was alight with a furious burning need.

"You look mutinous, darling. Have I told you how much I love how your porcelain skin flushes at my touch?" Torin skimmed a finger over her breast and down her stomach.

"Lovely, I'm sure."

"Ah, now, no need to get a pout on. Open for me, will you, love?" Torin laughed as Sorcha's legs fell open and then she lost all coherent thought as his devilish mouth found where she needed him most. Almost instantly, the wet press of his mouth against her sensitive skin sent her sharply back over the edge, careening into a burst of pleasure that seared straight to her soul. And still, he kept on, even though she was overly sensitive from his touch, and shocked her into another sharp rush of pleasure. Only when he'd sated himself, and Sorcha's head fell limply to the side did he untie her arms. Before she could even understand she was free, he entered her in one long thrust, the sharp hardness of him contrasting with her soft heat.

"Torin." Sorcha reared up, wrapping her arms around his shoulders, devouring his mouth with her own. He drove into her, his need undeniable, over and over, until her body became slick with need. "You feel so good."

He did, too, as though he was built for her, hitting the spot that excited her most. Expertly, Torin rolled his hips, holding her in place, as he drove her up the peak once more, harder, harder, until she cried out into his kiss, her body convulsing around his hard length. Torin groaned, driving sharply into her, as he finally allowed himself to take his own pleasure.

For a moment, they didn't move, their bodies pulsing together, as Sorcha tried to regulate her breath. Torin continued to nibble at her lips, still inside her, and slowly he began to deepen his kiss. Rolling, Torin kept himself firmly lodged inside of her, and Sorcha's eyes widened when she realized he'd hardened once more.

"Oh..."

"Fast recovery time, my love. A gift of the Fae." He arched his hips upward, driving into her, and Sorcha squeaked as he hit the perfect spot once more.

Hours later, when half the whiskey bottle was gone, and Sorcha's legs trembled from exertion, she put her hand up to stop Torin's next advances.

"I need a bathroom break. And some water. And like... six pizzas."

"Ah, your wish is my command. The first, let's use the cottage. The rest – I'll take care of." Torin handed her a shirt, pleasure having made his face go soft and relaxed. At least the tension lines no longer crossed his forehead so deeply, Sorcha thought as she tugged the shirt over her head.

A ping sounded, and Sorcha looked up. She'd forgotten her iPad that she'd left charging in her lockbox. The ping meant she had a new message. When another ping sounded, Sorcha forced herself from the mattress and she crouched by the lockbox, entering the code, before withdrawing her iPad. Gulping as she saw the number of messages that waited for her – she looked at the most recent notifications that kept rising on her screen.

"What's going on?" Torin asked, his voice sleepy.

"Ah, just my sister Mary. Says she's been worried about me. Best I just shoot her a wee message so she knows I'm safe." Sorcha popped the messenger app open and typed a quick message to Mary.

Well, that's a blessing, though it would have been nice to hear from you sooner. The whole of Ireland is talking about Smokin' Sorcha and her own family doesn't know if she's even alive. You could've dropped a line.

My phone was lost in the fire. Sorcha typed back.

Ah well, I suppose that makes sense. You'll need to call Ma at some point. She's sick of fielding questions about you. The rest of us are just annoyed, really. Once again, causing a big stir with one of your antics. Couldn't you just be normal for once?

Why? Being unique is much more fun. Sorcha pursed her lips.

Oh, there you go again, pretending like you're not the weird one. You haven't even asked after me. It's always about you, Sorcha.

Sorcha rolled her eyes, pushing down the automatic annoyance that surfaced.

Fine, Mary. How are you then?

Well, I'm grand, actually. Aside from all the negative attention you've brought us. I've got a new man. I think I'll be keeping this one.

Is that right? Glad to hear it.

Donal is just the sweetest. He's taken me to dinner several times, and we even have a special date in Dublin next weekend.

I'm thinking I'll let him go all the way – he's just too yummy to resist.

Sorcha's head shot up and Torin caught the iPad before it hit the floor.

"What is it?"

"Donal. He's dating my sister."

18

TORIN RUBBED HIS CHEST, the ache having spread more deeply through his body, making his movements slow this morning. He'd wanted to bring up the claim to Sorcha after the night they'd shared, but the moment had been lost when they'd learned of Donal's newest tactic. Since then, they'd barely caught a few hours of sleep and only because Torin had finally run a quick spell over Sorcha to get her to close her eyes for a few hours. She'd be of no use to anyone if she was exhausted, and she'd need to make good decisions if her family was involved.

He still didn't quite know how to broach the matter that she might not actually be blood related to her family. Watching her, as her finger tapped out a nervous rhythm on the steering wheel, he tried to gauge when an appropriate time to bring it up might be. After the third time he'd cleared his throat, she tossed an exasperated look his way.

"Just say it."

"You look beautiful this morning," Torin said, smiling at her.

"Aww," Bianca sighed from the back.

"While I appreciate the sentiment, that's not what has you clearing your throat repeatedly over there. Just say it."

"You're a little scary this morning, Sorcha. I would have thought you'd be a little less tense..." Bianca trailed off when Sorcha raised a single finger salute. "Hmm, Torin – I expected better of you."

Sorcha let out a whoosh of air that sounded a bit like a tea kettle about to blow steam, so Torin wisely bit back a chuckle.

"I suspect she's just a little on edge because of the whole family situation. And the princess thing. And, well, also the whole...family thing," Torin cleared his throat again.

"Is that what's bugging you? Meeting my family?" Sorcha glanced at him quickly, and then brought her eyes back to the road. They were following a winding country road, green hills rolling out on either side, sheep with dashes of spray paint on their sides dotting the fields.

"Me? No. Parents love me," Torin said, automatically and then gritted his teeth when Sorcha glared at him again. Maybe best not to bring up any other women's families that he had experience with then. "I was meaning that...well, since you are the princess, well, um, have you considered that you might not be...related to your family?" Torin stumbled through the rest and then waited, his heart hammering in his chest.

"Ohhhh," Bianca said. She came forward, and crouched between their two seats, laying a hand on Sorcha's shoulder. "Honey, I didn't even think about that. Oh, sure and that has to be a bit of a shock to you, isn't it then? No wonder you're tense. I'd be the same. You're close with your family?"

"Not really," Sorcha said. Her shoulder jerked, and her hands tightened on the wheel. "But I love them nevertheless."

"Do you want to tell us about them?" Bianca asked and Torin was grateful for her help in navigating this conversation. He tried to put himself in Sorcha's shoes, to suddenly discover he wasn't who he knew himself to be or that the people he loved weren't his own, and he realized how vulnerable it would make him feel. Uncertain. Likely not trusting his gut for a while. He'd have to make note of that, because if she was unsteady on her feet, it was possible she could make some rash decisions. Which is exactly what the Domnua wanted. If they killed her, well, it would bring them one step closer in their rise to power. Fear gripped him, and his eyes dropped to where the gold chainmail vest glinted dully on her chest. At least she hadn't argued with him this morning about wearing it.

"Stern father. Never happy. Always yelling. Tired mother. Six sisters. Never any space to breathe, or grow, or learn...or anything really." Sorcha's shoulders hunched as she recounted her history. "The truth is – it was a relief when I left. And, if I'm to be totally honest with you all? It's maybe a bit of relief to understand why I never fit in. At least there is some explanation. A better one than them not loving me, I guess."

"Well, if it's any consolation..." Bianca pressed a quick kiss to Sorcha's cheek. "I find you to be perfectly loveable."

"Yeah, Sorcha. You're the bee's knees!" Seamus piped up from the background and Sorcha barked out a sharp laugh.

"I'm sorry. He tries..." Bianca clucked her tongue and moved backwards in the van.

"What? Is that not a saying? I *thought* it was a saying," Seamus asked.

"It is a saying, Seamus. Thank you for the compliment." A smile flitted over Sorcha's face, and Torin was relieved to see some of her tension had eased. Maybe she just needed a little reminding that she could find family anywhere. Another note for him to tuck away for later, Torin thought, shifting in his seat as the ache intensified inside him. Soon he'd need to have a serious talk with her, and he needed to understand her in a way that he hadn't before.

His life was on the line.

And maybe hers.

"Do bees have knees?" Torin asked, causing Sorcha to laugh again. Good, if he could keep her smiling, then maybe things with her family would go smoothly. Not likely, though if he knew anything about Donal and the way his mind worked. He feared they were walking into a catastrophe. But until then, he'd do his best to keep a smile on Sorcha's face and remind her that even if her family wasn't her blood, they still deserved kindness. Well, maybe. He'd reserve judgment on that last part until he actually met them.

"It's not long now," Sorcha nodded to a sign directing them toward Abbeyfeale. "Our house is outside the town about twenty minutes or so."

Torin watched as they drove through town, a row of colorful buildings hugging the main street, and then continued on back into the countryside.

"Small," Torin commented.

"It is at that. But it was always exciting to go into town," Sorcha laughed, shaking her head so her hair feathered out around her shoulders. "At least it felt exciting at the time. Big nights out from our quiet nights in the country."

"Did you do that often?" Torin asked.

"No. Only for very special occasions. My father didn't want to pay for all of us to eat out – it was too much." Again, that awkward jerk of her shoulder.

"I suppose it was hard to support a large family," Torin

said. He didn't really understand it, as the Fae didn't use currency the same way that humans did. Instead, goods were shared with all, and needs were met before other material gains were sought.

"We made our own fun, when we could. We used to put on shows...in the backyard. I was the star, naturally, because I was the most talented with song and dance. Everyone else was my backup. Silly stuff, really. Just dances to the latest songs...or pretending to fall in love and be rescued by a prince someday." At that, Sorcha trailed off, glancing quickly at Torin.

"I think we all did that, didn't we?" Bianca chimed in. "We're brought up on fairytales, aren't we? It's fun to pretend."

"Until it's not pretend anymore. We forget that, don't we?" Sorcha's voice caught. "That a lot of fairytales aren't... well, not all of them have happy endings do they?"

Torin glanced at Bianca, feeling helpless. The stories of the human world were not his own, and he didn't know of what she spoke.

"Sure and children are a bloodthirsty lot, aren't they?" Bianca chuckled, seeming to sense the need to bring Sorcha's mood up again. "I swear I just loved all the pirate tales where they raided ships and murdered everyone. It's not so real, when we're kids, is it?"

"No, it's not at that," Sorcha agreed. "And now...well, here we are."

"And there's no place I'd rather be." Bianca's voice cut sharply through the melancholy of Sorcha's words. "Sure, this is scary, Sorcha. But you know what? It's also pretty incredible. You're one of the few humans, well – perhaps half-humans – that has knowledge of the greater magick in this world. *And* the next realm. I mean, how cool is that?

Sure, that knowledge comes with a cost. Magick isn't given lightly, Sorcha. And yes, we have to fight on the side of good. But, oh, just how wonderful is it to learn that there is so much more beauty and power to this world? It might not be an easy knowledge to carry. But it's not a boring life, Sorcha. And isn't that what you wanted all along? To get out of your tiny village and live a life with your eyes wide open?"

Sorcha didn't say anything, but the incessant tapping of her fingers on the steering wheel eased.

"This is it," Sorcha said, slowing to turn at a gravel drive that was barely visible from the road.

Torin wasn't sure what he expected, but it wasn't the simple one-story house with two run-down outbuildings. Ivy climbed up the wall of the main house, and one of the outbuildings had no roof at all. Various cars, mechanical parts, doors, and other random pieces cluttered the side yard outside what looked to be a workshop of sorts. Instead of the six sisters that Sorcha had spoken of, an elderly woman with slumped shoulders, wearing a beige jumper and dusty denim pants, straightened at their arrival. Deep lines furrowed her brow, and resignation instead of joy crossed her face when she saw Sorcha behind the wheel. Torin winced. It was so far outside his experience of visiting his own parents that he didn't know what to say. Instead, he reached across and took Sorcha's hand in his own, squeezing it repeatedly like she'd done when he was healing on his sickbed. Finally, she squeezed his palm back, acknowledging the comfort he offered.

"Well, she's an old battle-axe, isn't she?" Bianca asked, shocking Sorcha into a laugh.

"Oh god," Sorcha said, turning to beam at Bianca. "She really is. She'd hate you for saying it though."

"That's your mum, then?"

"It is. Well. Maybe not. I don't know." Confusion crossed Sorcha's face, and then she shook her head. "Either way. Yes. That's her."

"Well, she looks *lovely*." Bianca arched a brow and Sorcha laughed again.

"Cut her some slack. She's had to put up with my father all these years."

With that, Sorcha opened the door and Torin followed her lead, making sure to stay directly next to her so as to send a message to her mother.

"Mother," Sorcha said, stopping in front of the woman.

"Sorcha. Nice of you to stop by after all the problems you've caused us this week. We're the talk of the town." Sorcha's mother turned and looked Torin up and down. "Why's he so fancy?"

"He's rich, Mother. They dress nicer than we do." Sorcha's mouth quirked as her mother studied Torin's attire. He glanced down at himself, confused as to what was causing such a stir. He wore dark denim, leather boots, and a dark leather jacket. Maybe it was his belt buckle? Designed with the crest of his family, it also acted as protection for him and carried powerful magick. Otherwise, he'd considered his outfit relatively tame compared to what he'd usually pick if he was in the Fae realm.

"Is that right?" The mention of money brought an appraising gleam into her mother's eyes, and she held out a hand to Torin. When he brought it to his lips to brush a kiss over her fingers, a habit long held, her face wreathed in a smile, and she batted her eyelashes.

"Dear lord," Sorcha muttered under her breath.

"You may call me Aileen. Come, come. I'll get the kettle on." Aileen took his hand, tugging him along, and Torin sent a bemused look over his shoulder to Sorcha who just shook her head and sighed. He noticed that Aileen didn't even bother to greet Bianca and Seamus who fell in line behind Sorcha as they crowded into the house.

"Well, now, what's your name then?" Aileen asked. She'd stopped by a telephone sitting on a small tea tray by a worn armchair. The door they'd come through opened directly into a living area which held two shabby couches, an armchair, and a small coffee table. A threadbare carpet covered the laminate floor, and limp grey curtains hung at the window. There wasn't much in the way of adornment, or anything cheerful, Torin realized, as he glanced around the room. What was it like for an effervescent and imaginative child like Sorcha to grow up in such a utilitarian environment?

"His name is Torin," Sorcha said, and motioned to Bianca and Seamus. "And these are my friends Bianca and Seamus."

"And this one is...also a friend?" Aileen nodded at Torin, the phone cradled at her neck.

"I'm trying to convince your daughter to date me," Torin said before Sorcha could respond.

"It's the best you'd do, Sorcha," Aileen said, pursing her lips as she dialed a number on the phone. "I'd stop playing hard to get and take what he's offering."

Torin's eyes widened, and he wondered if anyone else heard what she muttered under her breath. *Before he realizes his mistake.* He was beginning to understand her mixed feelings for her family.

"Shannon, call the girls. Sorcha's finally brought a man home. And a fancy one at that," Aileen said into the phone, looking him up and down, "bring something to eat as well. Sure and I can't be expected to feed everyone when she shows up at the door with no notice. I don't have time to run to the shops now."

"Mother. There's no need, really..." Sorcha protested, but Aileen just gave her a look.

"Yes, they were having a sale on the tin of biscuits that I like earlier this week. Bring those as well." Aileen hung up the phone and motioned with her hands to the room. "Sit. Sit. I'll just get the kettle on."

Torin waited until she'd disappeared through a door to what was presumably the kitchen, the sound of cabinets squeaking open on rusty hinges and dishes clanking drifting out. He crossed to Sorcha and took her shoulders with his hands, forcing her to look up at him.

"She doesn't deserve you, Sorcha. Whatever relation or not you are to her – don't hang your worth on her opinion." Torin pressed a soft kiss to her forehead and was rewarded when she leaned into him. Outside, tires on the gravel sounded, followed by car doors slamming. Sorcha sighed and pulled away from Torin.

"Prepare for the onslaught. Best we go around back – there's a few picnic tables and the weather is holding. There won't be enough room for everyone in here."

"What's wrong with inside?" Aileen asked from the doorway where she wrung a dishtowel between her hands. "Are you too good for us now, then, Sorcha? This house had no problem fitting you and your sisters and all your friends growing up. Now it's not enough?"

"I never said that..." Sorcha pinched her nose. "I was suggesting we sit outside because the weather's warming and it's nice to take some time in the air when the rain is away."

"Well, then, I guess I'll have to haul all the tea out back."

"I'm more than happy to help you with that," Torin

volunteered immediately, and Aileen beamed at him again. He hadn't once seen her smile at Sorcha, and his heart hurt for her. No wonder she had to get out of this house – the environment so clearly dulled her shine.

"I'll just show the others out then," Sorcha said, turning from him, her face closed off. Had he miscalculated in offering to help? It seemed the respectful thing to do in the moment. It was like he was trying to walk a tight rope, balancing high above a pit of hungry alligators, and one false step would send him careening to his death.

"So, where did she find you?" Aileen asked, pulling mismatched cups from the cupboard. Voices filtered through the thin pane of the window over the kitchen sink, and Torin caught a glimpse of several women streaming past with bags in their arms.

"I found her, actually. At a festival," Torin said, keeping the details sparse.

"A festival," Aileen snorted as though the idea was ridiculous. "Who has time for such things? Was she working it? In one of those ridiculous costumes? Parading around half-naked for the world to see? Sure, and I know what you're after boyo."

"Ah, no. She was just there, enjoying the music, making friends…. fully clothed." Well, at least for part of the night, Torin amended silently and reached for the tray that now towered with cups.

"You're a working man then?" Aileen gave him another appraising look. "Sorcha said you were rich."

"Rich in life experiences," Torin said, smoothly. He refused to discuss anything akin to money with this woman who so clearly was angling for a way out of her depressing life. If only she realized that she could choose differently, then she wouldn't be stuck in the same routine she always was.

"Ah, well, listen to that. Rich in life experiences, the man says," Aileen laughed. She slapped the dish towel onto the counter. "Must be nice to afford to have new experiences. But maybe our luck is finally changing around here. I'd hope so...after all we've done for Sorcha. She owes us, you know."

"No, I don't know. Why would a daughter owe her parents?" Torin stood, tray in hand, choosing his words carefully. Would her mother give any more information on where Sorcha came from?

"We fed and clothed her, didn't we? Took her to the doctor when she got sick. Maybe it wasn't a grand life, but she survived. Her duty is to us as payment for that."

"I'm not sure that a parent and child relationship is transactional in that nature," Torin said, and a confused look crossed Aileen's face.

"I'm not sure what you're meaning by that, but she owes us. She's not like the rest of them."

"How so?" Torin asked, leaning against the doorframe. Aileen paused, seeming to realize she was revealing more than she wanted to, and waved her hands in the air.

"Ah, nothing really. Just a difficult child to rear. She never minded me one bit. Nothing but problems with that one since I met her. Right, then. Let's get these cups outside and hope one of my daughters was smart enough to remember my biscuits." Aileen nodded toward the door.

Torin turned and followed her down a hallway, her words echoing in his mind.

Since I met her...

19

"WELL, IF IT ISN'T SMOKIN' Sorcha..." Shannon, Sorcha's oldest sister drawled as she rounded the corner of the house followed by two of her other sisters, five of their children, and one roly-poly puppy. One of the kids scooped the puppy up and they raced into the field, barely waving at Sorcha before they were gone amongst a flurry of shouts.

"Knock it off, Shannon. It wasn't my fault," Sorcha said, irritation bubbling up. Her stomach tightened, and the old familiar burn of resentment filled her. These people had never understood her – nor had they bothered to try. She'd always put on an act with them, determined to keep the peace, but now? She didn't need to do that anymore. The problem was, there was a part of her that still desperately wanted their approval. Why? Was there really any point in seeking approval from people who not only didn't understand her, but didn't even bother to try? Their world view was so narrow that they weren't even equipped to begin to understand what Sorcha truly was.

A Fae Princess.

She drew her shoulders back and lifted her head, trying

to channel the confidence she felt when she was performing. Because that was all it was anyway, these times with her
family – a performance. When she wanted to get along with
them, she stayed quiet and subdued, allowing them to run
all over her. If she wasn't in the mood for it, she spoke up
and that is when arguments started. She'd never brought a
man here before, however, and introducing this new
element was unsettling. The dynamic had shifted, and
where Sorcha had thought perhaps her family might warm
to her more if she had a partner – something they understood – instead she felt even more isolated as the women all
but swarmed Torin.

"The radio reported that you had just come off stage
from performing a fire routine when the place went up in
flames. I mean, come on, Sorcha. Surely you can't be
suggesting that it was something else?" Shannon dropped
her bag of groceries on the table and began to unpack the
contents, nodding briefly when Bianca introduced herself
and Seamus.

"It wasn't me, Shannon. I take all precautions and am a
trained professional," Sorcha bit out.

"Trained by who?" Aileen put a jug of water and the tea
kettle on the table. "Is there a school that gives out degrees
in these things?"

"Actually…" Sorcha began, but her sisters had started
laughing, and talking over her, as three more women
rounded the corner of the house. The only sister missing
was Mary, and soon the noisy conversation grew so loud
that Sorcha hunched her shoulders and sat back, not bothering to try an interject anymore. If they wanted to believe
what the news said about the fire, well, that was on them. It
would have been nice to have one of them stand for her –
hell even just ask her what had really happened – but she

didn't know why she expected anything different. She was like a child that refused to learn her lesson, still touching the hot burner on a stove and expecting it not to burn her.

"Well, now, you're a handsome one, aren't you?" Shannon turned, a middle-aged woman with threads of grey lacing her blonde hair, weight from her last two pregnancies padding her hips. "I can't imagine why you've taken an interest in the likes of our wee Sorcha. What is it you do for work then?"

"I'm an advisor," Torin said, his face set in hard lines, "and I've taken an interest in Sorcha because she's perfection in human form – shining like a single crystalline drop of dew on a rose petal when the morning sun kisses it."

Silence greeted his words as all of the women in her family looked from Torin to Sorcha and then back to him. Shannon finally broke the silence with a loud laugh.

"It's a poet you are, as well, I see? Sure now, Sorcha's a lucky one to have caught your eye. I'm sure you've had many women lining up to date you with a smooth tongue such as yours."

"Ugh," Sorcha muttered. She'd plopped herself down on one side of the picnic table, and Bianca came to sit next to her. Leaning in, she bumped her shoulder to Sorcha's.

"Family can be difficult," Bianca said.

"Is there any liquor around?" Sorcha eyed the grocery bags hopefully. A soft breeze brought the scent of horses and damp fields, and the sun warmed her back. In any other situation, she'd enjoy a nice picnic right now. But, instead, she had to watch her sisters flirt with Torin. Most of them were married, for goodness sake, and there was Shannon blushing at something Torin said. When she leaned in and swatted his arm, looking coyly up at him from under her lashes, Sorcha tore her eyes away.

"I didn't see any. Got any in Betty Blue? I can grab it for you," Bianca offered, letting out a low whistle. Seamus, apparently not handsome enough for the women to fawn over, came to sit on the other side of Bianca. Leaning forward, he smiled softly at Sorcha.

"Don't let 'em get you down. You're a princess, remember?"

"Not like they'd ever believe it. I've only ever been a burden or an afterthought to them," Sorcha said.

"Well, to hell with them," Bianca said, startling Sorcha. "Why do you want to fit in here anyway? They're clearly unhappy. Look...your sister there with the wedding band on? I swear she's ready to climb Torin like a tree. Even your mother is having a flirt. People who are happy in their lives don't try to steal their sister's boyfriend. It's just not done."

"I wouldn't know. I've never brought anyone home before," Sorcha said. She didn't know these women, not really, Sorcha suddenly realized. The girls they'd been when they'd shared a bedroom together had matured into harsher versions as adults. Their edges had sharpened, and their hopes and dreams replaced with bitterness and judgment. They didn't look to the future anymore, instead they just muscled their way through the day. She could mope all she wanted about them not bothering to understand her, but the same could be said for her. She'd left them long ago – for good reason – but she hadn't really tried to stay in their lives all that much anyway. On a surface level, she performed her duties. She'd call once in a while, catch up on how the kids were doing, but did she ever ask what made Shannon happy? If she was working on anything new or had picked up a new hobby? She supposed she was just as guilty as them for putting a minimum amount of effort into their relationship.

Perhaps it was just easier that way.

Or, really, for the best.

People grew and changed. Families fragmented, the new parts never quite fitting back together again, and friends moved on. Maybe not everyone was meant to be in each other's lives forever. Some people stayed, and others served their purpose for the time they were there. In this new light, Sorcha studied her family. Would she ever be able to let go of her resentment of them?

"Hey, Shannon?" Sorcha asked, drawing her sister's attention away from Torin. Immediately, her other sisters converged on him.

"What?" Shannon asked, nudging off the top of a tin of cookies, her eyes automatically scanning the fields for her children.

"What makes you happy?" Sorcha asked, wondering if she could break through the wall her oldest sister had built around her.

"What?" Shannon repeated, her forehead creasing in confusion. She looked down at Sorcha. "What do you mean?"

"I'm just curious. We haven't spoken lately about things other than the kids. I was just wondering if you had a hobby you enjoyed, or if you had a dream for your future that lit you up inside?" Sorcha allowed a warm smile to bloom on her face, hoping to encourage an honest connection with her sister.

"Oh, well, isn't that nice, Sorcha? Isn't it nice that you have the time to dream? To have a hobby? Where in my day do you think I have a moment to myself, let alone to dream of the future? I'm barely getting by as it is, hardly enough time to feed all the mouths at my table. The future? That's what I'm cooking for dinner, and I'm lucky if I get that done in time. You always do this, you know? Come in and lord over us how you can just go anywhere you want and have all these dreams and aspirations. Well, you know what Sorcha? I can't. I'm stuck here, as I've always been, and I'll always be. And I don't take kindly to you reminding me of that, with your fancy boyfriend and your stupid traveling act. Go on with the circus or the travelers or whatever it is you're doing these days. Honestly, none of us really care. Just keep your name out of the news, we don't really have the energy to become the laughingstock of town. Again." Shannon slammed the top of the biscuit can down and stormed inside.

"Well, isn't *she* lovely?" Bianca asked, turning to look at Sorcha. "You poor thing. No wonder you ran far away. Keep running, darling. Your love is wasted here."

"I just need a minute…" Sorcha said, her voice raspy. She nodded to where her other sisters had drawn Torin away to show him something. Likely their boobs or something else equally embarrassing or ridiculous. "Can you keep an eye on him?"

"Don't go far, eh?" Seamus asked, worry creasing his face. "If Donal's about, well, we could have a problem."

"Just around the front to Betty Blue. I need a minute is all." Sorcha stood and slipped around the side of the house while Torin's back was turned. Tears burned in her eyes, and she stumbled past Betty Blue and toward the forest that lined their property. Her lungs had tightened, and she struggled with her next breath, the beginnings of a panic attack creeping up her spine. She'd never told her family about her anxiety issues or that sometimes she dealt with debilitating panic. Why bother? They wouldn't begin to understand, and she didn't need to reveal one more weakness to them.

Why couldn't just one of them – just one – try to be nice?

Even for a moment? She'd been half-tempted to toss a fire ball in the air and show them just who and what she was. Wouldn't that have been something to see? Maybe she should still do that...show her sisters exactly just how powerful she had become. The thought cheered her, pushing the anxiety down a bit, and she let herself daydream about going full warrior princess on her family. Oh, they'd lose their minds – that was for sure. But what fun it would be to see them scramble. Could she make them bow? Is that what princesses demanded of their people? Entertaining the idea of walking back and making her family stand in awe of her power, Sorcha pulled up short when she reached a bubbling brook. She'd forgotten this spot, and she pulled herself from her daydreams of forcing her family into hero worship.

Sorcha dropped down onto a fallen log by the stream, stretching her legs out in front of her, and let the stillness of the forest soothe her. Aside from the sound of the running water, the forest was silent – no birds chirping, no animals rustling in the brush, and no breezes brushing the leaves far overhead. That was odd, Sorcha thought. She stilled. Forests were *not* quiet. They were serene, but they weren't quiet. Her eyes darted around the clearing by the water, and the memory she'd had the night before rose unbidden.

You're a changeling from the forest...

She'd come from here. Somehow, someway, Sorcha had been found here. The truth of it slammed into her, and she stood, turning in a full circle to see if there was anything she could see that was unusual or out of place. Heart pounding, she stepped forward and looked down at the stream. It bubbled along, the water following rivulets of pebbles and stone, the occasional sunbeam glinting from its surface. At one point, the water dipped, as though streaming over a ledge, and Sorcha tilted her head.

The stream should continue forward, in the same direction that the rest of the water flowed. But not in that one spot. Instead, it swirled in a circle, counterclockwise, the water moving so fast it was impossible to see the bottom. She wondered...

"You finally found the portal."

A woman stood on the other side of the stream, dark hair coiling around her head, with eyes like shards of ice. She was beautiful in the way of a Great White shark – stunning to look at but deadly power radiated beneath the surface. Sorcha couldn't be sure, but she thought she might be in the presence of a Goddess. Slowly she raised her hands in front of her, holding them at her chest, unsure of how to proceed. Grateful for the chainmail vest she'd put on once again this morning, Sorcha focused on the woman, trying her best to also listen for anyone approaching from behind her.

The forest remained still.

Which made sense, now that Sorcha saw this woman. Survival of the fittest was an inherent concept in nature, so no wonder all the wildlife had fled.

"Is that what this is?" Sorcha asked, realizing the woman was waiting for her to speak.

"It is. One of many, of course, but special to us. You see... the Danula haven't found this portal yet. And it lets us come through to both their world and yours. It's one of the last few secrets my people hold. We'll protect it at all costs."

"Your people? You're...a queen, then?" Sorcha knew instantly she was correct about guessing this woman to be the Goddess Domnu that Bianca had been telling her about. However, she wanted to deliberately undermine her stature to see if the goddess was prone to vanity. If so, it was a weakness that could be used against her. Sorcha had spent a large part of her life watching others, reading their intent, and she'd have to use every ounce of her knowledge now if she hoped to escape this interaction alive. At the moment, her options weren't looking so great. She could attack, she could run, or she could jump into the portal.

"A queen? Please," the woman scoffed, flipping a strand of hair over her shoulder. "The title is beneath me. I'm the Goddess Domnu. Surely you've heard of me?"

Sorcha pursed her lips and looked into the air as though she was thinking hard and trying to remember any conversation about the goddess.

"No, I can't say I have. But I'm still pretty new to all this Fae world stuff. So you're not a queen then? Your dress is nice."

Rage flashed behind the Goddess's eyes.

Please don't kill me, please don't kill me, please don't kill me.

Sorcha kept her expression quizzical but interested. She hoped sliding in a compliment at the end would soothe some of her words to the goddess.

"My dress is made from the tears of those who betrayed me, their grief spun into shimmering threads of regret, and woven into a material that only a goddess can wear." Domnu smoothed her hands over her skirts. Sorcha hadn't been lying, the dress was stunning – a midnight blue shot through with crystalline shimmers – and now she better understood what made it so unique.

"That's...intense," Sorcha decided.

"Yes, well, strong emotions are the driver of change, silly human."

"Is that why you're here? What are you trying to change?" Sorcha just wanted to keep her talking, because if she was talking then she wasn't murdering, and Sorcha dearly hoped to stay on the right side of death this day.

"My people deserve to rule. We're stronger, smarter, and better than these other weaklings. Banished to darkness? Ha!" Goddess Domnu stabbed her finger in the air. "Life is so much sweeter up here. Humans are delightful playthings for us Fae, did you know that?"

"As a queen – can't you just make it happen?" Sorcha asked, baiting her.

Irritation snapped through the goddess and her hair rose around her head, hissing, and Sorcha's eyes widened. She hadn't realized the coils of locks were actually alive, but the new understanding sickened her.

"I'm not a queen!" Goddess Domnu shrieked, and if possible, the woods grew even quieter.

"No, you're not. But I am."

Instinctively, Sorcha ducked as she turned, bringing her arms in front of her face as Queen Aurelia stepped forward and shot a wave of magick at Domnu, sending the Goddess flying from the ground and crashing into the brush behind her. Sorcha sucked in her breath. The Goddess was *so* not going to like that.

"Stand back, Sorcha. It's you she wants." The queen, who had thus far seemed nice, but stern, to Sorcha now looked every inch a warrior. In lieu of a dress she wore metallic trousers and a fitted top, and upon closer inspection Sorcha realized it was a similar material to the chainmail vest she wore. Turning, Sorcha raced to a cluster of bushes and ducked inside of them, the branches poking her sides as she crouched and peered out from the leaves. Maybe it was a silly spot, but Sorcha didn't have much time to make a choice, and she wanted to remove herself from their battle so as not to cause a distraction. Nevertheless, she itched to go stand beside the queen.

The goddess reared up, firing magick, and the queen dodged as bolt after bolt of magick struck her. Sorcha couldn't even say what the magick was. She could just see small shimmery streams zipping through the air as the two women battled each other. A sickly feeling rose in her stomach when the queen stumbled, having taken another hit of magick, and the goddess laughed.

"You think you're stronger than me?" Goddess Domnu threw her head back and laughed. "I'm a goddess, you silly fool."

"And I'm of your sister's blood," Queen Aurelia gasped, crawling on all fours now alongside the stream.

"My sister is weak." Goddess Domnu flicked another wave of magick at the queen, bowling her over onto her back. Sorcha didn't even stop to think. A bolt of fire left her hands and struck the goddess in the head, her hair igniting. A lethal fury ripped across her face as she turned, zeroing in on Sorcha.

"You dare to attack me?" Domnu hissed. Her hair screamed as fire consumed it, and then the goddess was standing by Aurelia. Sorcha hadn't even seen her move. "Foolish girl. I liked this nest of hair."

With that, Domnu raised her arms at the same time the queen did, and their magick met in the middle, sending both women flying in an explosion of catastrophic proportions. Domnu winked out of sight, clutching her stomach, and Sorcha grabbed the branches, averting her face, as dirt and rocks flew through the air. When it was quiet once more, she turned, scared for what she would find. A bead of sweat trickled down her forehead, and Sorcha batted it away before it could get in her eyes. It was the red that caught her eye, and she realized that it wasn't sweat, but blood, that streamed down her face. Reaching up, Sorcha found the wound, and pressed her hand to it to try to stem the flow of blood.

Gingerly, she rose from the bushes, hand at her forehead, and crept forward. Goddess Domnu was nowhere to be seen. A shuddering moan rose from the forest floor and Sorcha raced to where the queen lay in the dirt at the base of three tall trees. The trees had broken her fall, it seemed, but now the queen lay limp, barely breathing.

"Queen...what can I do?" Sorcha dropped to her knees and reached for the woman's hand. Icy fear slipped through her as the queen shuddered out another breath, gasping as she tried to draw in air.

"You can't...die." The queen gasped.

"I...please, what do I do? How do I help you?" Sorcha blinked tears away, terrified at the ashen color of Queen Aurelia's face.

"It's...maybe too late. My son...please, tell him..." The queen squeezed Sorcha's hand softly. "I love him so. My people too. Tell them of my love."

"Wait...no, *you* tell them. You can't..." Sorcha gasped as the queen's grip went limp, her head falling backwards. "No, no, no. Aurelia. Listen to me."

"Wear this..." The queen pulled the gold circlet she wore from her hair. Panic gripped Sorcha when the queen fell backwards, no longer breathing. Without thinking, Sorcha began to pump the woman's chest, trying to restore a heartbeat. She counted off the pumps, as she'd been trained to do, her mind scrambling as she tried to figure out what to do.

A child's scream pierced the air.

Sorcha's head came up and she realized that her family

was under attack. Torn, she looked toward the house when more screams rose, and then back down at the queen's body. Her eyes darted to the portal.

It was the only magick she had available. Decided, Sorcha stood and picked up Queen Aurelia, hefting her lifeless body over her shoulders in a fireman's carry. Grateful, once again, for the muscles she'd honed through hours of training, Sorcha stumbled her way to the portal. With zero hesitation, she jumped into the stream, the queen on her back.

"The queen!" Sorcha barely had time to open her eyes before shouts greeted her. She didn't know where she was, but guards surrounded her.

"Take her. I have to go back. Goddess Domnu..." Sorcha gasped, pleading with a guard. "It was dark magick."

"We'll see to her, Princess." Already, the weight of the queen's body was gone from her shoulders, and Sorcha took one moment to make sure that the guards surrounded the queen, before she turned and jumped into the portal once more. The queen may be dead, but a princess still lived.

It was time to save *her* people.

20

THE PORTAL SPIT her out back at the stream, and Sorcha winced as she sloshed through the cold water and scrambled up the bank. At the top, she paused and scanned the woods. When a bird flitted by, a sigh of relief left her. Sorcha bounded down the path, racing back toward her childhood home, worry for the queen battling with concern for the others.

Torin.

She'd barely had time to think about the intimacy they'd shared the night before, nor how her feelings for him were shifting. And now, with their lives on the line, the past didn't really matter anymore. Did she really need to hang onto the fact that he'd left her one time? He'd found her again, hadn't he? And he'd shown up for her, over and over since. Now it was her time to show up for him, she thought, as she skidded to a stop in front of the house.

Quiet greeted her, and Sorcha did not like that at all. With a large family there was always noise coming from somewhere. Wary, she turned in a slow circle, her hands in the air, and tried to get a read on the situation. When nothing untoward happened, Sorcha turned back to where Betty Blue was parked. *Her lockbox.*

The staff.

Cursing herself for forgetting, Sorcha climbed up the little ladder on the back of the van and keyed in the code for the storage compartment that served as additional storage for her life. She'd secured the magnificent staff in the box the day she'd gotten it, not yet ready to incorporate it into her routine. Now, she prayed it was still there.

"Oh, thank you..." Sorcha gasped, seeing the wooden staff nestled in her down coat. The minute her hand closed around it, a wave of power flooded her, and she knew then that this was the Fire Fae's missing talisman.

Which meant the two things that were keeping the Domnua from fully controlling the Fire Fae were here – at least according to what Bianca had told her. The Domnua needed her out of the way. And they needed the staff. Realization of what a dangerous position she was now in dawned, but for the first time Sorcha didn't feel the beginning of a panic attack. Instead, calmness washed through her, and her senses sharpened – a cool clarity coming to her thoughts. Sorcha pulled off the circlet she'd slid up her arm when she'd rescued the queen and put it on her head. She hoped it wasn't a huge royal breach to wear this crown, but the minute she placed it on her head, courage filled her.

Sorcha dropped lightly back to the ground, staff in hand, and threw back her shoulders. *Now* she was ready to step into her own and fight for her people. Starting first with those who'd gone missing from the backyard of her home. Quickly rounding the house, her shoes crunching the gravel, Sorcha drew up short when she saw her mother quietly weeping at the picnic table. Hearing her steps, Aileen looked up and narrowed her eyes.

"Bastard child," Aileen said, venom in her voice. It was the sentiment hidden behind years of tense communication finally brought to the surface. Sorcha hadn't been wrong – this woman had always resented her.

"What happened?" Sorcha didn't have time to unpack Aileen's anger. "Where is everyone?"

"I should never have allowed your father...to..." Aileen hiccupped and scrubbed a hand reddened from years of manual labor over her face.

"To what?" Sorcha pursed her lips, continuing to scan the fields behind the house for any movement.

"To keep you...his lover's child..." Aileen hissed. At that, Sorcha's eyes widened. Her father? With another woman?"

"You're saying..." Sorcha tried to wrap her head around the thought of her father being intimate with anyone, let alone someone other than Aileen. He was a crude and caustic man, overbearing and angry, and without a charming bone in his body. It was a miracle that one woman had chosen to be with him, let alone now finding out that he'd had another on the side. Unbelievable, really.

"Yes, you. Demon spawn is what you are." Aileen made the sign of the cross, her fingers going to her necklace that held a simple silver cross. Touching it seemed to calm her, and she lifted her face to Sorcha. "I should've drowned you in the stream you came from."

"Well, now, that's a touch dramatic, isn't it then?" Sorcha batted away the sting of the words, refusing to let this woman sidetrack her from finding her friends – her true family. "Didn't think you were one for murdering babies and all."

"You always talked back to me. Not like the other girls. My babies. My angels. Never was there a better day than when you finally left the house. I'd have been happy to never see you again, but you still insisted on coming back."

"Trust me – out of a sense of obligation only. Now that's been removed, so I won't be fussing much with the likes of you in the future. Tell me what happened." Sorcha slapped her hand on the table, causing Aileen to jump. "I don't have time for this. Where is everyone?"

"The man took them." Aileen wrapped her arms around herself, tears streaming down her face. "My babies. I knew you'd bring us trouble one day. You were nothing but a ticking time bomb."

Sorcha sucked in a breath and studied the broken woman before her. It wasn't Sorcha's fault she'd been brought into this home, but it also wasn't Aileen's fault that she'd been incapable of loving her. Holding onto anger would get her nowhere. Leaning over, she forced Aileen to meet her eyes.

"I forgive you. You did the best you could with the hand you were dealt. I'm going to bring your family back to you. Understood?"

"You promise?" Aileen whispered, wiping her eyes.

"I'll do everything in my power to bring them home safe. It's the best I can offer."

For the first time, Aileen looked at her with respect in her eyes. The women measured each other, seeming to understand that everything had changed, and both coming to their own terms with it. Aileen took in the staff Sorcha still held and the crown of gold glinting dully in her hair.

"You always were the strongest of the lot."

"Be careful," Sorcha said, dipping her head slightly in acceptance of the compliment. Turning, she ran to where the field started and followed a low stone wall that hugged a dirt path that led to the first of the outbuildings. A soft whimper caught her ear, and Sorcha skidded to a stop when the puppy the children had brought with them earlier wandered around the side of the building. Spying her, it plopped on its hindquarters and began to cry in earnest. Poor thing looked exhausted, Sorcha thought, and scooped it up. Cradling the fuzzy warm body against her chest, she checked quickly for any wounds while the puppy lapped at her face with desperate gratitude. Backpedaling, she returned to where Aileen still sat at the picnic table.

"This one needs you. Water and cuddles. Protect him." Sorcha deposited the puppy in Aileen's arms, and the older woman automatically began to rock the dog, humming a mindless tune. Satisfied that the puppy would be seen to, Sorcha turned on her heel and jogged lightly back in the direction that the puppy had come from. At the first outbuilding, Sorcha plastered her back against the outer wall, the damp wood with ragged splinters scraping her shirt. She schooled her breathing, listening for anything amiss, her eyes scanning the land. Then she heard it – a sneeze – coming from the next outbuilding. This was an older building, with no roof, that her father had long ago given up on repairing. She'd spent many a day there as a child, hiding in dark corners and daydreaming of a different life.

Sorcha padded quietly to one corner of the building, and then turned, ducking her head into an opening in the wall where two doors had once been.

All her sisters, and their children, sat on the floor with their arms bound. Over them stood her one missing sister – Mary – and she held a gun in her hands. Where had Mary even gotten a gun? Guns weren't allowed in Ireland. For some reason that was Sorcha's first thought before the actual act of betrayal slammed into her. Why was Mary holding her own family at gunpoint? Had Donal managed to brainwash her? Or had Mary been one of the Dark Fae all along?

"You might as well be coming in then, Sorcha. I can see you out of the corner of my eyes," Mary said, her hand steady. Much taller than Sorcha, with thin blonde hair, and hunched shoulders, Mary had always been the sister with whom she'd had the most complicated relationship. For a while there, Sorcha had thought they were on their way to becoming much closer. But then Mary had gone off to Uni and frowned upon Sorcha's life choices. Now, Sorcha had to wonder if there had been other influences that had contributed to Mary's dislike.

"Mary. Put the gun down. You don't have to do this," Sorcha said, stepping slowly into the room. Well, half a room really. The sky opened wide above them, and in the distance, a low rumble sounded like the promise of a storm long before the rain began.

"I'm well aware of that Sorcha. The only thing I actually *have* to do is...capture you." Mary turned, the gun now trained on Sorcha. "I hadn't expected it to be so easy, nevertheless, here we are."

"Yes, here we are," Sorcha echoed Mary. The children whimpered, and her sisters hushed them, but it was almost impossible to keep a group of children completely silent. Perhaps Sorcha could use the distraction to her advantage. The magickal staff hummed in her hands. "But why, Mary? Why are we here? Your own sisters?"

"My own sisters who have done nothing for me. Nothing!" Mary said, anger flashing in her eyes. For the first time, the gun wavered in her hands. "I was the only one to go off to University. Did anyone care? Did anyone even come to my graduation?"

"I did," Sorcha said, softly.

"Sure, the one sister who isn't even related to us," Mary glared. Shannon's mouth dropped open and she looked up at Sorcha who gave a subtle shake of her head.

"How'd you learn that anyway? I just found out myself," Sorcha said, shifting slightly on her feet. If she could keep her talking and just move a few feet to the left, she'd be able to throw some magick her way.

"I've always known. I heard Mother and Father arguing about it one day. It's hard to keep secrets in a house so small," Mary said.

"And yet you kept that secret from us," Shannon piped in, and Mary's eyes darted down to her. Sorcha took the opportunity to shift a few feet to the left.

"Oh, hush, Shannon. Nobody cares about what you think. Just because you're the oldest doesn't mean you know best, does it? I mean, just look at you...taking right after Ma, aren't you? A few kids, a husband you don't like, same small town..." Mary's lip curled.

"That's rude," Sorcha said, wanting Mary's attention on her and not Shannon. At least she could defend herself. "Not everyone has the same vision for their life, Mary. You leave Shannon alone. It's me you want, isn't it? Why though – why you?"

"It's not my fault I'm the prettiest of the lot of you." Mary tossed her hair over her shoulder and pursed her lips. The gun shook in her hand, and Sorcha knew she was rattling Mary a bit. The girl certainly wasn't trained for a situation like this – at least not that Sorcha knew – which made her all the scarier, really.

"What does that have to do with anything?" Sorcha said, inching to the left again. Again, the low rumble sounded, and Sorcha wondered if a storm was coming in.

"It's why I was chosen – by Donal. I'm meant to be a princess," Mary preened.

"Is that what he's told you then?" Sorcha laughed, and Mary's eyes narrowed. The gun came up, this time focusing on her head.

"You know Donal?"

"Sure and I know him. He's a traitor and has very little power. You'll not be a princess like you're thinking. You want to know why?" Sorcha asked, raising the staff in front of her.

"Why?" Mary hissed, her finger going to the trigger.

"See the crown? I'm the Princess of the Fire Fae, darling. That spot has been filled."

Mary sucked in a breath and two things happened simultaneously – Shannon kicked Mary in the back of the knee, sending her toppling backward with the gun pointed to the sky – and Sorcha's blast of fire reached Mary. She hadn't wanted to hurt her, but there wasn't much that could be done in this situation. Sometimes, people were just bad inside. Her sister was one of those. She'd always been selfish, nasty, and difficult – and turning on her own nieces and nephews was evidence of that. Sorcha's magick hit the gun, knocking it to the ground, fire singeing Mary's hands.

She was crossing the room before Mary could react, kicking the gun out of the way, and bending over her sister. When she glared up at her and tried to jump up, Sorcha used old school tactics and grabbed her hair. Squealing like a cat tossed into a bathtub, Mary reached for her head, but Sorcha had already flipped her over and put a knee to her back.

"Shannon – can you move at all? I need something to tie her up with."

"I can stand," Shannon propped herself up and shuffled

across the room before kicking something back to Sorcha. She glanced down to see a roll of duct tape in the dirt.

"Come kneel on her," Sorcha ordered, not caring that Mary now whimpered into the dirt floor, her tears leaving streaks in the dust on her face. She had no mercy for traitors – particularly ones who didn't understand the stakes. Shannon cheerfully sat on Mary, while Sorcha made quick work of taping her arms and legs tightly.

"Let me..." Sorcha said, once Mary was secure, and she used the dagger at her belt to slice through the tape on Shannon's wrists. Instantly, Shannon was up and crossing to her children, their cries having grown louder.

"I have to go," Sorcha stood. Her sisters looked up at her with mixed expressions of shock and awe.

"You go. I'll be sure that Mary doesn't get loose."

"Do you know what happened to the others?" Sorcha asked.

"That way...that's all I know. They ran off." Shannon pointed across the field, and the rumble sounded again – this time much closer. She put an arm around her daughter and pulled her close. "Be careful, Sorcha. You may never have fit in with us, but there's nothing wrong with that. Don't let Mary's spitefulness distract you. She's a nothing. You, on the other hand, are a princess it seems. Own it."

"Thank you," Sorcha said, a quick smile flitting over her lips. She bowed her head to Shannon, and her other sisters chimed in to agree. No, they'd never be close – but a newfound understanding was born between them. "I'll be back as soon as I can. Ma's with the puppy bawling her eyes out behind the house. Don't let her near Mary or she'll likely convince her to cut you loose."

"She always did have a soft spot for Mary," Shannon shook her head. "Likely in their shared dislike of you."

Caught, Sorcha turned at the door. "You saw that?"

"Hard to miss it, Sorcha. You had a rough go of it. But I didn't have much to give you – still don't. But I'll try harder in the future."

"Thanks for that," Sorcha said and then she was out the door and bounding across the field, racing toward the noise she'd heard earlier. It wasn't a storm like she'd thought, as the sky remained sunny and cloudless. No, something much more sinister waited, and the staff Sorcha held heated under her palm. It seemed to be warning her of impending danger, and Sorcha glanced down to see the tip – an intricately designed heart – glowing softly. Sorcha crested a hill, her heart pounding, and stopped.

"Oh, shite," Sorcha said, her stomach knotting.

Below her, an army of Domnua stormed across the field, led by Donal. The rumble had come from their sheer numbers, and the ground trembled lightly beneath her feet as they advanced. Sorcha's heart froze. In front of the army stood Bianca, looking tiny and defenseless against the mass of Dark Fae, with Seamus and Torin flanking her. Fearless, and foolhardy, Sorcha thought and dove into action. She raced down the hillside, trying to get closer, but the Domnua were far ahead of her. She could only watch as they began to fire off magick before they'd even reached her friends. This was bad, Sorcha gasped, fear almost paralyzing her. Understanding dawned that she wouldn't get to them in time.

But it was her they wanted, wasn't it?

Without another thought, Sorcha threw herself to the proverbial wolves.

21

"HEY!" Sorcha screeched at the top of her lungs. "Hey! You idiots! I'm right here! I've got the talisman, too!" Sorcha brandished the staff high above her in the air.

It was like a record screeching to a halt, and the entire army stopped, pivoting at once like some sort of weird mechanical dolls being controlled by a remote. Sorcha saw the panic in Torin's eyes as Donal switched direction as well and bore down on Sorcha.

Right, so, she might have needed more of a plan than just distracting them. The staff heated under her hand, the worn wood ridges almost burning her palm, and she looked at it.

Of course.

The talisman of her people. It was telling her to lead them. Call her people and fight this battle. She was the princess, after all, wasn't she? Shouldn't that come with a few benefits like summoning her own Fae army at a whim? Stabbing the staff into the ground, Sorcha closed her eyes and focused on the small ball of light deep inside her that signaled her power. Tapping into it, she allowed the power to flood her body, opening her heart and soul, and tipping her head back, she shouted to the sky.

"Fire Fae! I command you to fight this battle. We need you. Now!"

Pandemonium erupted.

Flames shot from the head of the talisman, creating a line of fire that shot straight to sky, and the ground heaved beneath her feet. Stumbling, Sorcha went down to one knee, so focused was she on the wooden staff that now seemed to be a flame thrower of sorts.

"Okay, I can work with this," Sorcha said, and turned the flames on the first round of Domnua that leapt at her, taking them out in one fluid stroke of fire and silvery carnage. In a weird way, Sorcha was grateful the Domnua didn't bleed the color red. It would have made it much more difficult to kill them, she thought, as she took down another row of the army in a silvery explosion. Instead, it still seemed so surreal to her that she was here – in her own backyard – battling magickal beings.

The next line of Domnua skidded to a halt, their eyes widening, and Sorcha glanced over her shoulder to see what had scared them. Glee shimmered through her, and she raised the staff higher in the air. Her people had come.

Hundreds of Fire Fae streamed across the field, a wall of flames surrounding them, looking like a tornado of fire racing across the field. Smoke billowed to the sky as they darted past Sorcha and straight into the army of Dark Fae, cutting a dangerous path. Shouts sounded as the Fire Fae consumed the army, their sheer power and force of fire over-whelming the Domnua, and Sorcha cheered. Racing ahead, she followed the Fae into battle, searching for her friends.

"Bianca!" Sorcha shouted, finding the pretty blonde with dirt streaking her cheeks, cheerfully stabbing a Domnua.

"Sure and you're a sight for sore eyes, aren't you then?" Bianca gasped. "I thought we'd lost you for a second there."

"I'm sorry," Sorcha said, whirling and hitting an approaching Domnua with her fire stick. "I shouldn't have gone away from the house. I'm not even sure why I did…"

"The Fae are tricky when they want to be. Likely compelled you to do so," Seamus said over her shoulder and Sorcha grinned up at him.

"Glad to see you in one piece."

"Same for you. That sister of yours is trouble…" Seamus said, easily lopping off the head of a Domnua next to Sorcha with a grin.

"So I found out. Where's Torin?" Sorcha asked, taking down a group of approaching Domnua with her newfound flamethrower.

"That's a handy tool, isn't it?" Bianca nodded her approval.

"Seems to be. I've had it all along…I didn't know," Sorcha said, scanning the battle, trying to find Torin. The Fire Fae were a force to be reckoned with, and already the Domnua retreated under their relentless attack. Sorcha couldn't blame them – fire was no joke – and a wall of it rose in front of them. Through the flickering flames, she spotted Torin in a headlock with Donal.

"Oh no…" Sorcha breathed. "I see Torin. I have to go to him."

"Go on. We've got this. The worst of them are handled. Your Fae are kicking ass!" Bianca charged another Domnua, her eyes alight with adrenaline.

Sorcha was already moving, the acrid taste of smoke on her tongue, the heat of the fire dancing over her skin. Would she be able to reach Torin? Just because she was the Princess of Fire Fae didn't necessarily mean she could walk through fire, did it? She really hadn't had any time to get a rundown of the rules that came with being a Royal in the Fae realm. Giving herself a mental pep talk, Sorcha tried not to let her fear get the better of her.

Plunging through the wall of fire, Sorcha stumbled to the other side, her face slick with sweat. Using the staff to catch her fall, she blinked through the smoke that burned her eyes.

"Ah, perfect," Donal said, his voice at her side, and then his arm was around her neck, pinning her in place. The smoke had temporarily blinded her, and in doing so, she'd walked right into Donal's trap. "Miss me, Princess?"

"Eat dirt," Sorcha said, bucking her head back. Unfortunately, due to her short nature, she just butted her head into his stomach instead.

"You're not as nice as your sister," Donal decided, holding her in front of his body. "She was much more welcoming to me. I can't say I enjoyed her charms much, but she didn't need a lot of convincing to join my side. Like a starved dog looking for table scraps, that one."

"You took advantage of her," Sorcha seethed.

"It's hard to take advantage of something given freely. Women aren't so tough to read, you know. Some like to play hard to get. Others are just desperate to be wooed. Mary came to me of her own choice."

Sorcha widened her legs and swung the staff backwards between them, hitting Donal directly between his own legs. Instantly, his hold loosened on her throat, and she danced out of his reach as he dropped to his knees.

"Silly men...you're all the same," Sorcha taunted him, happy to see him gasping for breath as the wall of fire surged behind him. "Thinking your cock is your biggest strength when in the end its your greatest downfall."

Donal's head reared back, and he raised a hand, the dagger already flying through the air before Sorcha could react. A soft moan sounded at her shoulder. Whirling, Sorcha saw Torin crumple to the ground, the dagger in his throat, his tawny eyes full of pain.

"No," Sorcha gasped, his own pain rocketing through her, their connection still strong. "Torin! No..."

Why had she taken the time to taunt Donal? She should have killed him on the spot. Hadn't she seen what they had done to the queen? Fury clouded her vision and she turned back to Donal as he stood, laughter on his face, fire at his back.

"Whoops..." Donal said, shrugging a shoulder. "I meant that for you, but I guess my aim was a bit off."

This time, Sorcha didn't hesitate. The Fire Fae's most powerful talisman, filled with the power of a thousand fires, pointed at Donal and she unleashed its power, refusing to hold anything back, and her rage screamed from her in a blazing bolt of power. Donal disintegrated on impact, his smile disappearing in flames, a blight on humanity destroyed.

"Torin," Sorcha said, dropping to her knees by his side. "Please, please...I can't lose you."

The wound was ugly, made more so from the guilt that ran through Sorcha, and she stroked Torin's cheek, unsure if she should remove the knife. Feeling helpless, she turned her head.

"Bianca! Seamus! We need help!" Sorcha shouted, returning her gaze to Torin. "Tell me how to help you."

"My pretty Sorcha..." Torin beamed up at her, sadness and pain in his golden eyes. "My favorite surprise. I never thought to know you..."

"Torin. Please, save your energy. Help is coming. Tell me

what to do," Sorcha begged, tears streaming down her cheeks.

"I loved you since the moment I laid eyes on you." Torin's words came out on little gasps of air. "Much like this...through the flames that danced around your head. The ruler of my heart, the light of my soul." His eyes fluttered closed, and Sorcha's heart stopped.

"Torin! No, you can't let go. You have to hold on." Sorcha pulled the shirt away from his neck, pressing her hands to his chest to see if he still breathed.

"Shite," Seamus said as he dropped to her side.

"Do something!" Sorcha shrieked. "I don't know what to do. How do I help?"

"Hold on, just hold on..." Seamus ordered her, digging in a pouch at his side. "I have the elixir here somewhere."

"Give him space now," Bianca said, tugging Sorcha's arm to move her a bit to the side.

"I can't...I can't look at him...not like this..." Sorrow rose – for Torin, for the queen, for the loss of everything in her life that she had thought to be real – and tears blinded her. "I need more time with him."

"Shhh, shhh. Let Seamus give him the elixir. It's extremely potent and meant to work wonders. A Fae can only use it once in his lifetime, that's how strong it is."

"Will it..." Sorcha swiped a hand over her eyes, coughing as a gust of wind brought smoke to them. "Does it work?"

"We'll see. Let's just give him time," Bianca said, her voice firm.

Seamus unstopped a small gold bottle and, leaning over, he nudged Torin's lips open and poured the precious contents in, holding his mouth closed. Much like when Torin had been hurt before, Sorcha watched his throat to see if he would swallow.

"Wait, didn't Prince Callum already give him an elixir? Isn't it too late?" Sorcha asked. Her grip on the staff grew almost painful, but she couldn't let the talisman go – not if they were still at risk. She'd let her guard down, and she wouldn't do so again until she knew they were all safe.

"No, that was just regular Fae medicine," Seamus said, reaching over to close his hand around the dagger at Torin's throat. "Look away ladies."

Sorcha squeezed her eyes shut, gripping Bianca's hand tightly, and was rewarded by a soft moan.

"He's..." Sorcha leaned over Torin, ignoring the wound that rapidly closed in his neck, and pressed a soft kiss at his lips. "Torin, come back to me."

But he didn't. Instead, his eyes remained closed, his chest rising precariously with each breath.

Seamus looked at Sorcha, concern creasing his face.

"Something's not right. We need to get him home, as quickly as possible. I'm not sure I can manage to transport all of you to the portal at the cove. It's a longer journey than I may be able to do with a wounded person."

"There's a portal here," Sorcha grabbed Seamus's arm and shook it. "By the forest. It's where I was when I went missing."

"There's a portal here?" Seamus eyes widened and he was already lifting Torin into his arms, moving so quickly that Sorcha barely registered the movement. "How far?"

"Over the field...by the house. Into the forest."

"Give me better details," Seamus demanded.

"The stream in the forest. About a fifteen-minute walk from the house. To the north."

"Ladies, hook arms with me. I can transport that far at least. Torin needs more help than I can give."

Sorcha hooked her arm around Seamus's waist, and

Bianca did the same, creating a little huddle of people. Seconds later, the sucking sensation started, and Sorcha leaned into it, trying to hurry the transportation along. Moments later, they stood by the stream, sunlight filtering through the leaves overhead.

"It's just down here..." Sorcha said. Grabbing Bianca's arm, she led her down the path, dread slipping through her. What if it wasn't there anymore?

"I see it." Seamus said.

"Where?" Bianca demanded.

"It's just there – in the water. Where the stream swirls counterclockwise. Follow me in." Seamus splashed through the water and jumped feet-first into the portal without another glance. Sorcha appreciated that about him – no time wasted – and she took Bianca's hand.

"It'll be okay," Bianca promised.

"You can't be sure of that," Sorcha said, anxiety clawing its way up her throat.

"No, but I choose to believe."

Together, they jumped.

22

TIME SEEMED to both slow down and speed up, and before Sorcha could register much of anything, she was once more in the gilded tower room, with a sorrowful Prince Callum at Torin's side.

"He's had the *beathra*?" Callum asked, his face set in hard lines as he studied his friend. Torin's chest rose, but not without struggle, and Sorcha's heart twisted. There had already been so much pain – in such a short amount of time – that Sorcha turned away from the bed and walked the side of the room to collect herself. The last thing the Fae needed was her weeping over Torin's sickbed, but all of her emotions slammed into her at once.

"Hey…" Bianca said, having followed her to the wall. Sorcha dropped to the floor, no longer caring what anyone thought of her, and buried her face in her hands. "Give it time."

"It's too much…" Sorcha gasped through her hands. "I… it's just too much. My life – my entire life has been upended. I no longer have the career that I love. My family isn't actually my family, and I still don't know if they all lived or what will happen with Mary. The queen..."

"What happened to the queen?" Bianca whispered, shooting a furtive glance over her shoulder at Callum.

"She didn't..." Sorcha couldn't say the words and Bianca's face fell.

"No, please tell me..."

"I'm sorry. I tried to save her..." Sorcha said, tears streaming down her face. "And now...this. I can't lose him. I was finally understanding what we had together. Every night he came to my dreams, did I tell you that? I've grown to look forward to it, to laughing with him, loving him..."

"You love him?" Bianca asked, narrowing in on the important part.

"I do. I really do. He's a dream come true, really. A real-life fairy prince come to life. And I failed him."

"You did no such thing, but you are now," Bianca said, her voice firm. "Look at me."

Sorcha looked up at Bianca's earnest face.

"You've had yourself a good cry. Now, dust it off and get back by his side. He needs you right now – the time for tears will be later. Understood?"

Sorcha drew in a long breath, and then another, pain shuddered through her. Was she strong enough to watch Torin die? She didn't know, but she also knew that she wouldn't want to be alone if she was in his position. Rising, she wiped her tears and crossed the room to where Callum murmured with Seamus. Another man – whom she recalled from the battle at the beach – joined them.

"Nolan," Bianca nodded to the newcomer. "You'll remember Sorcha. Torin's fated mate."

Fated mate.

The words slammed into her, both a promise and a threat, and Sorcha swayed on her feet. Could it be...Sorcha shook her head and looked up at the men who clustered around the bed, sorrow clinging to them like burrs in wool.

"Is it..." Sorcha's voice rasped out, and she cleared her throat as everyone looked at her. "Is it not working?"

"It should work," Callum said, his hands crossed tightly over his chest. "I just can't understand what else would be harming him right now. Is it possible the Domnua have a new magick? That the knife carried a toxin we don't yet know?"

"Maybe," Nolan said. He was a large man with intimidating features, and Sorcha felt the punch of his confidence as though it was a physical thing. "But our poisons witch is fantastic. Surely she would know if they'd introduced something new?"

"I...um..." Sorcha tried again, casting her eyes down to where Torin's breath rattled in his chest. "Is it possible that..."

"That what?" Callum asked, his voice sharp.

"I haven't claimed him..." Sorcha rushed out, unsure of what their response would be. "I didn't know what it was or how to do it...and was uncertain at first. He told me..."

"A fated mate denied his claim. Just like his sister..." Nolan gave her a look of absolute disgust, tearing her heart in two.

"I didn't know...I promise you, I didn't understand," Sorcha pleaded.

"It would make sense," Prince Callum shook his head, sadness dancing across his handsome features. "Is it possible you feel that way now? Or are you certain you don't wish to claim him?"

"I can still claim him?" Hope bloomed, shiny and pure, deep in her chest.

"Of course, until his last breath," Prince Callum leveled a look at her. "But don't claim him if you don't mean it. Lying has its own consequences in the Fae world."

"I mean it...I promise." Sorcha held up her hand. "What do I do?"

"Why didn't he reject the claim?" Nolan interrupted. "Why wouldn't he just let the claim go?"

"He needed his powers to protect Sorcha or the Domnua would have gained ruling of the Fire Fae. This is their princess," Seamus nodded to Sorcha.

"Ah," Nolan said, his stormy eyes assessing her. "And now he's unable to speak...and therefore can't reject you now."

"I don't think he wants to," Bianca interjected, squeezing Sorcha's palm. "He loves her."

"If that's the truth of it – then claim him," Nolan spit out.

"How?" Sorcha asked. "Is there a ritual?"

"You need to tell him that you do – and if possible – sing your heartsong. It adds a layer of magick to the bond, and he'll need everything you have to give him."

"Step back," Bianca said, walking around the table and nudging the royals back as though they were annoying boys clambering around a snacks table. "You need to give her some room or she won't be able to think straight. Go on now."

Ever grateful for Bianca, Sorcha waited until the group had crossed the hall and turned to Torin. Not caring about propriety, she crawled into the bed next to him, snaking her arm under his neck and wrapping herself around him so that her body pressed to his. His breath came – but achingly slow – and fear made her mind go blank. She didn't know their heartsong, did she? Please help me, Sorcha begged silently. The queen appeared in her thoughts, just an image of her smiling face, pink hair shining in the sun – and she threw out her hand at Sorcha as though tossing her a ball to catch – but instead it was a memory. Sorcha's mind jumped back to their first night together and the words came to her in a flash.

The flames will dance,
Fire lights the dark,
To give love a chance,
Takes only a spark.

Sorcha gasped the words out in a tremulous song, her lips hovering over Torin's, love pouring from her heart.

"I claim you, Torin of the Fire Fae. I claim you now, in the future, and into the next realm. Forever mine, sweet Torin. I claim you," Sorcha repeated the words over and over, not sure if she'd made it in time, as his chest shuddered heavily with one last breath and then stilled.

"Sorcha..." Her name on his lips was a kiss from the heavens.

"Oh, thank you," Sorcha collapsed against Torin, weeping, as he shifted, pulling her tightly to his chest.

"You claimed me," Torin said against her lips, and then she knew nothing else but his love rolling through her like lava pouring out of a volcano heating every dark crevice it found.

A throat cleared behind them.

"Should we leave you two alone?" Seamus asked.

"We should probably check on him," Nolan argued.

"Or maybe we'll just see ourselves out," Bianca ordered.

Sorcha smiled against Torin's lips, cradling his face in

her hands, laughing when he pulled away from her kiss to give the group behind them a thumb's up. And then his attention was back to her.

And she was lost to him, their bond born in fire and solidified in love.

23

It had been a week since Sorcha had brought Torin back from the brink of death, and he'd devoted most of his time to thanking her in increasingly creative ways. Sorcha didn't seem to mind, particularly when the gifts were something magickal and new to her. Torin delighted in showing her his world, enjoying how her face would light up with each new thing she discovered, and he wanted nothing more than to shelter her in this cocoon of contentment they'd created.

And their nights...well, those were a feast for a starving man. Making up for lost time was the first thing on Torin's agenda, and he'd sequestered them in the tower room for an entire day after she'd claimed him to show her just how grateful he was that she'd chosen to share her love with him. There was nothing he didn't want to learn – the way her skin pinkened beneath his kisses or how her eyes went soft with satisfaction after he pleasured her. He was drunk on her, he was certain of it, and more than happy to satiate her every need.

The power of their bonding, well, no wonder fated mates claimed each other. Torin rubbed at his chest, the

dull ache having disappeared with her claim, instead
replaced by a lightness and effervescence that made him
want to bound around the room. His energy seemed insa-
tiable, and his magickal powers had grown to new levels.
He'd been told this could happen with fated mates, and now
he understood why waiting to find the perfect mate
mattered so much to his brethren.

As much as he'd wanted to keep Sorcha in his home,
she'd insisted they take one small trip to check on her
family.

"Why do you want to go, my love?" Torin asked for the
tenth time that day.

"I've told you already – I don't think I could live with
myself if I knew they were hurting or needed help. At the
very least we need to check on them."

"I'll send a guard," Torin said. He leaned down and
nibbled at the sensitive skin beneath her earlobe, brushing
back a lock of her hair. She smelled of citrus today, a light
scent that made him want to explore further. When he ran
his hand up her side to lightly cup a breast, she laughed and
danced away from his arms.

"Later for that. You promised," Sorcha said, looking up
at him from under her eyelashes.

He had promised, much to his annoyance, but he wasn't
one to go back on his word. "If there's trouble – we leave
immediately. Understood?"

Sorcha nodded her agreement, following him to the
portal. The discovery of the portal had been shocking for
the Danula, and between Donal's betrayal and the
newfound portal, they'd launched an investigation.

Tomorrow, they'd celebrate the life of the fallen queen.

"I understand. I just left them in such a precarious position, it would be nice to see what happened," Sorcha tugged

him toward the portal entry, nodding to the guards who bowed deeply in acknowledgement of her title.

There was a lot to learn when it came to how Sorcha would step into the role of the Fire Fae's princess, and they'd decided right away to return the talisman to a very grateful Bran. Though he'd seemed surprised that Sorcha hadn't wanted to hold onto their most powerful item, he'd readily agreed to their plan of allowing Sorcha the time and freedom to learn more about the ways of the Fire Fae. In fact, the people had respected her more for not immediately coming into power and throwing her weight around, and now she had a devoted following of Fae. For her part, she wasn't certain how much responsibility she wanted to take on, and still talked mournfully of her lost career. Torin hated hearing the sadness in her voice, but he said very little about it. He didn't want to push her one way or the other when it came to something she was passionate about and trusted she would find her own way in carving out a path for herself. One thing he'd learned about Sorcha, she was fiercely adaptable and highly creative – and he was certain she'd design something new for herself.

"I don't know that I'll ever get used to this," Sorcha mused when they appeared near the stream by her child-hood house. A light drizzle misted the air, and morose clouds hugged the sky.

"It has its perks for travel, that's for sure," Torin agreed, keeping his hand in hers while scanning the forest. He opened up his senses, testing for magick, and didn't find any traces other than the portal. Good, he thought. He'd already been beating himself up this week for not being quick enough to help her with Donal. His powers had been severely drained at that point, and he'd foolishly decided not to revoke his unanswered claim before going into battle.

At that point, the sickness had filled him – making his movements slow and weak – and he'd become a liability. His pride had stopped him from revoking it, but now he knew something else had as well – his heart. He'd *needed* her to pick him, as much as he'd needed his next breath, and in the end, he'd landed exactly where he'd hoped with her.

They left the woods just as a dusty station wagon rolled to a stop in the gravel driveway. Two doors slammed and Sorcha stopped in her tracks, waiting to see what her reception would be. Torin came to her back, his hands on her shoulders, and watched the two women cross to them. The mother and one of the sisters, Torin thought, though he struggled to remember their names.

"Shannon..." Sorcha addressed her sister, and she trembled lightly under his hands. "I don't mean to cause any problems, I promise. We're just here to check on you." She didn't address the mother, but Torin didn't blame her after what Sorcha had told him.

"Thank you for coming back..." Shannon looked up at Torin and then back to Sorcha, her tired eyes filled with kindness. A breeze rippled her blonde hair around her face, and Shannon shifted, tugging at the strap of her purse. "I... we, were worried about you."

"We're okay," Sorcha said. "We, um, eliminated the threat. So, hopefully you should be safe. I wouldn't advise your children to play in the forest near the stream though."

Sorcha's mother sucked in a sharp breath, her eyes darting to the trees, and then back to the ground.

"And we'll be thanking you for that tip, won't we, mother?" Shannon nudged her mother.

"Oh, um, yes. Thanks. Your...your father sends his regards." Aileen nodded sharply, and then turned and went back to the car to start unloading what looked to be bags of groceries. Shannon's gaze followed her retreat before looking back to Sorcha.

"It's the best she can offer," Shannon explained.

"It's more than I expected. I'm a reminder of something painful for her," Sorcha said, and Torin squeezed her shoulders. He hated knowing that such a brilliant person hadn't been showered with love as she'd grown up. He planned to spend his days making up for it, that was the truth of it.

"That's fair. Fairer than you have the right to be, but I'll be accepting the kindness on her behalf. Um..." Shannon worried the strap of her purse between her fingers. "You're alright then?"

"I'm good, Shannon. You might not be seeing me much anymore, but I'll check in here and there if you'd like." It was a peace offering, and she wondered if Shannon would take it.

"That'd be grand. I'd worry for you if I didn't get word of you once in a while. You're still my little sister, Sorcha, even if you're...whatever it is you are."

"Fae. I'm Fae, Shannon." It was the first time Torin had heard her speak the words, and the pride in her voice warmed him.

"Well, now, isn't that something. I supposed something was afoot with you when you shot that fireball at Mary," Shannon shook her head. "She's gone, you know."

"I meant to ask..."

"Sure and she's run off, left all her stuff behind. Her flat mate is right angry about it, too. But it's only been a week. If she's here and causing a fuss – do I need to let you know?"

"I don't think she'll be a danger anymore, not with Donal gone. But if so..." Sorcha glanced up at Torin, uncertainty in her eyes.

"Head out to the stream. Look for the portion where the

water swirls counterclockwise. If you throw a red scarf inside, we'll know to come," Torin said, and Sorcha leaned backward into his chest, and he wrapped his arms fully around her.

"Let's hope I don't have to do that," Shannon measured them with an uncertain look. "I know Mary thinks I have a horrible life, but there's nothing wrong with wanting simple things. I've made my own peace with it, and I'm hoping it stays that way." It was both a warning and an acceptance, and Sorcha nodded.

"Simple is good. For me? I needed more – which makes sense now that I know what I am. I need to consume – art, travel, performances – it's a part of who I am. And I think understanding what you need is the biggest gift we can give ourselves."

"Alright then, go on before you make me weepy," Shannon said, waving her hand in the air. Sorcha moved forward, out of Torin's arms, and the two women stood awkwardly in front of each other before hugging quickly. Stepping back, Sorcha took Torin's hand, and they left without another word, turning their backs on her childhood home and the memories it held.

"Do you want to try and find your father?" Torin asked as they ducked into the woods.

"No, I really don't. We were never close and there's nothing to be gained from speaking with him now. He likes what he can understand, and I'm not something he can wrap his head around. He's never been able to control me, and he's never been able to accept me. It leaves us at a stalemate, and I suspect the both of us will be much happier without addressing it."

"In that case, can I take you home, my love? To our

home – the one where you belong and are loved deeply – so I can show you just how much you mean to me?"

Sorcha looked up at him, her eyes shining bright with love, and smiled.

"Yes, Torin – take me home."

Together, they jumped.

EPILOGUE

"From dust to ashes, and back again, our souls reunite with their home – the earth from whence they came. It's no more a goodbye than it is a welcoming, and our earth greets our queen with great joy, quiet acceptance, and resounding love as Queen Aurelia is planted once more to bloom with our future brethren."

Sorcha stood next to Torin, high up on a cliff over-looking the castle, a selection of royal friends and family surrounding them as Queen Aurelia was laid to rest. The officiant – a large woman, round in every way, wore a figure-hugging silk green gown and a golden circlet of branches twined through her brunette hair that fell in curls to her waist. Confidence radiated from her, in a way that spoke of power, and Sorcha leaned into Torin.

"Who is that woman?" Sorcha whispered, watching as she dribbled liquid over Queen Aurelia's grave, a thicket of bushes rising immediately from the ground. From the bushes, radiant golden flowers uncoiled, their petals flut-tering down in long hanging strands, and already little glowing fairies flitted between them. Their light caused the bush to glow from within, and Sorcha smiled, though her heart ached for the loss of a very powerful woman.

"Her name is Terra. She's in the same role as I am, but for the Earth Fae."

"Terra...meaning Earth in Latin, no?" Sorcha asked, leaning into Torin's warmth as a chilly breeze rippled down the mountainside. Prince Callum and his love, Lily, approached the bushes and bowed their heads. Sorcha felt for him. She'd essentially just lost her mother, as well, though hers still lived. It stung, so she could only imagine how it felt when the relationship was a strong one.

"During this joyous time where we celebrate the queen's return to the Earth," Terra smiled out to the crowd, and Sorcha was struck once again by the sheer presence of this woman. "We anoint our new ruler. As we are a matriarchal society, the responsibility for ruling will someday fall to Lily, Prince Callum's betrothed. However, am I to understand that won't be the case?"

Prince Callum turned and looked out at the crowd. He wore a suit of gilded gold, and he held his head high.

"My love has asked for me to rule in my mother's stead, as my father has abstained from power. When Lily and I celebrate our nuptials in due time, we'll discuss if she is willing to take over the throne. Until then, I am your new king."

"Loinnir Ri!" The crowd shouted and Sorcha looked up at Torin in question.

"Loosely translated – light king," Torin whispered at her ear. "We use the singular word – light – as a cheers of sorts. So, they are toasting the new king."

"Thank you, my brethren. My mother..." King Callum looked down to the ground and collected himself before continuing. Lily squeezed his hand, and Sorcha appreciated the break in protocol. People should support each other in times of sadness, and that was the truth of it. Too often emotions were kept well-hidden. "She was a unique woman of great strength. I'm lucky to have had her in my life, and even more so now as my guiding star. As is our custom, we will now celebrate the joys she brought to us during her time in this realm."

Torin had explained to Sorcha earlier this week that Fae funerals were not remotely somber – but instead they celebrated until the wee hours of the morning. Life was a fluid concept to the Fae, with souls dancing between realms, and they felt people's journeys should be honored with great joy. Learning that, Sorcha had planned something special. She hadn't known the queen long, but since the woman had died defending Sorcha – and her people – Sorcha thought it was only right that she acknowledge the sacrifice made in the best way she knew how.

A man still stood by the grave, his head bowed, and something in the way he held himself caught Sorcha's attention.

"Who is that?" Sorcha asked, as people turned to leave. She nodded discretely toward the man who lingered with his back to the crowd.

"Him? That's the king. Well, Callum's father." Torin said, tugging her hand to lead her away. Sorcha couldn't take her eyes off the former king, drawn to him for some unknown reason. When he turned, his eyes meeting hers across the crowd, it hit her.

It was him. The man from the thrift shop. It had been the king who had given her the enchanted staff that ominous morning weeks ago.

Shock and confusion slammed into her, but Sorcha had no time to process this revelation before she was swept up in the crowd. As the group of royals streamed down the mountainside, trumpets blared, sounding their arrival. The Danula people streamed outside the palace walls, many holding instruments, and a lively song bounced through the air. Her heart soared, taking in the jubilance of the people, and Sorcha was once again reminded how heartbreakingly beautiful life could be.

"We haven't met." A melodious voice drew her attention. Terra, the rotund woman who'd caught Sorcha's interest earlier walked next to her. They were nearly the same height, something Sorcha appreciated, as she so rarely met people as short as her. "I'm Terra, Royal Court Advisor to the Earth Fae."

"It was a beautiful ceremony, Terra. I'm Sorcha, and I'm still getting used to saying this – but I'm Princess of the Fire Fae."

"A child of prophecy, born in flame, forged in light," Terra murmured. Upon closer inspection, Sorcha saw her almond-shaped eyes were a lovely shade of green with tiny golden flecks dotting the irises.

"Something like that, I suppose."

"The Earth is crying..." Terra said, a wrinkle marring her brow as she frowned. "The rumblings have started."

"What do you mean?" Sorcha asked.

"I fear we've only maddened the Domnua. Like hitting a hornets' nest with a stick. They'll see the loss of our queen as a chink in our armor."

"You think they'll push harder now?" Sorcha asked, worry slipping through her.

"Yes, I do," Terra pressed her lips together. "This night we'll dance. But on the morn? We'll fight."

"Already?" Sorcha's heart picked up speed.

"It's already begun, Sorcha. But we'll take this night to

celebrate our queen and laugh in the Domnua's faces. Joy is a powerful weapon, Princess. Use it wisely," Terra nodded and then was called away by another royal. Sorcha stared after the woman, her motions fluid and with a grace that spoke of deep strength.

"Sorcha. I'm ready for you," Bianca came to her side and tugged at her arm.

"Where are you off to?" Torin asked, grabbing Sorcha's other arm, and she smiled playfully up at him.

"Girl talk," Sorcha said, and her hand tingled when he brought it to his lips and pressed a kiss to her palm.

"Don't stay away too long. I want to dance with you tonight. Remember when you danced for me when I was ill? Nothing lights me up the same way as you, my love." Heat bloomed low and liquid at his words, and Sorcha paused, lost in his eyes.

"That's for later, you two lovebirds." Bianca pulled her out of her stupor and Sorcha reminded herself that she had more important things to tend to first. Blowing a kiss over her shoulder, she followed Bianca inside the castle walls and behind a row of tents that led to a stage set up in the courtyard. Already a band played, and the Fae who had their own instruments joined them out on the field. It was one wild and raucous party, with bonfires blazing in the corners, dancers everywhere, and voices raised in song. The Fae didn't lie – they really did love to party. Sorcha gulped down the nerves that threatened and focused on her breathing exercises. She owed this tribute to the queen.

Sorcha climbed the stairs behind the stage and quickly changed into the costume that Bianca had brought for her. Swallowing, she waited behind the curtains as trumpets sounded once more, silencing the crowd.

"Sorcha."

Sorcha turned at the voice, caught on wave of emotions as the former king stepped to her side.

"I..." Sorcha didn't even know what to say. She tilted her head to look up at the man.

"I don't believe we've been formally introduced. I'm King Gregor, well, I suppose it's just Gregor, now. Thank you for caring for my wife in her last moments, I've connected with her since and she's aware of the aid you attempted for her."

"You've...connected?" Sorcha raised her eyebrows, uncertain what to think.

"Yes, the Fae have a way of communicating with those who have passed on. Their soul never really leaves you see, only slipping into another realm where it enjoys a time of renewal before rebirth."

"Why did you give me the staff?" Sorcha rushed out before she second-guessed herself. "Did you know what would come of it?"

"I understood the possibilities. The future is never written completely in stone, as I'm sure you know. But both I, and the queen, knew the potential for what would happen. We decided together that the benefits far outweighed the risks. The staff was meant to come to you when I gave it to you. Now, learning Donal's involvement, I'm even more content with our decision to pass it off to you when we did. He was too close and the staff in his hands would have been catastrophic for the world."

"Oh," Sorcha said, struck by the difficulty of the decision they'd had to make. Tears slipped into her eyes. It seemed having power went hand-in-hand with making heartbreaking choices. "I'm so very sorry for your loss. I didn't know the queen long, but she's left a lasting impression on me."

"As she did with most. It was an honor to be her

husband. Now, my dearest – don't be sad. Today is a time for celebration. Please, go on. I hear you plan to honor my love."

"I do...I hope that I make her proud." Sorcha lifted her chin as nerves fluttered through her stomach.

"You already have."

Trumpets sounded once more, and a cry rose from the crowd that waited. With a last bow to the former king, Sorcha ducked through the curtains and onto the stage, bracing herself as a cheer rose from the thousands gathered before her.

"A gift for our queen from the one who shared her last moments."

Steeling herself, for she'd never danced in front of such a large crowd before, or for something so meaningful, Sorcha burst forward in an almost violent movement, bounding across the stage. She paused as the light found her, and then threw her hands to the sky. The music began, both urgent and sharp, her movements echoing it as she streamed across the stage in a series of complicated steps, leaving a trail of fire in her wake. On she danced, her sorrow and rage echoing in her movements, her body translating the ferocity of battle and a life lost. As the flames grew higher around her, the music changed, reaching an impossibly tremulous crescendo, before exploding into several seconds of silence as Sorcha dropped to the floor. Now the music slowed, a delicate dance of light and laughter, as Sorcha reared up, arching her body backwards as she radiated joy and love as the tempo picked up speed once more. On she twirled, a desperate joyous race against time, as the fire followed her across the stage until she dove into the middle, consumed by flames.

Drums shook the field, and the fire exploded to the sky, and Sorcha curled into a ball, ripping her outer costume to reveal a simple body suit of glittering gold. When the flames dropped away, she huddled in a ball, before arching slowly and gracefully upwards, until once more she stood – proud – her arms reaching to the sky.

A phoenix, exploding in flame, rising once more from the ashes.

So too, shall love rise once again, Sorcha thought, tears flooding her eyes, for light shall always conquer dark.

Do you want to read more about Torin & Sorcha? Well I have excellent news there is an extended epilogue.

Get your free gift here:
www.triciaomalley.com/free

CHORUS OF ASHES: BOOK THREE IN THE WILDSONG SERIES

CHAPTER ONE

DIVIDED WE FALL.

Terra watched her people celebrate the life of their queen, and took heart that love lived on. As the Earth required it to do so. Without love, the Earth would die, drying out to a wispy husk, nothing more than a broken shell on a forgotten beach. Even now, power hummed through Terra, deeply rooted in the ground, and she felt its call.

It was never easy for her, to be around this many people. Instead, she was a woman of the wilds, the forest and hills her friends, comfortable keeping her own company. For she was never alone, not really, as the energy of the natural world flowed through her in a delightful song. She could spend hours conversing with a flower, learning its music, her thirst for knowledge of the natural world keeping her constantly entertained.

Content that her people celebrated the queen appropriately, Terra turned and made her way from the castle, crossing a field where luminous miniature flower sprites danced among the foliage. Her silk dress fluttered behind her, the material soft against her skin, and Terra hummed a little sound of pleasure. Naked was her preferred way of being in nature, but if she must be clothed, silks were next best. Finding a spot by the little stream that meandered along the side of the field, Terra dropped to the ground and crossed her legs beneath her, immediately placing her fingers into the spongey moss. The scent of dirt, and fresh grass teased her nostrils, and she breathed it in the same way a baker would scent her muffins.

Her happy place was here, but her people weren't happy. Even now, the rumblings of the Earth Fae's anarchy vibrated through her palms, their complaints growing, and Terra sent a wave of soothing magick into the dirt. Perhaps, she'd calm them for a bit, but the prophecy was already in motion. Elementals divided. Children of the prophecy lost.

And a man she was meant to claim.

"Show him to me," Terra ordered, leaning over the stream. The water shifted, shimmering as it swirled over the rocks, and then an image appeared in the surface.

A large man, muscular shoulders contained in a crisp business jacket, studied a sheath of papers at his desk. His brow creased, annoyance flashing through his chestnut eyes, his brown hair neatly combed. Terra wanted to muss up his hair, and to see him wild and wanton, walking barefoot through the woods.

A sigh escaped Terra's lips, and she reached out a finger, aching to trace it over his lips.

Her fated mate. Her sworn enemy.

∼

Don't miss out on Terra's story where she has to decide if
love is worth it all.
Chorus of Ashes.

AFTERWORD

AUTHOR'S NOTE

Thank you so much for joining me on this new journey through the Fae realms in Ireland. It's quite fun to dip into the Elemental world of the Fae, and I try to mirror a bit of each element's personality in my characters. Recently, I was spending time with an Irish friend of mine and he was talking to his two small daughters and told them to always give a warning before they tossed the bucket of water they were holding. He said it without thinking, but it made me smile – the prevalence of Fae mythology and history is still very much alive today in the Irish culture. And, to explain – many Irish people are taught to give a warning before tossing a bucket of water out the back door lest they hit a fairy with it.

Thank you to my now *husband*, Alan, for supporting me while I wrote this book, planned a long-distance wedding, and tried not to panic over leaving our sweet dog behind for almost a month. I'm happy to say the wedding was hands-down the best moment of my life, and Blue stayed happy and healthy the whole time we were gone.

To see wedding photos – you can go to
www.triciaomalley.com/free

Thank you to Dave & Rona for taking the time to help me shine up my books – as well as for the excellent butler service during our recent bout with Covid while in Scotland.

Thank you to my awesome Beta Readers who are my next line of defense in wrangling this book into top form. You all are the best!

And, as always, a huge thanks to my lovely readers who share in my delight of all things magickal and mystical. Sparkle on!

WILD SCOTTISH KNIGHT

BOOK 1 IN THE ENCHANTED HIGHLANDS SERIES

Opposites attract in this modern-day fairytale when American, Sophie MacKnight, inherits a Scottish castle along with a hot grumpy Scotsman who is tasked with training her to be a magickal knight to save the people of Loren Brae.

A brand new series from Tricia O'Malley.
Wild Scottish Knight
Wild Scottish Love

ALSO BY TRICIA O'MALLEY

The Isle of Destiny Series

Do you want to learn more about how Bianca & Seamus fell in love and helped battle the Dark Fae during the Four Treasures quest? Read the complete Isle of Destiny series in Kindle Unlimited!

Stone Song

Sword Song

Spear Song

Sphere Song

A completed series in Kindle Unlimited.

Available in audio, e-book & paperback!

"Love this series. I will read this multiple times. Keeps you on the edge of your seat. It has action, excitement and romance all in one series."

- Amazon Review

The Wildsong Series

Song of the Fae

Melody of Flame

Chorus of Ashes

Lyric of Wind

"The magic of Fae is so believable. I read these books in one sitting and can't wait for the next one. These are books you will reread many times."

- Amazon Review

A completed series in Kindle Unlimited.

Available in audio, e-book & paperback!

The Siren Island Series

Good Girl

Up to No Good

A Good Chance

Good Moon Rising

Too Good to Be True

A Good Soul

In Good Time

A completed series in Kindle Unlimited.

Available in audio, e-book & paperback!

"Love her books and was excited for a totally new and different one! Once again, she did NOT disappoint! Magical in multiple ways and on multiple levels. Her writing style, while similar to that of Nora Roberts, kicks it up a notch!! I want to visit that island, stay in the B&B and meet the gals who run it! The characters are THAT real!!!" - Amazon Review

The Althea Rose Series

One Tequila

Tequila for Two

Tequila Will Kill Ya (Novella)

Three Tequilas

Tequila Shots & Valentine Knots (Novella)

Tequila Four

A Fifth of Tequila

A Sixer of Tequila

Seven Deadly Tequilas

Eight Ways to Tequila

Tequila for Christmas (Novella)

"Not my usual genre but couldn't resist the Florida Keys setting. I was hooked from the first page. A fun read with just the right amount of crazy! Will definitely follow this series."- Amazon Review

A completed series in Kindle Unlimited.

Available in audio, e-book & paperback!

The Mystic Cove Series

"I have read thousands of books and a fair percentage have been romances. Until I read Wild Irish Heart, I never had a book actually make me believe in love."- Amazon Review

A completed series in Kindle Unlimited.

Available in audio, e-book & paperback!

Stand Alone Novels

<u>Ms. Bitch</u>

"Ms. Bitch is sunshine in a book! An uplifting story of fighting your way through heartbreak and making your own version of happily-ever-after."

~Ann Charles, USA Today Bestselling Author

<u>Starting Over Scottish</u>

Grumpy. Meet Sunshine.

She's American. He's Scottish. She's looking for a fresh start. He's returning to rediscover his roots.

<u>One Way Ticket</u>

A funny and captivating beach read where booking a one-way ticket to paradise means starting over, letting go, and taking a chance on love…one more time

10 out of 10 - The BookLife Prize

CONTACT ME

I hope my books have added a little magick into your life. If you have a moment to add some to my day, you can help by telling your friends and leaving a review. Word-of-mouth is the most powerful way to share my stories. Thank you.

Love books? What about fun giveaways? Nope? Okay, can I entice you with underwater photos and cute dogs? Let's stay friends, receive my emails and contact me by signing up at my website

www.triciaomalley.com

Or find me on Facebook and Instagram.
@triciaomalleyauthor

Made in the USA
Las Vegas, NV
08 February 2024

85415599R00152